Math's hands moved over her with the sun-block lotion, covering every bare inch of her shoulders, neck and back...and then some.

Elain felt his fingers slide just under the edge of her swimsuit, around the top of the band across her shoulder blades. His touch was like electricity running over her, and her starved body leapt to respond to the touch it needed. She could say nothing, do nothing, hypnotized by the stroking, like a cat.

She knew she should stop him—how could she get involved with a suspect?—but if she allowed herself to move a muscle it would not be to get away from him.

"Are you asleep?" he asked softly.

Was he kidding? Asleep? She had never been so awake in her entire life....

Dear Reader,

We've got one of our most irresistible lineups ever for you this month, and you'll know why as soon as I start talking about the very first book. With *The Return of Rafe MacKade*, *New York Times* bestseller Nora Roberts begins a new miniseries, The MacKade Brothers, that will move back and forth between Intimate Moments and Special Edition. Rafe is also our Heartbreaker for the month, so don't get your heart broken by missing this very special book!

Romantic Traditions continues with Patricia Coughlin's *Love in the First Degree*, a compelling spin on the "wrongly convicted" story line. For fans of our Spellbound titles, there's *Out-Of-This-World Marriage* by Maggie Shayne, a marriage-of-convenience story with a star-crossed—and I mean that literally!—twist. Finish the month with new titles from popular authors Terese Ramin with *A Certain Slant of Light*, Alexandra Sellers with *Dearest Enemy*, as well as *An Innocent Man* by an exciting new writer, Margaret Watson.

This month, and every month, when you're looking for exciting romantic reading, come to Silhouette Intimate Moments—and enjoy!

Yours,

Leslie J. Wainger
Senior Editor and Editorial Coordinator

Please address questions and book requests to:
Silhouette Reader Service
U.S.: 3010 Walden Ave., P.O. Box 1325, Buffalo, NY 14269
Canadian: P.O. Box 609, Fort Erie, Ont. L2A 5X3

DEAREST ENEMY

ALEXANDRA SELLERS

Published by Silhouette Books
America's Publisher of Contemporary Romance

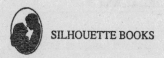 SILHOUETTE BOOKS

ISBN 0-373-07635-5

DEAREST ENEMY

Books by Alexandra Sellers

Silhouette Intimate Moments

The Real Man #73
The Male Chauvinist #110
The Old Flame #154
The Best of Friends #348
The Man Next Door #406
A Gentleman and a Scholar #539
The Vagabond #579
Dearest Enemy #635

ALEXANDRA SELLERS

was born and raised in Canada, and educated in England—Royal Academy of Dramatic Art, 1971; School of Oriental and African Studies, 1992—where she now lives with her husband. Her first novel was published in 1980. She loves cats, but is allergic to them.

For my mother,
Mildred Joy Quincey Lewis Sellers,
with love.

Chapter 1

The village sat at the meeting point of a river and its tributary, clustered beside the bridge that gave it its name, Pontdewi. The main road continued over the bridge on its journey towards the sea ten miles away. Elain took the turning, the only one in the village, onto a narrow side road that led south, following the smaller river.

She was suddenly in another world—climbing the side of an ancient, mossy river gorge overhung with beech and oak. Below her on the right, the water chattered and sang on its way over the rocks and between the trees. On the left, tiny grass-carpeted, stone-fenced fields—green dotted with the white of sheep, and sprinkled with trees—climbed towards the forest. On that side, they were the invader plantation forests, the unnaturally regular ranks of conifers dark under the misty sky, but on the right, climbing the hill from the river, were ancient oak and ash and beech, the trees native to the country. Soon the conifer plantations disappeared, and the deciduous trees closed in, so that she was driving through a wonderland of green.

The forest, with its arched branches meeting in a canopy close above the road, and the subdued light filtering through, suddenly seemed timeless to her, as though Arthur and his knights might as easily come riding through the trees as another car down the narrow, precipitous road towards her. Perhaps she would paint that, she thought as she drove—a small red car on the road, oblivious of the ghosts of medieval knights among the trees ... Arthur Pendragon's standard flying above. ...

She almost missed the turning, a dirt track closed by a gate that was marked with a small sign, Cas Carreg. Beneath, there was another sign reading The White Lady Hotel, and underneath, *Y Ddynes Wen*. This track led down to the narrow river and across it over an ancient stone bridge, shrouded in mist. Then she was climbing again, and suddenly the forest fell away on her left and she was on a ridge overlooking a lushly beautiful valley. Below her, white sheep and black cows grazed on green pastures, and stone-fenced fields and farmhouses sprinkled the valley floor. Beyond were shadowy heather-covered hills, their tops shrouded in mist.

Enchanted, Elain slowed to a crawl, her eyes half on the track, half on the breathtakingly serene vista below and beyond. On the other side of the car, the ancient forest thinned and gave way to thick green grass and moss-covered stones, the road turned away from the ridge, and then, above her on the hillside, she saw the house.

It was solidly built of grey stone and mortar, with several high square chimneys that looked like turrets. Two wings ran at right angles to each other, one long and low and the other higher and square. It stood over the valley like a sentinel. Behind it, farther up the hillside, she could just see through the sprinkling of trees what looked like a ruin from an earlier period; off to the left there were outbuildings.

Covered with thick ivy that glistened almost black in the mist, the house looked ancient, imposing and sheltering. There was another gate across the road, that had to be opened and closed again behind her. Before driving on, she stood for a moment in the soft mist, simply accepting the peace of the place. There was no sound except the distant bleating of a sheep, and the wind rustling the branches of the trees. Above the ruins, a black horse and rider galloped across the brow of the hill.

In a century gone by, the farmers must have come up from the valley floor for protection at the now-ruined fortress whenever attack threatened.... She almost saw them, dragging precious possessions, scrabbling up the hill— women with their skirts tucked up, their muscular legs mud-streaked, a red scarf around a pair of shoulders . . . crying children, a terrified goat with its mouth open, red tongue hanging out, its belligerent feet digging in against the pressure of the rope around its throat . . . the fortress huge and dark on the skyline . . .

"Am I awake?" Sally had demanded plaintively. "Did you say *Wales?*"

Her ash blond hair was fanned around her head in a nimbus of tousled, broken rays, and she sat blinking at the morning sunlight that fell across the breakfast table as if it were an alien life-form. When Elain's laughter carolled out, she winced.

"Wales," Elain repeated, stifling her laughter but still grinning irrepressibly.

"Why?" Sally asked in groggy surprise. Wales might have been the other side of civilization, instead of just a few hours away to the west. "I mean—it's very beautiful, Elain, but why so suddenly? And—" she added feelingly "—why first thing in the morning? Have you found some long-lost cousins, or something?"

"No, I'm going for Raymond." Elain tossed her red hair back and poured the coffee. She couldn't stop smiling. Unlike her actress roommate, Elain liked mornings. When Sally was between acting jobs—or "resting" as it was called in London—she worked in a nightclub. Elain's on-and-off temping work was generally nine to five.

More than once over the eighteen months the two Canadians had been sharing this apartment since their graduation from two prestigious London arts colleges—Sally from the RADA actors' course and Elain from the Slade School of Art—Sally had offered to get Elain a hostessing job in the club where she worked. "A night job would leave your days free for painting. Anyway, it's better money," Sally had always pointed out. "Come down and talk to Harry."

What she said was true, and at first Elain had been tempted. It would have been terrific to be able to paint all day instead of working for a living. But then she saw the costume Sally wore, and there wasn't a chance. She never told her friend the reason, and Sally laughingly told their friends Elain was "prim." Elain wasn't prim, and the dress wasn't vulgar. But it was low-cut, and she knew no nightclub manager would ever hire her to wear it. She saw no reason to submit herself to the humiliation of being told that by Harry.

So she had slogged away at her temporary office jobs, and squeezed in what painting she could at the weekends, until one day she had stumbled into luck. Her temp firm had sent her on a two-week assignment to a private detective named Raymond Derby. He had found her so quick and intelligent that after the first week he had told her she was wasted on his typing and filing and asked if she would be interested in trying an assignment as an undercover operator.

He had a client, a clothing manufacturer, who was losing stock to internal thieves. Would Elain be willing to go to work for the client—under cover as a temporary secretary—and try to find out what was going on?

The pay was more than double what her agency paid her. Elain had jumped at the chance. The thieving employees hadn't been quite so careful to hide from a temporary secretary what they hid from their bosses, and Elain had collected the evidence fairly quickly.

That had been the first of many jobs she had done for Raymond. She had never had to work full-time again. On average now, she worked only two weeks a month, and that, combined with the artwork commissions that were, even in the middle of a recession, steadily increasing as her work became known, paid the bills. So Elain had plenty of time for painting. But this latest assignment was the best of all. Elain had been almost jumping up and down with excitement as she dragged her sleepy roommate from bed to tell her the news.

"You're always so bright in the mornings," Sally complained mildly, staring at her cup of coffee as though uncertain whether it would save her life or poison her. "I didn't get to bed till four."

Elain laughed and ran a hand through her thick hair, pulling it down over her left cheek in a characteristic gesture. Elain's hair, a fellow artist who worked in wood had once told her, was the colour of clear-stained mahogany. With the morning sun on her head, there were red-gold highlights spangling the glowing auburn that fell around her shoulders, like diamonds in a gauzy scarf. "I'm sorry. But I had to wake you—I'm leaving in half an hour and I'm not sure how long I'll be away. And, anyway, I had to tell you —you'll never believe it!—I'm going under cover as an artist!"

A slow smile transformed her roommate's face as she took it in. "Really? What kind of a case is it—coke being smuggled in tubes of titanium white? I wish someone would send *me* under cover into the West End as an actress!" she added parenthetically.

"Suspected arson," Elain said, spreading butter thickly on her toast. "A hotel, right near Snowdonia National Park, Raymond says." She took a large bite and then wiped a drop of melted butter from her lip and licked her finger. "I'm supposed to try to get a room in the hotel. I'll pose as an artist wanting to paint the mountains." She smiled again, and her deep grey eyes went distant. "And the green hillsides covered with fat, woolly sheep. And the oak forests, and the sky. And the old Celtic fortresses, and the standing stones. And the—"

"Hello, hello!" Sally carolled, waving a hand in front of her friend's eyes. "If the hotel was burnt down, Elain, how will you get a room there? And if it wasn't burnt down, how can there be arson?"

"Fair question. I asked it myself." Elain munched for a moment, and swallowed. "Raymond says one wing of the hotel was pretty badly burnt. The rest is perfectly intact. People are still living in the wing that wasn't damaged." She shivered suddenly, and Sally's eyes grew concerned.

"What is it? What's the matter?"

Elain shrugged and shook her head. "Nothing. Just someone walking over my grave." But she had lost her appetite, and she set down her toast and reached for her coffee.

"Did someone die in the fire? Is that it?" Sally knew that Elain had lost both her parents in a fire long ago. She also knew there was more to it than that—not from anything Elain had ever said—but Sally wasn't the friend to push for confidences.

Had someone died in the fire? Or been hurt? She hadn't asked Raymond about it. How on earth could she have forgotten such a basic question? "I don't know. I didn't think to ask." She looked at Sally, unaware of the look that had entered her eyes.

Sally bit her lip. "Who do they suspect of the arson? Welsh nationalists?"

Everybody knew that certain Welsh nationalists used arson as a form of protest, but it was usually the empty "summer homes" of the absentee English that were the targets of such attacks.

Elain shook her head. "No, it's insurance fraud, Raymond says. They suspect the owner himself, a guy named—" she paused and reached for the notebook she had written Raymond's instructions in "—named Mathonwy Powys. Is that a weird name, or what? I don't even know how to pronounce it."

"Emphasis on the second last syllable," said Sally absently. She had toured Wales in *Private Lives*. It had been an unhappy company and the rain had never stopped.

"Anyway, that's why I've got to be right inside the hotel."

Sally frowned. "It sounds a bit dangerous to me, Elain. Do you think—?"

"It's no more dangerous than a couple of other jobs I've done." Elain shrugged. But it wasn't really true. She had never before been asked to live in with an investigation, and presumably the suspected arsonist, if he was one, had a lot to lose. And he was the owner.

"And how are you going to get a room? Won't you look kind of suspicious right from the start, going to a burnt-out hotel and asking to stay?"

"Raymond says that area of Wales is really booked up in high season and maybe I can pretend I've tried everywhere else."

"Be careful how you use that one. In small places, all the hotels always know who's got room and who doesn't." With months of theatrical touring under her belt, Sally knew everything about temporary accommodation in the British Isles. She put on a high-pitched, middle-aged voice with a cockney accent. "Ohh, I am surprised to 'ear you sigh Mrs. Beadle is booked up, dear. She was sighing only yestidie that she 'ad empty rooms this week."

She was a very good mimic. Elain laughed, and felt her worries lift. It was foolish to let bad memories colour the present. Of course she would be safe. "All right. I'll think of something else."

"Pretend you had a reservation and it got lost in the fire," Sally suggested. She stood up in her rumpled pyjamas, stretched and bent to kiss the top of Elain's head. "Be careful, and remember I'll miss you. Don't be too long finding the evidence."

"I never thought of that!" declared Elain, much struck. "If I manage things right, I could be painting in Wales for months! Oh, yes, I can see it!"

Sally laughed and wandered off in the direction of the bathroom. Elain quickly tidied away the breakfast things in the large sunny kitchen, humming as she did so. It was a lovely flat, and she would miss it as well as Sally over the next little while.

If you craned your neck you could just see the river from one corner of the sitting-room window. Sally, the actress, had been thrilled with the idea of living in fashionable Chelsea, and Elain, the artist, loved being near London's picturesque river. With her easel and paintbox under her arm, she could walk to the Chelsea Embankment in ten minutes, and from there half an hour's stroll along the Thames would bring her to Westminster Abbey, Big Ben and the House of Parliament.

Now, Elain was thinking as she quickly rinsed cups and plates to the sound of Sally's voice singing "I made my mind up back in Chelsea," under the shower, she would have the mountains and valleys of Snowdonia National Park to paint. Her breath quickened in excitement. She did love London, but there was no doubt the air pollution and traffic and graffiti and filth on the pavements got to you after awhile. She needed some country air, and Raymond had said that the nearest village would be a mile away. In Canada, that would have meant nothing, but in this tiny, overcrowded island kingdom, a mile from the nearest village was the back of beyond.

And there was another reason she was drawn to Wales. More than a century ago, her great-grandfather had been born there. That was almost all she knew about him, but she had always meant to find out more. Now, perhaps, she could. It made another good reason to take the job, in spite of...

Anyway, fears ought to be faced, or so everybody said. Even those you'd lived with for twenty years.

In the act of wiping her hands, Elain frowned and shook her head. She suddenly had the curious feeling that there was another reason for her going, one she knew nothing about.

* * *

The rider had changed direction and the horse was cantering down the hill towards her. Elain watched dreamily for a moment, and then realized that whoever it was was not simply riding down the hill, but was making directly for her.

Her mouth opened slightly and a curious sense of danger and foreboding came over her as the horse drew nearer. Unconsciously she tensed, as if for battle, and she felt goose bumps lift the skin of her arms and back. Suddenly she was afraid of what would happen if she let the rider reach her.

Elain turned abruptly and climbed back into the car, setting it in motion almost before she had the door closed. Out of the corner of her eye she saw the rider turn his mount away and spur it to a gallop again.

The track led around the house, and now she could see that one half of the long wing had no glass in the windows, and the stone was scorched black in places. The ivy, too, was brown, giving the place a curiously autumnal air, as though the death of the building were a part of the cycle of the seasons.

Elain parked her car in the curving drive and got out once more. The mist, wet on her lips and her face, was turning into a light rain, but still she stood and gazed at the house. The grey stone was darkened with rain and the clouds had thickened and completely blotted out the sunlight, but there were lights shining golden behind the arched mullioned windows on the ground floor, and the strongest impression was one of welcome. It looked like home.

''How long ago did you send in your cheque?''

''Months ago. March or April, I think,'' said Elain. This was the part of her job that she hated: starting out with lies.

The woman, short, thickset and middle-aged, attractive in a slightly florid way, flipped through her cards again. ''The thing is, if we'd got your cheque, we'd have sent you a confirmation. And if you were booked, we'd have sent you a letter to cancel. We've had a fire, you see.'' She had a lovely lilting accent, which Elain found charming.

"Yes, I saw traces of it. I'm awfully sorry. But it was contained, wasn't it? Don't you have any guests at all staying? Is it possible for me to—"

"I'm afraid we're all too much at sixes and sevens at the moment. We do have a few guests, but they're all our regulars—people who have been here before and know us, or people who live here more or less permanently."

"But you do have room?"

"Well, there are—"

"Please let me stay." She was dimly aware that her urgency wasn't entirely on Raymond's client's behalf. Somehow she had already fallen in love with this beautiful place. "I promise not to be demanding if things go wrong. I want to paint Cadair Idris." The mountain called Cadair Idris was nearby, Elain knew, and if everything hadn't been shrouded in mist, she would probably have seen it as she drove. "I've been driving all day. It will take me ages to find a room anywhere else. And it's getting late...." That, of course, had been deliberate. It would be harder to turn someone away at seven-thirty in the evening than at three or four in the afternoon. And the rain that was coming down now was an unlooked-for bonus.

The woman pressed her lips together thoughtfully. "You're from Canada, are you?"

"That's right." Elain thought it better not to add the information that she lived in London. "You've got a very good ear for accents."

"My nephew is in Canada. I visited him there last year. In Vancouver, he is, working in construction engineering." Elain relaxed as they chatted, knowing she had all but won. "Well, I'll just ask," said the woman after a minute. She turned into her office and exchanged a few words with someone in a guttural but strangely musical language, one that seemed curiously familiar to Elain, as though she had heard it in a dream, or in another life. "He's out at the moment," said the woman, coming out again. "Really, I don't know what—" She lifted her head as the door opened behind Elain. "There you are, Math. Here's a young woman from Canada, an artist she is, who sent a cheque for a reservation and we never got it. She's wanting to know if we can put her up.''

''Hello,'' said a male voice, and Elain felt a prickle of superstitious dread between her shoulder blades, knowing the man heading towards her must be her prime suspect. ''I'm Ma—'' He paused as she turned, and for a moment out of time, they stared at each other. Then slowly, reluctantly almost, as though a smile was not his first response, Mathonwy Powys smiled at her. He reached for her hand, and just as reluctantly, she gave it. ''I'm Math Powys.''

He was taller than she. Elain was used to looking directly into most men's eyes, but she had to look up to meet his gaze, and although he was slimly built, he had broad shoulders and muscular arms and hands. He was dark, with very thick black hair falling over his forehead, and deep black eyes that seemed to see and take in everything. His nose was broad and thick, strong without being well-cut, his mouth wide and square, with full, generous lips. The kind of mouth that smiles easily at women. The kind of mouth that always made her nervous.

He was wearing the grey shirt and faded jeans she had seen earlier, but she didn't need that clue to tell her this was the man on the horse. She would have recognized him even if he had changed; the sense of threat, of personal danger, was the same.

She wanted to run. Every instinct warned Elain not to ask to stay, but simply to turn to go at once, while she still could. Her heart was pounding in her throat as if it would choke her, and she could feel it even in her hand as he touched her, could feel her pulse where it pounded against his warm, strong palm.

She drew her hand back, and made up her mind. She could not, would not get friendly with this man. He was dangerous. She would tell Raymond to find someone else. She would get away from here.

Because Mathonwy Powys had done it. She was sure that this feeling of deep, dark mistrust was telling her that—that

he was guilty, just as they suspected. And never until she
looked into those all-seeing black eyes had she been so
afraid of the consequences of getting friendly with someone only to betray him. He was ruthless, she knew that. Her
heart was pounding as if she were meeting an old, deadly
enemy, or...or... With him looking down at her she felt
hunted, as though she had already betrayed him and he were
after her.

No! she protested silently. It wasn't fair that her luck
should turn against her like this.

"I'm afraid we've had a fire," he was saying. Thank God
he was going to say no! It would be easy. She would just pick
up her things and go. She would drive back to London—or
at least out of Wales—before she slept tonight.

He was looking deep into her eyes, frowning slightly now,
as if bemused by what he saw there. "But we can't drive you
out into the storm," he said. That was a laugh, she thought,
because whatever might be kicking up outside was nothing
compared to what was building for her here, if she stayed.
"If you're willing to put up with a certain amount of in-
convenience, I think we can find room for you."

"Oh, well, I wouldn't—" she began, but he reached out
to take her wrist in his hand, and that shut her up as if he
had clapped a hand over her mouth. He smiled, and she
sensed a determination in him that sent hot and cold waves
of irrational fear over her.

"I insist," said Math Powys.

He knows, she thought in panicked dread. *He knows why
I've come. And he's not going to let me get away.*

Chapter 2

"I'll show her up to Llewelyn's Room, Olwen," he said, and bent to pick up her easel and two of her suitcases. "Send Jan along, would you?"

If she had had no luggage she might just have been able to get away. But she had been the author of her own undoing, she thought, as she helplessly watched him take the key and walk down the hallway. She had deliberately brought in all her luggage before ringing the bell at reception, in the kind of psychological manoeuvre Raymond had taught her: establish a beachhead. Now it was rebounding on her.

"But I . . ." she began, and then felt something she didn't understand at all. An inner immobility assailed her, a frozen lethargy, as if she were somehow unwilling to rescue herself, as though some buried part of her were determined that she . . . what? Face the threat, the danger? But why? *Why?* she cried helplessly to that inner self. But there was no answer, only the seal on her lips, the weight on her limbs, that made resistance impossible.

"Llewelyn's Room," said Olwen approvingly. "That's not Llewelyn ap Gruffydd, of course. He's too far back. But that's what the room's always been called."

Elain tore her gaze away from the retreating back of Math Powys. "Really?" she said, though she had heard nothing. "Could I use a phone?" She must talk to Raymond. If she explained to Raymond, he would tell her to come back.

"Right over there," said Olwen. An old-fashioned black phone sat on a little table between two armchairs beside the door. Her heart sank. "I'll have to dial the number for you in the office. It's a very antiquated system we have here." She smiled and sensed Elain's hesitation. "But you'd better go off now with Math, and see your room. Dinner's almost ready. I'll tell Myfanwy about you."

Elain picked up the small bag and her paintbox and followed Math Powys as if to her doom.

The lift looked like something out of a thirties English movie, and Elain couldn't help being affected by its old-fashioned charm. She loved the movies of that period. Sally had a huge collection of films on video, and it was always the old black-and-whites that Elain watched. Math Powys set her bags down and held the gate open for her, and when she was inside with him and the gate was closed and it was too late to get out, she realized how small it was. It had been designed to fit into the stairwell, and it was about the size of two coffins.

"You're an artist, are you?" He had the deep, mellifluous voice that is the hallmark of the Welsh, but without the strong, lilting accent.

Elain nodded, thanking her stars that that was the truth. He was a man, she felt, who would have seen through that kind of lie in about five minutes. He had pushed the button, but it seemed to be taking the lift a long time to respond. "That's right," she said awkwardly. Under the pressure of his nearness, the old, tongue-tied feeling of social ineptness came creeping over her.

With a reluctant clang, the lift began to rise.

"You'll find plenty to paint around here. But you know that, or you wouldn't be here. Have you stayed at the White Lady before?" He was just making conversation, and yet her heart was pounding in her ears. She felt sweat beading her brow and under her arms. She even felt dizzy. This was a ridiculous overreaction. What was wrong with her? Of course he didn't know why she was here.

She licked her lips and her fingers combed the hair beside her left ear. "No," she said.

He smiled and turned as the lift leaped a little, bounced down again, and stopped. "It's usually better not to bother with the lift unless you have luggage," he said drily. He opened the clanging gate and picked up her luggage again, then preceded her along a short wainscotted hall to a door at the end, and opened it.

She stepped into another century: grey, rough-hewn stone walls hung with a needlework tapestry; a dark-stained wooden floor with a couple of small carpets; an old portrait in oils of some seventeenth-century beauty; an antique chest of drawers; a free-standing full-length mirror on an oak pedestal and an unstained oak chest at the foot of the bed. The bed, against the one wall of ancient wood panelling, was covered by a green tapestry spread that matched heavy curtains at the windows. There were two arched, leaded casement windows cut into walls that were at least two feet thick, and a small stone fireplace that hadn't changed in hundreds of years. Elain stopped dead, a few feet into the room, and gazed around her, mouth open.

"Oh, how beautiful!" she breathed, because she loved old things, and the room breathed a timeless peace that her soul had hungered for without knowing.

"Yes," said Powys, nodding. "This room has been restored. Most of the others are still semi-modernized. I've been working on the restoration one room at a time."

He set down her bags and crossed the room to the deeply recessed windows. They faced out over the valley, where rain-clouds now darkened the sky. Off to the right a swirl of greys and pinks behind the rain meant the sun was setting.

He opened one of the windows. The song of a single blackbird immediately came in on the wind and, too loud to be from the valley, the crying of sheep. He stood looking out over the valley for a moment, not heeding the raindrops that blew onto him. Then he turned. "Cadair Idris," he said, and smiled an invitation to come and stand beside him.

It was beyond her to go and stand beside him in that intimate space. Elain pretended not to notice the invitation, crossed to the other window and opened it, gazing out at the scree-topped mountains that stood across the valley, barely visible in the mist. What parts were visible were coloured deep purple. "Where?" Elain asked, and then wished she hadn't, for he came and stood beside her to point out over her shoulder.

"That long shape," he said. "The peak is just covered."

He was not touching her, though she felt as though he were. Her skin was crawling with awareness, with hostility. "It doesn't look very high," she said rudely. It was true. The Welsh mountains were not high, nothing like what would be called a mountain at home, she knew. But it was said they had a kind of perfect proportion that made any term other than "mountain" impossible.

He glanced down at her. "No," he agreed. "You can climb it in a couple of hours. Do you like walking?"

"Not as much as the English do," Elain said, her tone suggesting that that was a failing on the part of the English. She was sounding sullen and narrow-minded, a Canadian who couldn't see virtue in anything that wasn't just like home.

"The views from the top are spectacular. On a clear day," he added with a grin.

"Oh, yes?" She hated this. Why didn't he get away from her? She wanted to shove him away, but was afraid of touching him.

"But don't stay with him all night."

She glanced up at him. "What? With whom?"

"With the giant of the mountain, whose name is Idris. *Cadair* means 'chair' in Welsh. The mountain is the chair of

Idris. He's a friendly soul, but if you stay on the mountain overnight, tradition says, you come down in the morning either mad, or a poet.''

She felt an uncomfortable sense of being enchanted against her will. "Really? Have you done it? Stayed overnight on the mountain?''

He hesitated and then looked at her with a smile in his black eyes, inviting her to share the joke with him. "I have, as a wild young man.''

"Was it for a dare?''

He hesitated again. "Not quite.''

She couldn't help asking, "And did you go mad?''

"I hope not.''

"Are you a poet, then?''

"Olwen says we have a new guest and sheets are wanting, Math. Is it in here you're wanting them?''

Elain blinked and whirled as the voice intruded into...what? Had she so easily been hypnotized? She glanced up at him in dismay, but he had already turned away to the young woman who was standing in the doorway, sheets and towels over her arm. "Yes, that's right. This is Jan," he said to Elain. "She'll generally see to your needs in the housekeeping department. Jan, this is..." He paused. "I'm afraid I neglected to get your name," he said, as though his lapse surprised him.

"Elain," said Elain to both of them. "Elain Owen.''

"Elain," he repeated, making a move to take her hand but recovering easily when she avoided the touch. "Would you like to come downstairs for a drink before dinner while Jan makes your room ready?''

"If first I could...''

"Of course. Jan, perhaps you'll show Elain where the bathroom is. I'll see you down in the sitting room, then, when you're ready, and you can meet the others.''

With a nod at them both he was gone, leaving a curious void behind, as though he had taken all the energy of the room with him.

"Owen," said the girl, when she had set down the sheets on a chair and was leading the way out of the room. She emphasized both syllables, in a more musical pronunciation than Elain had ever heard before. "That's a Welsh name. Are you Welsh, then?"

"My great-grandfather was born here."

"And do you have people here?" She stopped and opened a door, but waited while Elain replied.

"I don't know. I'd like to think so."

"In this part of the country, would they be?"

"I don't know," she said again.

"This is the bathroom," said Jan, opening the door wider to expose a very handsome old bathroom with a Victorian-looking white tub and sink surrounded by dark mahogany wainscotting. It was another century altogether from the bedroom.

"Goodness," said Elain, in mild astonishment. Above the sink hung a large, mahogany-framed antique mirror, giving a muted, kindly reflection. Her creamy skin and auburn hair seemed to have been brushed over with softly tinted shellac, so that she herself looked as though she belonged to that other world.

"The toilet is next door," said Jan, setting down clean white towels. "I'll leave you now, shall I?"

All this ancient splendour was getting to Elain. "Do people change for dinner?" she asked in dismay, glancing down at the jeans and wrinkled shirt she had been wearing since nine that morning.

"Vinnie always does, of course. The others do when they like, or not, as it suits them. Tonight you'd be better not to change, because with so few guests everyone eats at once, and Myfanwy—that's the chef—will get upset if people are late. They'll be sitting down in fifteen minutes."

So much for her plans to squeeze in a quick bath to wash off the travel grime. "Right," said Elain, closing the door as Jan left.

She washed her face and hands, and back in her room again, rummaged in her case, changed her shirt for a loose light cream cotton sweater that hung almost to her knees, kicked off her travel sneakers, slipped bare feet into her loafers, combed her hair and quickly renewed eyeliner and mascara. She was quick enough that Jan was still making up the bed as she left, quick enough to have all thoughts of the man downstairs driven from her mind until she was lightly tripping down the wide stone staircase that encircled the lift.

Then she caught her lip between her teeth, and her light steps slowed. It had happened before, this feeling of instant dislike for someone without there being any apparent objective reason for it.

Did the man downstairs remind her of Stephen? His eyes were a little like Stephen's, perhaps...yes, maybe these two had some similarity, shared some common trait, that had nothing to do with looks or profession, if she could find it.

It was like a sixth sense trying to tell her something, when she just couldn't hear clearly enough to get the message. What had—

"There you are," said his voice, and she came to with a start to find herself standing a few steps up from the main floor, and a dark figure at the bottom, silhouetted against the light. "We're just in here."

The hall was broad, though the dim light from the deep windows falling onto the centuries-old grey stone of the floor didn't go very far. Above her the staircase stretched up three floors, dark and mysterious and full of the whispers of another age. Math Powys stood in front of her, and as she looked into his dark face, he, too, seemed to be a shadow from another age. *I've known you before,* Elain was thinking suddenly. *We were enemies then, too. We've been enemies from the beginning.*

There was a huge stone fireplace at one end of the large room, which looked as though it could roast a whole sheep, and probably had done in the past. It was primitive and

roughly beautiful, its mantel an axe-hewn beam of stained
oak, holding up a mountain of stone. On both sides there
was dark, antique panelling. Owen Glendower, Prince of
Wales, might have stood there with his warriors, in full armour, eating a hasty meal of meat and bread, and red wine
in pewter tankards, as he rested briefly from his assaults on
the English overlords....

A small group of people was sitting in the sofa cluster
nearest the fireplace. They had all looked up at her entrance, and Powys led her towards them. The rest of the
room, barring the leaded windows, was disappointing: the
stone walls all plastered over, an interior wall covered with
faded wallpaper, old-fashioned crystal chandeliers, everything done to diminish the power and strength of the original, to bring it down to size, to make it coyly comfortable.
She was back in the thirties movie.

"This is Elain Owen," Mathonwy Powys said. "She's just
arrived. Elain, meet Vinnie Daniels." The oldest occupant
of the room, a very slender white-haired woman in pearls,
a silk blouse and a grey pencil-slim skirt, sat with her legs
drawn elegantly sideways, the pose of a woman who has
lived her life with beautiful legs. They still were, Elain saw.
In the legs, as in the face, bones were what counted, and
Vinnie Daniels's ankles were perfect.

"How do you do, Miss Owen?" she said in a warm, crisp
voice, reminding Elain of Deborah Kerr. A perfectly aged
Deborah Kerr, playing a countess. "How very nice to meet
you."

"How do you do?" she returned, taking the woman's elegantly proffered hand. It was all delicate skin and bone, but
she got a good firm grip out of it, Elain noted. The denim
of her jeans was growing hot on her calves; there was a
glowing fire in the fireplace. She had stood too close to the
fire because she was trying to keep away from Math Powys,
yet fire was something that she usually avoided.

Two women in their sixties were sitting side by side on the
sofa. "Rosemary and Davina Esterhazy," said Powys, not

making absolutely clear which was which. Elain bent to take the hand of the one on the right.

"I'm sorry—Rosemary, is it?" she said.

"That's right!" said the woman, slim but squarish, her shoulders held very straight. She took Elain's hand in a firm, no-nonsense grasp. "Now, isn't that interesting, Davina! She got it right, first time! I wonder if she has the Gift? Do you have the Gift, dear?" Sharp, assessing eyes fixed on her face with a detachment that was curiously at odds with her words. Elain, getting into this now, immediately cast her in the part of the humourless school headmistress, one of those actors whose name she could never remember.

"I shouldn't be at all surprised," said Davina, before Elain could say a word. She was smaller and less military than her sister, her fine hair slipping out of its pins to halo around her head, and her figure fuller, softer and more rounded. "I felt something the *moment* she entered the room," she declared, her delivery almost theatrical.

Elain almost laughed aloud. She sounded exactly like Margaret Rutherford playing the psychic, Madame Arcati, in one of Elain's all-time favourite films! Elain gazed at her. Was she going to complain that Elain was "interrupting her vibrrrations"?

"You can always tell when another person has the Gift," Davina explained to them all. "It's like Mind speaking to Mind, isn't it, dear?" She smiled compellingly upon Elain, daring her to refuse to be endowed with the Gift.

But Elain managed to hold her own, made an apologetic face and shrugged. "I don't think I'm very psychic." She smiled. Not for worlds would she have told them about Owen Glendower and his nobles.

"Oh, I think you are." Madame Arcati raised a hand to her temple. "I'm quite sure of it, my dear. If you haven't realized it yet, that merely means that you have not been made aware of your own potential. We must see what we can do while you are here. I have had a little experience in training the, uh . . . non-initiates."

Math Powys grinned appreciatively. "Before you get into telepathic communication, meet someone else in English." Everybody laughed, and he turned to another chair, where a young man with puffy eyes, pale skin and a wry smile was nursing a large whiskey. "Jeremy Wilkes. Our resident poet," said Math. A large black Lab lying beside the poet's chair raised its eyes and gazed at Math. "The dog is Bill."

"Mostly unpublished," the poet said at the same time, taking Elain's extended hand. He smiled at her with a certain amount of tired charm, the twinkle in his eyes sharing appreciation of the scene just past with her. "Hello. How on earth have you managed to end up in a burned-out hotel like this?"

She gave that a smile and a shrug. "Have you spent the night with the giant, too?"

He raised his eyebrows in real shock. "I beg your pardon?" With a little zing of surprise, she realized that Jeremy was a good deal older than she had first imagined. His face looked young, but the skin was sagging and lined; he must be forty at least. When he was an old man, she reflected, he would look like a pickled child.

"You know—the mountain."

"Elain has just heard the legend of Cadair Idris," said Math Powys. Elain's imagination stopped short of being able to cast him.

Jeremy Wilkes jerked his head as he got it. "Oh—oh! Oh, yes, I have, actually. I must tell you sometime what happened to me up there. But, more's the pity, I think I came down mad."

That made them all laugh, and then Elain sat in a chair beside Jeremy while Powys offered her a drink and moved off to pour it. The dog got up and followed him.

"Math's been telling us you're an artist, Miss Owen," Vinnie began, her voice quiet but beautifully pitched. "That must be so interesting! I do envy people with talent. Tell us, what do you paint?"

Elain sighed with relief. If someone had asked instead, "What brought you to Wales?", she would have been starting with a lie again, and she always hated that.

"The sort of thing I mostly paint is called magical realism now," she said, taking the glass of wine that Math offered. He went back to leaning against the dresser, and the dog settled down at his feet.

Rosemary frowned. "I thought that was a literary term. Taliesin writes magical realism. *Wounds Which Bleed Profusely*. And Gabriel García Marquez."

"*A Thousand Years of Solitude*," interjected Jeremy, nodding. He sighed. "Fabulous book."

Elain nodded. "Yes, I think the literary term was borrowed by artists. Or art critics."

"Surely it's a hundred," said Rosemary. Everybody stared at her. "*A Hundred Years of Solitude*," she expanded impatiently. "Surely not a thousand."

"Yes, that's not what I meant," said Jeremy. "I wasn't quoting the actual *title*. When I say a thousand years, I mean that's the *feeling* the book gives. You know, all that history, all that solitude." He waved a hand.

It wasn't a book Elain had ever read, and what he said was meaningless to her, but Rosemary clearly had. "I don't see—" She broke off, frowning at Jeremy as if she would like to sort him out but had tried before and knew it wasn't worth it.

It was left to Math to pick up the pieces in the silence that the poet's curious gibberish had produced. "What is magical realism in art?"

She never felt very comfortable with words, and anyway, his interest made her nervous. "Oh, well, if I were to paint the fireplace, for example," she began, babbling slightly, "with all of you sitting here, and then an overlay of Owen Glendower and his men in armour...you know, as if to say—" She broke off, smiling and shrugging. "Well, I'd rather paint it than talk about it."

"What a very lovely idea. I do hope you'll paint that. I should love to be in a picture with Owen Glendower. Such a fine warrior and general," said Vinnie. "I hope you'll make him look very Welsh, and very masculine."

"Not this fireplace," said Rosemary. "Not Owen Glendower. Wrong period."

And under that clinical tone, the vision that had been taking shape in Elain's head abruptly shattered and fell back into that strange sea from which it had arisen. She closed her eyes to hide her fury with this wanton destruction. It was her own fault. She knew better than to babble out ideas while they were still forming. It was because she was nervous that she had neglected to obey her own hard-learned rules.

"This wouldn't be earlier than 1550, would it, Math?" Rosemary went relentlessly on, sounding even more like a very old-fashioned schoolteacher. "Glendower was probably dead by 1416. If he was around here during his years of conquest, it was up at the old fortress, I should imagine."

"This house was begun in 1547, according to the records," Math agreed softly. "There are signs that there was a building on the site contemporary with the fortress, though, and the age of the fireplace has never been established. It may belong to the original building. In any case, as the present house was built with stones taken from the fortress, Owen Glendower almost certainly *has* stood near the stones of the fireplace, even if they were in some other shape at the time. The Lord of Cas Carreg was one of his earliest supporters in the North-West." He smiled at Elain as he spoke, but the look in his eyes was not quite a smile. With a little shock, she realized he was trying to give her back her vision. How had he understood? "By tradition he certainly slept here."

The fire belched a puff of grey smoke straight at Rosemary, punctuating his speech, as though the stones themselves had cried, "So there!" Rosemary coughed and groped in her sleeve for a hanky, blinking her suddenly burning eyes.

"How stupid!" she cried.

Elain gasped and bit her lip against a smile of astonishment, but the rest of the company was not so restrained. They burst out laughing as one, Bill sat up and barked, and Vinnie leaned towards the fireplace and called, "Hello, my dear!"

"Jess putting you in your place, Rosemary," said Jeremy with some relish, as she coughed again and waved the smoke from her face. "Again."

"Oh dear. She really does seem to have taken against us, doesn't she?" Davina murmured.

Elain found herself staring at the fireplace. "Who's—?" she began.

The door opened and Jan stepped in, looking harassed. "Myfanwy says she's kept dinner back twenty minutes already and if she keeps it any longer it'll spoil, and if you don't come now she's leaving," she told the room firmly.

"Right. We're coming now," said Math, setting down his glass and straightening up. The rest of the company shot to their feet like privates at the entrance of the general's adjutant.

As they moved from the room, the black Lab firmly leading the way, Vinnie came up beside Elain and took her arm. "It's all right, dear. It's just our resident ghost in action. But you'll be fine. I can tell she likes you already."

She was in a movie, all right. And she was beginning to wish she'd read the script in advance.

Chapter 3

The first course was carrot soup, with a dollop of cream and a sprig of fresh parsley decorating the centre of each bowl, and it was delicious. The plumbing might be Victorian, and the hangings date from the war, Elain thought, but it looked as though the food was going to be first class.

The dining room was a large space that ran through the main floor from front to back, with windows at either end overlooking the valley and the ruins. All the walls here had been masked with plaster, and the wallpaper and hangings were faded, as in the lounge.

It was sprinkled with tables for two and four, but they sat at a large table at one end of the room, in a niche created by the placing of a handsome but rather chipped wooden screen. They were beside yet another fireplace, and with the wind-driven rain beating against the windows, the fire was surprisingly welcome for a summer evening.

Their table was round, and to Elain's relief, Vinnie was between her and Math. "We're not always so cosy," Vinnie explained. "At first, after the fire, we suspended non-resident dining, but Myfanwy is the best chef for miles, and what with the demand from all around and Myfanwy getting bored and sulky cooking for a mere handful every day, Math was virtually forced to reinstate the public dining room. But on Mondays we have always had Residents Only Dining. In the old days it was to give the head cook a break, you see. The underlings could cope with a smaller group."

"And here we are," said Jeremy, rather theatrically, from her other side. Elain was still trying to place him in her cast of actors.

"My dear, I wonder if you could paint a portrait of the ghost," said Davina abruptly, leaning across the table towards her with dizzy Madame Arcati enthusiasm. "Do you think you might be inspired to do that, ah, Elain?"

Elain blinked. "I...don't know. Who is it? When did she live?"

"Her date is not very certain, although there have always been stories in the village," said Vinnie.

"They say it's a girl," added Jeremy. "Sometimes I'm convinced it's a man. It's got Althorpe's sense of humour to a T."

"Who's Althorpe?" She looked down at the dog, lying by the fire. No, the dog had been introduced as Bill.

"Good God!" exclaimed Jeremy. "Althorpe! Viscount Althorpe!' Elain still looked blank. "The Princess of Wales's brother."

"Well, of course, Earl Spencer now," Vinnie interposed softly.

"Oh, of course," said Jeremy, clapping his hand to his forehead. "The last time I spoke to my dear cousin, it was still Althorpe. He's a cousin on the mater's side," he said in parenthesis to Elain, looking at her to be sure she was properly impressed. "Not nearly so well-connected on Father's side, I'm afraid," he added, apparently in ritual English self-deprecation, but it wasn't lost on Elain that, once having established cousinship with Earl Spencer, he didn't have to worry too much about the impact of his father's shortcomings. "And now, in any case, much in disgrace with fortune and men's eyes."

Sydney Greenstreet, she said to herself. *He's been on a diet.*

The second course was grilled salmon with boiled buttered new potatoes and snow peas, all cooked to perfection.

"Myfanwy normally takes Mondays off," Vinnie explained. "But she's just been away for a week, so she's cooking tonight. Her mother is very ill, and Math made her take a week off to go and visit. Mondays we generally manage to cobble something together among ourselves."

"We positively begged Myfanwy to cook tonight. Not that she was unwilling," Davina said.

"Yes, you were lucky not to arrive last week. It might have been baked beans on toast," said Jeremy. He shuddered at the memory.

"How ridiculous. It was never that bad," said Rosemary repressively. "Math's steaks were certainly delicious." She paused, but no one spoke. Elain wondered what Rosemary had cooked when it was her turn. Rosemary turned to her. "Do you cook?"

"Umm," said Elain hesitatingly, "cheese sandwiches? Mushroom soup?" She could cook, she enjoyed eating food too much to neglect the means of preparing it, but somehow under Math's watchful gaze, she superstitiously wanted to keep biographical information to herself. As though if she told him too much, he might manage to steal her soul.

Everybody groaned in mock resignation. "Not another sandwich-maker!"

"As you see, we've developed a bunker mentality since the fire," said Math with a grin. "It's us against the world. Usually we all muck in on Monday nights, but last week we took turns."

"Math has had to let the sous-chef go, you see," Vinnie said quietly to Elain. "With not taking guests for the summer."

"Unfortunately," said Davina clearly and precisely, "the enemy is in the bunker with us."

Elain turned so suddenly to look at Davina that her hair snapped around her head and hit her mouth. Everyone else seemed largely unmoved, although Vinnie shifted uncomfortably.

"Oh, not that again!" said Jeremy.

Elain's heart was beating wildly, and she had to close her eyes in order to contain the impulse to look at Math and see if he had noticed her guilty reaction. For one panicked moment, she'd imagined that Davina was talking about *her*.

"What is it? What do you mean?" she asked, hoping no one had noticed that betraying pause.

"Everybody thinks the ghost is an innocent prankster," Davina told her gravely. "But I think this ghost has Tuhned."

"Tuhned?" Elain repeated.

"Yes. You know," she urged as Elain still looked blank. "Tuhned ugly. Sinistuh. They do, you know."

"Oh, *turned!*" Light dawned, and Davina nodded.

"That's what I said. Tuhned."

"Do they really? I've never heard that before. What makes a ghost turn?"

Madame Arcati waved a negligent hand. "Oh, there may be many reasons. One doesn't always know. I have sensed with this one—" she put a hand to her forehead "—perhaps a restlessness, a frustration, if you will, with being locked on this plane for so long."

Well, there were stranger things in the world, though she did make Elain want to giggle. Elain looked directly at Math for the first time since they had sat down. "Have you thought of bringing in an exorcist? Would your vicar—"

Davina's horrified sucked-in breath cut her off. "Oh, one mustn't do that! Not under any circumstances!"

"Why not?" asked Jan curiously. She had come in to clear the second-course dishes. "That's what my mother says, too."

"You cannot exorcise a ghost if it is Tuhning," Davina said flatly. "It is extremely dangerous."

Elain was prepared to go so far, but this was a bit beyond her tolerance level. "Come on, when's the last time a ghost was really dangerous? Isn't that just for the movies?"

"It is most certainly not 'just for the movies,'" Davina told her repressively.

"I see." She turned to Math. "Have you tried to have it done? An exorcism?" He shook his head. "Why not?"

"Because I like her. Most people do. She's a tradition—she's been in the house for generations. I've been here three years. It would be presumptuous of me to tell her to go."

"You think the ghost is a woman?"

"Without a doubt."

"Why?" she asked curiously.

"Because I have got to know her, and she is very female," he said with an appreciative smile. Elain didn't know why his tone should send goose bumps up her back, but it did. She visibly shivered, but not for the reason they all thought.

"There's really nothing to be afraid of," said Vinnie. "I've lived with her for many years, and she has never once been malicious. Sometimes childish, but she has such a marvellous sense of humour that one always forgives her." She turned to Math. "It certainly would be a great pity to send her away."

"I feel like pinching myself," said Elain in charmed amazement. "Is this an act you put on for newcomers? You aren't seriously telling me you all believe that there is a real, live ghost in this house, turning or otherwise?"

Rosemary sighed. "Ah, the limited colonial mind. Of course, in Canada, I suppose you haven't any buildings old enough to have ghosts. Here in Britain, my dear, we have been building permanent structures rather longer than you have. Many of the great houses of England have ghosts and, I should imagine, numbers of lesser houses. It is stupid to ridicule something simply because you have no experience of it."

Elain sat silent under the unpleasant little hail of words. She had not really been ridiculing their ghost, but now she was, as usual in the face of mockery, absolutely tongue-tied. She blushed and wished she could answer the attack, but she only felt that unbearable shyness she knew so well, and the certainty of being on her own.

She wasn't sure why she looked at Math just then. Perhaps because she felt him looking at her. There was a smile of understanding in his eyes, and he leaned towards her over Vinnie. "You can always paint her portrait," he murmured.

The relief was like lightning through her, entirely unexpected. She went off in a gale of uncontrollable and very infectious laughter.

It caught the table's attention, although Davina had been saying something about the supernatural being misnamed—it wasn't "super"natural at all, just something within the as-yet-undiscovered laws of perfectly sound science.

"What is it? What's the joke?" demanded Rosemary. Clearly she disapproved of talking in class.

Elain bit her lip and shook her head, choking back giggles. Math said calmly, "I was suggesting that Elain might paint you."

Rosemary tried to pretend not to be flattered by this. "Really? Paint me? I can't think why!"

"Because she is an artist of colour and shape, and not of words. That puts her at a disadvantage when she is insulted over the dinner table."

Elain and Rosemary gasped together. Rosemary's chest was suddenly beet red under the scoop-neck collar of her dress, and Elain watched transfixed as the blush crept slowly up her neck and into her cheeks and then to the roots of her coiffed blond hair. For a moment, the older woman sat staring at nothing. Then her gaze fell onto her plate, flicked back up to Math, and then to Elain. She touched her neck lightly, as though she wore pearls.

"I certainly didn't mean any insult, my dear. I hope you'll forgive me. It is a habit of ours, I'm afraid, to chafe Canadians and Australians a little as 'colonials,' but I hope you can accept that it is entirely good-natured.''

Elain was now more embarrassed than ever. "Yes, yes, you didn't...I just..." She subsided into silence as Jan came around the screen with the dessert trolley.

In the silence that fell as she passed around servings of something made with fresh peaches and clotted cream, Jan asked brightly, "Did you tell them about looking for your family?" Clearly she was no ordinary employee. Elain was going to have to cast her in the movie, too. "Elain's got people she'll be looking up while she's here, did she tell you?"

Everyone ohhed at this.

"Really?"

"Where are they?"

"You mean, you're Welsh?"

When she could get a word in, Elain said, "My great-grandfather was born in Wales in 1879. His name was Arthur John Owen. That's all I know. I thought of looking him up, if I could."

"Elaine isn't a Welsh name, of course," said Vinnie. "But there is a Welsh name, spelled without an *e*. Then it's—"

"My name is spelled without the *e* on my birth certificate," Elain interrupted excitedly. "I've always wondered why."

"Is it? Then it should properly be pronounced El-line, shouldn't it, Math?" Vinnie said.

"That's right—E'lain," he said, subtly emphasizing the first syllable so that the name rhymed with Pennine. "It means 'hind' or 'fawn.' But it's rare as a name."

"St. Catherine's House is the place to look up births," said Rosemary. "You should go to London."

Elain's face fell. "Really? I could have done it when I was there! I didn't know!"

"You were in London?"

"Yes! I should—" She broke off. What had she told them? Hadn't she said she'd come here straight from Canada? She couldn't remember. Nervously she glanced across

Vinnie to Math. It was stupid to think, as she had, that he already knew, but he looked very intelligent. She would have to be careful. "Yes, I was in London for awhile. But I didn't realize I could look up Welsh birth records there."

"You can look them up here, too," said Math. "The population records back to 1837 are in the National Library in Aberystwyth."

"How far away is that?"

"Not far. A couple of hours' drive."

"Maybe I'll do that, then."

"So you're Welsh, Elain. I suppose we might have guessed." That was Davina. Elain had had about enough of Davina's sixth sense for the moment, but she grinned cheerfully.

"Really?"

"That red hair, of course. It's a Celtic trait."

Elain laughed and stroked it forward over her ear. "Yes, I've been told that. But my great-grandfather is very dark in his pictures. A black Celt, I've been told."

"Like Math, then."

She looked at him. His Welsh lineage was unmistakably drawn in the heavy black eyebrows and eyes, the cheekbones, the nose, the full mouth, but it was not his Welshness that made her so nervous. She didn't know what it was. "Are you descended from the lord of the fortress up there, who supported Owen Glendower?" she asked, trying to make it light. "Or perhaps from the man himself?"

He was watching her as though something about her made him curious, interested him. "No. From down in the valley. Farmers and miners in my blood. What was your great-grandfather?"

"A builder," she said. The conversation seemed to be about something else, not least because no one else was speaking. They were all listening to this exchange. "He built houses. And his father before him."

"He emigrated to Canada?"

"That's right. And there he became a minister of the church, and then was elected to Parliament."

Dearest Enemy

"I suppose he was a very fine speaker," said Vinnie Daniels. "The Welsh are."

"He died when my mother was fifteen or sixteen. I never heard him, of course, but my grandmother said he was a magnetic presence in the pulpit." She looked at Math. She could imagine him in a pulpit, hypnotizing his listeners with that deep, dark voice.

A voice she would be hearing a lot of, if she stayed and did the job. A voice she would be getting down on tape. Elain blinked. As if drawn by her gaze, he was watching her now. She shivered a little.

In the morning a wasp was sunning itself on her windowledge. She watched as it cleaned its proboscis and head and then wiped its hands. Like a cat, she thought. The wasp flew away on a breeze, leading her eyes down over the valley.

It was a beautiful morning. The sun hadn't reached the valley yet—it was still climbing up behind the hills—but it was shining full on the White Lady. She had left her curtains open, and so had been awakened early by its slanting light. She had washed quickly and dressed.

In the night, she had decided to stay and do the job, decided she'd been tired from the long drive and foolishly overwhelmed by the place and the man. There were so many good reasons why she should not leave: the chance to paint, Raymond's certain fury, the money, reluctance to look like a fool...and that other, inexplicable thing that both repelled and drew her at once....

Elain checked her recording equipment and put it on, and still breakfast wouldn't be for an hour yet. She decided to go exploring. She wanted to see the ruined fortress.

Someone was up and about, she could hear the clanking of pails or dishes somewhere, and the front door was open. She was out of the shadow of the house in a minute, and then the sun was very bright, and promising a hot, cloudless day.

It took about five minutes to reach the fortress ruins, and it was uphill all the way. Elain thought again about the farmers in the valley. It must have taken them at least a half hour of steady climbing to reach the fortress—more if you were laden with children and food and precious items like the family Bible. And wouldn't they have been burdened additionally by panic? When the English came fighting Owen Glendower, Prince of Wales, and his lords and knights, had they burnt and pillaged his villages, too?

It wasn't a large fort, as the castles of Wales went, and most of it was in very poor condition. Elain thought Math had been right last night—many of the stones had been taken away to build the house, and perhaps some had even been pillaged for fences and the houses in the valley. There was now only a small line of stones in one short section of what once must have been a considerable perimeter wall. The shell of the central keep was still mostly standing, along with one outer building that was part of the short strip of remaining wall.

Elain climbed an ancient but solid stone staircase inside the central fortress. It was cool inside, and shadowed, although at midday the sun must pour in overhead. She stood at the top of the stairs looking out one of the tall arrow-slit windows. She could almost imagine the castle as it had once been, dark and damp around her.... She felt the presence of a woman who had stood here long ago, looking out, watching and waiting...for what? For the return of her warrior husband from battle? Yes, a man she loved deeply, a strong, rugged man who had gone off with his prince and—had she heard that the battle had gone against them? And then stood waiting, waiting, for the thunder of hooves that meant he was alive and coming back to her... or that a messenger had come to tell her he was slain. How the sound of those hooves would have reverberated through the stone, so that she felt them through her bones, into her spine, and in her heart, and she would wait for the sound of his voice...his or another's—

"Elain? Are you in here?"

She leaped as if she had been scalded, and nearly fell off the stone platform as she whirled. A horse snorted and blew,

and she looked down over the edge of the stone stairs to see
Math on a big black horse in the shadows below, looking
enquiringly up.

"Hello," she said lamely. He was grinning with the
pleasure of the exercise, and the enormous vitality of horse
and man seemed to reach out and touch her.

"I thought I saw you come in here." He swung out of the
saddle and let the reins drop. The horse immediately
dropped its head and began munching the green grass that
carpeted the castle floor. Math came to the foot of the
staircase and stood looking up at her.

She felt a curious impulse inside, completely at odds with
her own feelings for Math, as though the spirit of that other
woman still infected her, and this was her knight. Deliberately she slowed her pace as she descended the stairs, because otherwise she might have run. And she didn't think
she could explain to Math that it wasn't *her* running to *him*,
but another woman to another man long ago, a man who
had never arrived till now, and that woman thought she
recognized in Math...

There was a moment of silence as she reached the ground
and they stood looking at each other, as though something
else ought to be happening.

Then he said, "Care for the guided tour?"

It was her job to say yes. She had decided that the irrational fear she had experienced last night had been just
that—irrational, but still she wished she could walk away
from him now. With Math, something was before her, like
a chasm she couldn't see. Even in the bright light of morning, it frightened her, though she had been sure it would not.

"Yes," she said. "Thank you."

The horse's rich black coat was sweaty from his gallop,
but she couldn't resist patting the glowing neck. His head
bounced abruptly up and he pressed his nose against her
chest, almost pushing her over. Laughing, Elain stepped
back to get her balance.

"My, he's a friendly beast," she said.

"Sometimes," said Math.

The horse was still pushing at her. "Does he think I've got some sugar for him?"

"He may think you *are* sugar. Watch out."

He was smiling and it meant nothing; it was the kind of harmless, flirtatious remark any man might say to any woman in such circumstances. She had long ago learned to cope with such remarks. Yet she felt some kind of internal shock at Math's words. The huge physicality of the horse, the smell and feel of sweat on his thick pelt, were abruptly overwhelming. And it was his evident desire to press his nose against her breast.

She gasped and stepped back, the heat rising in her cheeks, knowing she was looking foolish. To hide her reaction, she bent her head and began to poke at the wire between the Walkman fixed to her belt and the headset around her neck, as if she thought the horse's actions might have pulled the connection loose.

As she did so, she surreptitiously pushed a button, and that little movement seemed to put her back in control. She looked up with a smile and pushed her hair out of her face. "All okay. What's his name?"

He was looking at her so steadily that she almost turned the machine off again, guiltily convinced he knew what she had done. But that really would have looked guilty. She bit her lip and smiled.

"Balch," he said.

She frowned. "After the city?"

"It's Welsh for proud. Spelled with *ch,* as in the Scottish word 'loch.' Balch."

"He's very handsome." The horse was eating grass again, and she risked putting out a hand to pat his neck again. This time he lifted his head and snorted softly in her ear. Elain laughed over the very physical tide of panic rising up in her. "Right! Let's go! I know when I'm not wanted!"

Math raised an eyebrow. "You're sure about that?"

She pretended not to hear, looking up through the open roof of the fortress and asking about the age of the building and who had built it. There wasn't much left of it, but they went into the various "rooms," although no doors closed them off anymore. Math described what each space might have been. As he spoke, she had the sense of seeing the inhabitants in the bustle of their lives. It was true what they said about the Welsh—his voice, as much as the place, seemed to lay an enchantment on her.

"And who lived here?" she asked, as they came out and began walking towards the other, smaller structure.

"The builder would have been a small lord who paid allegiance to Llewelyn in the thirteenth century. The valley probably belonged to the castle."

She looked around, smiling. The sun had lifted over the brow of the mountains, and the valley was bathed in the golden light of sunrise. She felt a sense of oneness with all those who had stood on this spot over such a long time. "There has been a steady line of people watching that sunrise from this spot for seven centuries," she said, half to herself, half to Math.

"Much longer than that," he said softly. "There has probably been continuous occupation here well back into prehistory. There was a fort before this one, perhaps from the time of Arthur. Before that, the Romans were here—we turn up Roman arrowheads every now and then. And before the Roman period, the Celts were here."

Her ancestors, as well as his. Perhaps that explained the strange push-pull she felt. "What did they build?"

He pointed. "There's a mound just over there, beyond the keep walls, with traces of bank-and-ditch fortifications. It was probably an early hill-fort from the first or second century B.C. or A.D."

She looked at him. "Are you a historian?"

He hesitated. "In a manner of speaking."

"What made you buy a hotel?" The tape was whirring away at her belt, and she felt a cheat. She had such negative feelings towards Math, whenever she came out of the daze his voice induced in her. Normally she wouldn't be talking to someone she disliked so much, pretending an interest in his life. Like Stephen, her tutor at art college. She had insisted on changing tutors, though they had talked and talked about how good he was for her, what good work she produced working with him. She'd never pretended an interest in Stephen. She'd hated talking to him.

"I was looking for somewhere in the country, and Vinnie happened to be selling up. My family comes from close enough to this spot that they probably paid allegiance to the lord of this castle." He smiled. "I found that difficult to resist."

"What does a historian do?"

"Some teach. I write, mostly." He didn't seem to want to talk about it any more than she did.

"What do you write?"

"Articles, books."

"About Wales?"

"Sometimes."

"May I read something sometime?" she asked, not even knowing why she wanted to. Something to do with coming up against her own distant past, perhaps, and wanting to understand it. Nothing to do with wanting to know him.

He was silent, looking down at her.

"Oh, well, if you'd rather I didn't, it doesn't matter," Elain said, alive to any rebuff.

"On the contrary, I'm flattered by your interest."

But she didn't believe him. "What would it have looked like, the hill-fort of the ancient Celts?" she asked, staring towards the mound. It didn't look like anything to her. Just a small hump of land covered with scrub and heather. "What would their life have been like?"

"They generally built in dry stone with timber framing. There are artists' reconstructions in some books I have, if you'd like to look at those," said Math as if he understood why she was asking. "They grew barley and wheat and flax. As they built strong fortifications, with sophisticated defences around the entrances, life was probably interrupted regularly by tribal war."

"Did the farmers come up from the valley for protection?" she asked slowly.

"I suppose people came up from the valley for protection in times of war regularly for two thousand years."

She might paint it as a panorama through time—the Celtic hill-fort, the Roman garrison, a castle of one of Arthur's nobles, then the fortress, with Llewelyn's, and later Owen Glendower's supporters, going off to battle....

She said dreamily, "There was a woman up there in the fortress, looking out."

"Yes?" said Math softly.

"Not a ghost, just..." She paused. "She was waiting for a man who never came back."

"Didn't he?"

She didn't tell him that she, too, had once waited for a man who never came back, and that perhaps that was why she had felt the woman's presence. "How high would they have built in Arthur's day? Would they have got up there, to the second storey? It might have been the battlements in an earlier fortress, mightn't it?"

He said nothing, letting her dream.

"I couldn't tell what period she was. Five hundred years ago, or a thousand?"

"Women have waited for men who never came back from the day war was invented, I imagine."

"Yes, but she—who was she? I want to paint her."

He looked at her closely for a moment. "Are you saying you think she was our ghost?"

The question startled her out of her reverie. "What? Oh! No, I wasn't... No. Anyway, this one's not a ghost. She just...stood there so long she left a trace. Do you know what I mean?"

"I do," said Math.

"I feel that, sometimes. Usually I can't put a finger on it so firmly. I just feel something and want to paint it. But her—I really *felt* her, not just as an idea, but as a personality."

She could feel the picture forming in her mind now, and realized she didn't need to see the woman more clearly than she did at this moment, because she would be... an eye behind the grey stone of an arrow slit? Or a distant figure on the ramparts. Something like that. It was something else that mattered, not the colour of her hair.

They were walking across the thick green grass of the ancient courtyard to the smaller ruined structure set into what was left of the perimeter wall. This one had several wooden boards and a Danger No Entry sign nailed across the door space. Elain paused to peer through the bars. "Is it falling down?"

"There's a bit of subsidence. It's been out of bounds since the war, when someone fell into a hole and broke a leg. It's probably a well, so whoever fell in was lucky to get out again. We have tourists coming up here from time to time, so I don't risk leaving this open."

Elain pushed her head between two boards and looked in. It was a much smaller structure than the central keep, and here there were no subdividing walls. "What do you—ohh!" She broke off as the board she was leaning on gave way under her hands, and fell forward with a little scream of surprise.

It might have been worse—if she'd fallen against the board below, she'd have been badly winded at the very least—but Math caught her around the waist from behind and held her firmly as the board clattered to the ground. "I think you'd better keep away from this part," he said as, flustered, she stepped back and straightened up. "I don't want you spending the night down a well."

"I wasn't trying to climb inside!" she said. "The damn board gave way under my hands! I'm not an idiot!"

She was reacting more than his comment called for. She felt nervous and discomfitted. His hand had hit her Walkman as he caught her, and had he felt the vibration that meant it was recording? His hands were still wrapping her waist, his left arm across her back, his right on her right hip. She looked over her shoulder up into his face. His eyes were very dark.

"Sorry," she said, before he could speak. Her heartbeat was suffocating her, but she had no idea why she was so afraid. If Math knew who she was, even if he were guilty of arson, he would hardly hurt her. That would be worse than stupid.

And it was stupid to feel he must be physically dangerous to her. So why was her heart hammering as if there were an imminent danger of him hitting her over the head and throwing her down the well?

Chapter 4

"She's at it again," Rosemary announced.

"Is she?" Jeremy yawned. He didn't like getting up early, but the reduced guest list at the White Lady meant reduced staff, and that meant there was no one to sneak breakfast to his room at ten o'clock any more. His aristocratic cousinship had never impressed Jan.

"That woman—that ghost," Rosemary enlightened Elain for free as she poured a cup of coffee and firmly stirred it. "Soot from the bedroom chimney fell right in my face this morning. I tell you, she's malicious." Davina was nodding in emphatic agreement, her mouth too full of hot buttered toast and jam for her to speak.

Jeremy reached for the coffeepot. "Whatever were you doing in the chimney?" he asked in mild surprise. Elain choked on a crumb and began to cough.

"There—I thought I heard a bird caught in the chimney. I looked to see."

"Maybe it was the bird who knocked the soot in your face," Elain offered. Rosemary seemed so unlikely a person to be arguing for the existence of a ghost ahead of all rational explanation. When Rosemary irritably shook her head, she asked, "Why do you care so much about the ghost? What are you afraid of?"

Davina swallowed. "Well, you see, my dear, we feel quite certain that the ghost deliberately caused the fire. We are afraid there may be another incident, perhaps fatal this time. There was, thank God," she added, her voice dropping to a lower pitch, "no one killed in the fire."

Elain's hand had already found the On button on her Walkman. Meanwhile she raised her eyebrows. "You think the *ghost* caused the fire? Is that possible?"

"Of course it's possible. It isn't only poltergeists, you know, who are capable of manifestation on the physical level. Ohh, no. There are those who may be said to have poltergeist properties and propensities, but who are a different, more complex spirit form than the term 'poltergeist' implies. These are the ones who are at particular risk of Tuhning."

The coffeepot had come round to Elain, and she poured herself a cup. "Are you a medium, Davina?"

"Ah. I didn't realize you didn't realize. My dear, I am a psychic. I am attuned to spirit presences."

"Like Madame Arcati."

"I *beg* your pardon?"

"You know, that fabulous film with Margaret Rutherford playing the—"

"I am well aware of who Madame Arcati is," Davina said icily. "I am not a medium."

"I've got a roommate in—" Elain cleared her throat "—who's a real film buff. She's got a huge collection of videos. I got really hooked on old English films of the thirties and forties. I love Margaret Rutherford, don't you? Especially in *Blithe Spirit*."

"Would you pass me the butter, please, Jeremy," said Davina.

Rather belatedly, it dawned on Elain that she had offended Davina. "Well, of course, it's a comedy," said Elain lamely. "But she did do it, didn't she? I mean, she really worked it so the wife came back." Then she remembered that that wasn't quite true. Hadn't it been the maid, who was unconsciously psychic?

"Quite," said Davina.

"My sister takes her work very seriously," Rosemary said, apparently taking pity on Elain.

"Are you here professionally? I mean, did Math call you in to give advice or something?"

"No." It was Rosemary who answered. Clearly Davina needed time to recover. "We came to the White Lady for the first time a few years ago quite by chance, on holiday, and heard about the ghost then. Last year we returned for another holiday. We often spend our summers in Wales, and we particularly like this area. At that time, although we said nothing, my sister became slightly alarmed at what she felt were changes in the ghost's emanations. But it was early days to deliver a warning, especially as she hadn't been consulted professionally and no one even knew that she was a psychic. It's not something we talk about, of course."

"Of course," said Elain, thinking that they were certainly talking about it now.

"We came back this year because my sister is researching a book on the ghosts of Britain. She wished to include this one, and particularly to note whether the changes of the kind she expected had indeed occurred. If, in fact, this ghost was Tuhning. We arrived to find the place a ruin."

"So no one had called to warn you, either?"

"You see, we had been travelling." Davina took up the story. "There was nowhere we could be contacted. When we arrived, there was still the smell of smoke." She shuddered. "It was dreadful. I don't think I've ever been so horrified in my life. It burnt so quickly! One forgets how fast old places, even stone buildings, catch. How lucky the whole place didn't go up!"

"That was mostly Math's doing," Jeremy interposed. "I helped, of course. It was damned hot work, it was indeed, until the fire truck arrived. I, for one, certainly despaired of our being able to contain it."

"How did the fire start?" Elain asked, gently placing her hand on her Walkman to be sure that it was running. Once she had got a wonderfully incriminating conversation going and discovered later that she had somehow turned off her tape. Once was enough. "How does a ghost start a fire?"

"It started in the cellar of the other wing," said Jeremy. "Underneath the lounge. The insurance people were poking around for days trying to decide how."

"What did they say?"

"I don't know what they said exactly, but they still haven't paid the claim. Math wants to get to work rebuilding, but until they pay he can't."

"Don't they know how it started, then?"

"Apparently there was some petrol stored in that part of the cellar, which no one knew about." This was Rosemary. "Two large cans. They had been there since the war."

Vinnie Daniels came into the room like a fresh breeze, making Elain aware how close the atmosphere had become. "Good morning, everyone," she carolled. "I'm afraid I overslept." She sat down beside Elain, smiling kindly as she picked up a delicate cup and saucer. "Would you be so kind as to pour coffee for me, my dear?"

"Of course." Elain filled the porcelain cup, and offered her cream and sugar. "We've just been talking about the fire. It seems amazing that that stored petrol didn't go up long ago."

Vinnie spooned a quite startling amount of sugar into her cup and stirred vigorously. "What is amazing is how it got there in the first place. I am sure there was never any petrol stored in the cellar. Certainly not as long ago as the war, because my father cleared it out when he bought the place in 1948," she said briskly, as though repeating something she had said before. She looked at Rosemary, and then at Elain.

"Perhaps you don't know, my dear. My father bought the house after the war and converted it into an hotel. My husband had been killed at Arnhem, and so I came here with my parents. I sold to Math three years ago when it began to get too much for me."

This certainly cleared up a couple of points that had been confusing Elain. "But you still holiday here?"

"I live here permanently," Vinnie replied. "It's the only home I've known for nearly fifty years. Math agreed to let me stay on until I die."

"There may have been petrol there that you didn't know about," Rosemary insisted. "That old part of the cellar is so dank and small I suppose no one ever went into it. The insurance people found the cans after all. Or the remains of them."

"There were no petrol cans in that part of the cellar," Vinnie repeated firmly.

Rosemary frowned at Vinnie as though the older woman might be going senile. "They were of a design last manufactured in 1942. Isn't that what Math says the man told him? How on earth can that be explained away?"

"What do you think happened, then, Rosemary?" Elain asked.

"One of the cans must have begun leaking. I think heat or a spark ignited the petrol."

"And spirit presences are quite capable of generating heat on this plane," said Davina.

"Oh, absolutely," Jeremy offered. "They generate cold, as well. Ghosts often cause cold drafts and cold spots, don't they? Althorpe has got ghosts, of course. I used to meet one as a child."

"Children often do," said Davina, beaming on a prize student.

The insurance company was going to have trouble swallowing all this, Elain thought with an inward laugh. But Raymond wanted a thorough job, and if that included ghosts, it wasn't up to her to edit them out.

"Do you think the ghost used to live here? When she was alive, I mean?"

"Undoubtedly," said Davina.

"There is no question that this used to be her home," Vinnie agreed. "Quite unmistakable."

"Oh, of course." That was Rosemary.

"But why would she want to burn down her own home?" Elain asked Davina. "Where would she go?"

This question seemed to catch Davina off guard. "Well, she—" she began, and broke off.

"Exactly," said Vinnie with a snort. "There is no reason for her to become sinister, and none at all for her to attempt to burn this house to the ground. She has, in any case, far too much sense of humour to do anything so stupid."

"It is the intelligent ones who are most likely to Tuhn," said Davina nervously, almost pleadingly. Clearly, Vinnie's determined common sense made her uncomfortable.

"I should think that a most unlikely proposition. In any case, how could it be proven?" said Vinnie, calmly drinking her coffee.

"Perhaps Davina should devise an IQ test for ghosts," Jeremy suggested.

In her room later, Elain played the conversation again on her Walkman. The advent of the "personal sound system" had, Raymond often said, been a real blessing for undercover operators. It meant you could walk around permanently wired for sound without looking suspicious.

Elain's Walkman looked like, and on one level was, an ordinary cassette tape player, in which Elain always carried a language-learning tape. She generally made sure people knew she was studying Italian, a not unreasonable preoccupation for an artist who hoped to go to Italy one day to paint. The sound of voices from her Walkman, if anyone overheard, wouldn't seem odd.

But the machine also had a secondary cassette deck, with an independent, disguised set of controls; it was on this that Elain recorded conversations.

When she was working for Raymond on a case, she always carried the Walkman, with the headphones—that contained the mike—around her neck or on her ears. People generally got used to thinking Elain a person always glued to her Walkman, and ceased to see it.

She was getting pretty proficient at Italian, too.

She made notes of the conversations she had had, playing the breakfast-table tape all the way through, but there wasn't much there that would interest Raymond's client. They must already know what had caused the fire, and anyone less likely to buy into the theory that a ghost had manifested sufficient spark to set the petrol alight than an insurance company, Elain couldn't imagine.

A more interesting issue was Vinnie's insistence that there had been no petrol cans in the cellar. Was it this denial that had made the company suspicious of Math Powys?

She noted the date and time on the label and dropped the tape into a pocket of her small valise; she never wiped any recording until the case in question was completely finished. You never knew what might turn out to be evidence.

Then she picked up the other tape, the one she had made up at the fortress talking to Math. There was nothing on that of any relevance, but she would keep it, nonetheless. She noted the date and time on another minuscule label and pressed it onto the tiny cassette. Then, about to pack it away, too, she paused, and instead slipped it into the player and rewound it.

"What's his name?" she heard her own voice, loud as usual because of her proximity to the mike.

"Balch."

Why had she begun recording here? There had been no chance of turning the conversation on to the fire just then. What had made her feel she ought to push the button?

"...Welsh for proud."

The resonance of his deep voice lost nothing for being right in her ears. Elain shivered and turned the machine off. She wasn't going to listen to that voice any more than she had to.

* * *

"They're all out of a movie," she said. She was calling from the pay phone in the village. There was no phone in her room, and the lobby phone was impossible.

"Really? Which one?" said Raymond.

Elain laughed. "That's what I'm trying to figure out. I think the title should be *It's a Mad, Mad, Mad, Mad World*, or has that been done?"

"Been done. What's mad about them?"

"Well, you know, they're all eccentrics. Now I've heard of the English eccentric, Raymond, but as far as I know, you don't get a whole passel of them in one place, do you?"

"Depends on the place. Bedlam probably had a few more than its share."

The trouble with Raymond was, he could always go you one better. And he had the dry delivery that was part of what she liked about the English sense of humour. Elain wasn't verbal, she got tongue-tied. Perhaps that was why she admired articulateness so much in others.

"And there's a ghost," she said. "Name of Jess. A few centuries old, I understand."

Raymond sniffed. "Oh, well, not a suspect, then."

"But that's where you're wrong," Elain gurgled. She outlined Davina's theory of the fire.

"Nice," said Raymond, "but not good enough. I doubt if we could legally prove the ghost was acting as a party for the insured, even if she was."

She said suddenly, "Vinnie Daniels is the previous owner, do they know that? She says the petrol cans weren't in the cellar. Is that what made the insurance company suspicious?"

"No," said Raymond. "They're not saying, exactly, but I think it was a tip-off."

So he had an enemy, then. One way or another, there was someone who wanted Math Powys hurt.

In the afternoon she took her easel and paints up to the ruined fortress and settled down in the warm sunshine to paint. She sat looking down the hill to the White Lady and the valley beyond. On the other side, Cadair Idris rose up against the sky. It was true what they said about the Welsh mountains. They might not be high, but they were perfectly proportioned, perfectly beautiful. There was no other word for Cadair Idris than mountain.

This was the view the woman in the keep would have had, as she walked the battlements, or stood watching out the tiny window. Except for the house immediately below, the view probably hadn't changed very much since the days the woman had watched and waited. Had there been sheep on the hillsides then? Fewer of the fields would have been cleared, and there would have been no conifers, though there would have been many more acres of forest—oak, ash, beech, elm, rowan, larch…. Almost she could see the army of green beauty marching across the valley….

She put the woman on a battlement with her back to the viewer, the broad panorama spreading out before her. As she painted, she thought of the woman's wait—how long did they have to wait in those days, before they knew? Was it days, or weeks, or even months before one learned the truth? If her man had gone on the Crusades, it might have been years. Years of waiting, believing…willing him home, as if her own determination would bring him out of harm….

As she painted she remembered her own time of waiting: those long, painful days and weeks when she had repeated over and over like a mantra, "He said he'd come. He promised." They had tried to be gentle with her at first, telling her he would never come again, not because he didn't want to, but because he could not. When she had refused to accept this, they had become frightened, and in their fright they had become cruel, shouting at her that he was dead, her father and mother were dead, and she could never go home again.

This woman must have known the truth in her heart. But for her, too, perhaps, there was a sense of not breaking faith with the one who had promised, for whom only death could have caused that promise to be broken. He would have come

if he could, and therefore she had been doomed to wait and
hope and believe.... Because not to believe was itself a betrayal. *Come home. Come back.*

And because there was nothing else to do but wait. There
was no other life if he did not come back. There was only
waiting... because when you loved that much, nothing else
counted. Nothing except to wait, and to will him to come.
Elain frowned down at her canvas, concentrating on the
shape of the woman's back, her hands on the stone parapet
in front of her...they had been married in heaven—she must
have pleaded that with the gods, as she yearned and willed
him to be safe. *You gave him to me, bring him to me
now... come to me, come to me, beloved, come back....*

She heard the scuff of foot on stone and looked up, her
brush automatically lifting from the canvas. He stood in
front of her, his eyes dark, his face drawn, frowning intently down at her; and for one strange, wild moment she
believed she had done it, that after all this time she and the
woman had willed her lover home.

"You called me," he said, and his voice was hoarse.

Elain's eyes stretched wide, her lips parting as reality
trembled around her. "Math!" she whispered.

"What is it?" he said. "What's the matter? You called
me."

She was stunned, confused. Her brain seemed inert, it
wouldn't function. For a moment she gazed down at the
hotel on the hillside below. "No," she said. "How could I
call you?"

They stared at each other, he with his hands loosely at his
sides, she with a brush falling from nerveless fingers. She
saw him move closer, and felt how he was bound to her
through time and space. Her palette fell onto the grass as he
reached for her, and under his hands she stood up and
swayed into his arms.

How strong he was, his arms wrapping her so tightly she
would always be safe. She lifted her mouth and his kiss exploded through her body, a thousand separate shocks to a

thousand separate nerves, in the same moment. Sensation ran across her skin in a shivering tremor as if she were hot and cold at once.

She felt an overwhelming sense of urgency, both clear and cloaked at the same time. She moaned and opened her mouth under his, while her hands found his shoulders and pressed and held, and her whole being trembled with the joy of the power she felt in his body.

His hands cupped her head, and he lifted his mouth and tilted her head back and kissed her throat, then the line of her neck from ear to shoulder. She whimpered, and heard his voice murmuring phrases meaningless to all but her secret ear. His mouth found hers again, and he wrapped his arm around her. Then he lifted his head and, smiling darkly down at her, bent and slipped a hand under her knees. In another minute she was in shadow, the shadow of the keep. He carried her over the carpet of grass, and then her feet were on the ground, and he was drawing her gently down beside him on a bed of soft, lush green.

Chapter 5

The grass was soft under her back, as though the earth itself embraced her. Everything was right, even the blackbird that sang somewhere above her head, the sheep that called in the distance. *"Yr wyf i yn dy garu di,"* she heard in her ear. *"Fy nghalon i."* Every creature in the world spoke the same words, and with her secret ear she understood them all.

"Math, Math," she cried softly as, above, the blackbird answered her mate, and on the hillside, the lamb the ewe. His hand trembled as he stroked her neck, her shoulder, her cheek; and her heart shook in reply. They were in some other world, where there was only grass, and sunlight, and music. Her heart sang, and his mouth made the melody against her skin.

His hair was so thick under her hand, like the grass under her body—nature's richness and fertility proven for her. He kissed her mouth as though he were drowning in the kiss, and lifted his lips again. He turned her head to one side, and kissed her left ear, her cheek. "How beautiful you are," he whispered, as though he were scarcely conscious of his own words, but with a little shock, Elain became conscious of them. His kisses and his voice followed the curve of her neck from her ear down to her shoulder, and then he was unbuttoning the top button on her shirt, and pulling aside the fabric to kiss her shoulder, her chest . . . her breast . . .

"Beautiful, my be . . ." she heard, and then all her blood was cold in her veins. In an eyeblink she was ice from fire. She was starving where before she had been offered abundance.

"No," she whispered in panic. "No, *no.*"

He lifted his head at once, and smiled gently at her, his eyes filled with the light of passion, his arms trembling with it. "What is it?" he asked, and she saw how his will was called into service to rein in a nearly all-encompassing passion.

No words of explanation came to her. She pushed at him. *"No!"* she cried. His body was still the length of hers, his right arm still embraced her. She felt his body tense in every muscle, his hands tighten on her.

"I see," he said. He swallowed, and his hair fell over his forehead, and there was a fire in his eyes as he looked at her that terrified her. But he closed them, and when he had opened them again, the light was gone. His arms loosed her, and he sat up away from her.

She was shivering with aftershock, as though she had been in an accident. She sat up and dropped her head forward, feeling chilled and sick. "I'm sorry," she whispered. "I'm sorry, I can't."

He heaved a breath. "All right," he said.

She began to cry. How had this happened? "I can't. I'm sorry."

"Yes, I see." For a moment he was silent as she wept. Then she was astonished to feel him draw her in against his chest. He held her gently, as a father might, comfort without possession in his hands. "It's all right," he said. His voice shook as though he, too, might be weeping, but he stroked her hair and let her cry against his chest, and told her it would be all right.

* * *

When he left her she stood in front of her easel, staring
down at the valley. The light was still good. She did not feel
in the least like painting, but the thought of meeting anyone if she went down to the hotel now made her stoop to
pick up her fallen palette and seat herself in front of the easel again.

The palette had defied the laws of perversity by falling
paint side up. She picked up her brush. She had been concentrating on the woman; the background of the valley was
only sketched in. She would paint that; in this mood she had
no patience for the delicate work on the woman. Watching
the valley, she bent and reached for a tube of cold titanium
white, and then for lamp black and Payne's grey, and
squeezed some out onto her palette. Then she began to paint
the valley.

She painted a lifeless, cold valley, a valley that might be
green to other eyes, but seen through the eyes of the woman
a valley of endless, barren winter, a valley where the Goddess never visited, where seeds never sprouted. She painted
a valley of emptiness, where the sap froze in the trunk and
blood dried in the vein. Where the ewe called but no lamb
answered. Where the blackbird flew without a mate. Where
the sun shone coldly in a grey sky. Where all the seasons
were one, and that one, unmoving winter. Where not even
rot occurred, for even decay is a sign and promise of life.

The tears dried on her cheeks as she painted, and she did
not cry again.

Later still, when she packed to go, she missed her Walkman. Reluctantly, unwillingly, she turned to the fortress behind her and moved to the entrance. The sun was lower in
the sky, and the tape recorder lay in the line of a long sweep
of sunshine that poured in through the door. She wiped her
hands on her jeans and stepped over to it.

She picked it up and fastened it to her waistband, found
her headphones and put them around her neck. She looked
around her then, and down at the green bed of grass that

covered the keep floor like a carpet, and wondered what had happened. What had possessed her, and him? Had it been the waiting woman's desire that she felt?

Elain turned and went back into the sunshine, and in curious detachment lifted the lid of her carrycase to reveal the picture. Her own painting seemed new to her now, as though she herself hadn't painted it. She saw its ugly bleakness in distant surprise, a kind of ugliness she hated and never allowed herself to paint, raw and cold and angry and beaten. She hated ugliness. If her paints had not been packed away, she would have taken a brush and obliterated the picture with bright red streaks of denial: there *is* life, there *is* beauty, even though there is none in me. And it will, it must triumph.

Yet even as the impulse flooded her, it abated, and she heard the thought in her, quiet as it was: *that's my life. I've painted my own life, barren as dead water.*

The sun was behind a clump of trees, and she shivered in their shadow and dropped the lid back. Who had almost made love to Math, and who had painted this picture? She must find out. She must think.

They were drinking tea in the garden, and called her to sit with them. Elain smiled and chatted for a moment, then excused herself, saying she must get her paints put away, and took her teacup with her to her room.

There she opened the windows wide and flung herself down on the bed. It was going to be too much for her. She should never have come here. When Raymond had said there had been a fire, she should have made an excuse.

Something was on the move in her, something strange and incomprehensible, and whatever it was, she knew it would no longer be held down.

She had awakened because she could not breathe. She remembered choking, gasping, but it was dark and she did not know that it was smoke that choked her. There was a roaring noise that she had never heard before, that terrified her.

She staggered to the door and opened it, and then it wasn't dark any more, but bright with red light and a sea of flames coming up the stairs.

Something bright fell on her, hot and terrible against her chest. Her hair caught fire and she screamed. Then her father was there, beating her head and shoulder with his bare hands to put out the flames, snatching her up into his arms and carrying her back into the bedroom. She felt his chest move as he coughed, felt how he swayed as he raised a foot to kick out her window.

Someone called out below. There were people running. "Jump! Jump!" she heard.

"Richard!" her father called. "I'll drop Elain out. Can you catch her?" Then there was the cold night air, and she clung around her father's neck.

"No!" she cried, loving him more in that moment than her heart could bear. She could feel it tearing with the intensity of her love, a child's heart too small for the strength of love that flooded through it. "You jump with me!" she begged. "You come, too!"

He had hugged her tightly, just for an instant. "I've got to go and get your mother," he said. "Then I'll come, Elain. Then I'll come."

"Promise!" she had cried, but she was already dropping through the icy air, and her cry was swept away by the wind. Arms caught her, and then, as the man who caught her fell back, she was in the snow, choking, and her face and chest were burning and freezing at the same time. Then they were carrying her away, and the house was a torch behind her, and she screamed, "Daddy! Daddy!" as the roof gave way with a roaring that was straight from hell.

She awoke in another kind of hell, one that was white and sterile and empty except for pain. Strangers came and looked at her through a glass, and talked among themselves and wrote things down. No one touched her. When they did, they put gloves on. They made sad faces and shook their heads when they looked at her. She thought it was because she was dirty or ugly that they could not bear to touch her, to look at her. And all the time she was drowned with pain. Breathing was pain. Moving was pain. Consciousness was pain.

After an eternity, there were faces she recognized at the glass. Her grandparents, crying and trying to smile at her. "Oh, my poor baby," said her grandmother, making that same sad face. Her grandmother never touched her, either. That was when she knew how terrible a thing she had become, because her grandmother always touched her, hugged her, loved her. Her grandparents never even came inside the horrid white cocoon they had put her in. They stood outside and waved and wept.

"Where's my father?" she said to the people in white, but they didn't answer, turning away in embarrassment. "Where's Daddy?" she asked her grandparents. "He promised to come."

"He can't come right now, sweetheart," they said. "He can't come."

"He went for Mommy," she said. "Did he find Mommy? He said they would come."

"He can't come now," her grandfather said, because her grandmother was weeping too much to speak.

"When will he come?" she asked, and to this there was no answer. After awhile the question changed. "Will he come?" she asked then. But even to this question there was never a reply.

In her child's heart she answered the question as she wished it answered, as it *must* be answered. "He will come," she told herself. And when the words had no power to comfort her, she said them more loudly, more determinedly. "He *will* come! He will!"

One day her grandfather stood there with one of the people in white. "It's going to have to be done, I'm afraid. We've left it as long as we dare, and it's not recovering. The damage is too deep."

After that there were different kinds of pain. The skin of her leg hurt high near her hip, and now there was a white bandage there, too. "It went very well," said the man in white to her grandfather. "I expect the graft to take."

Then she was in the bed she sometimes slept in when they visited her grandparents. People came to visit, and when they looked at her they smiled sadly and shook their heads. "She was such a beautiful child," they said to her grandmother. "What a dreadful pity."

There was something wrong with her hair. She couldn't understand that. Her mother used to comb her hair every morning and every night, and she always combed it all the way down her back, and they would laugh and measure where it came. Every night her mother would press her back to tell her where her hair was now, and she remembered how the pressure had changed over time, moving slowly from the centre of her back down to her waist....

Now her grandmother only brushed over her scalp, and never showed her the mirror when she was through. It hurt when she combed, but even so, Elain said, "Why don't you comb it all, Grandma? Why don't you comb down my back?" Her grandmother wept then, dropping the brush and putting her face in her hands and sobbing aloud. She was sitting on the lid of the toilet, and Elain turned and put her arms around her. "It's all right, Grandma," she said. "It'll be all right when Daddy comes."

Her grandmother had let out a terrible sob then, and wrapped the child in her arms. "Oh, my darling, your daddy isn't coming, my sweet, he can't come ever again. Oh, my sweet, your poor hair, your poor face!" She put her hand under Elain's chin and kissed her tenderly, her lips wet with tears. "Oh, my darling, I wish he would come, too, but he can't. He's with your mother, and with God."

"How long is he going to stay with God?" Elain asked.

"Forever, my darling," her grandmother said softly. "He won't ever come, my dearest. But you have us now, and we have you, and we love you very much."

She understood that her hair and her face were ugly now, and that was why her father wouldn't come back. Her father had always called her his little beauty, and it was for her father's sake that she and her mother had shared the secret joy of her growing hair, because her father had loved her long, shining hair. Her mother used to tie ribbons in it, and when her father came home she would run to the door to meet him. And he would come through the door and look at her, and say, "Oh, my, aren't you beautiful tonight! Are those ribbons in your hair for me?"

"Put ribbons in my hair," she said to her grandmother. "Then my father will come."

But the charm did not work. Her grandmother was right. They never came back.

A window banged in the breeze, and Elain rolled over to look at her watch. If she was going to change for dinner, she would have to hurry.

She stood under the shower, willing it to wash away the memories, but the British shower that will do that doesn't exist. This one was particularly bad, the water coming out grudgingly, hot and cold not well mixed, so that half her scalp was scalded and half simultaneously frozen. But the last few years of similar showers had made her practically immune to such deficiencies. She turned it full on and stood with her face under the gentle bipartite stream and vigorously pretended.

Back in her room, she dried herself, avoiding the full-length mirror until she had on bra and pants. Then she stood looking at herself for a moment. She had long, curving, neatly muscled legs; slim but rounded hips that ran up to a small, firm waistline; her breasts...

She was being an idiot to think what she was thinking about Math, she told herself ruthlessly. Even if her whole history didn't stand up and cry out against the risk, the fact was that she was investigating Math's connection to arson! What a fool she would be to let herself get involved. Somehow the only man to have got under her skin for years was the very one she could not allow herself to even hope to trust. She smiled ruefully at the way life was.

But she was bloody lucky things were the way they were, she reminded herself ruthlessly. Under any other circumstances, she might have been tempted to run the risk. She had enough self-knowledge to see that. That was why she had been so afraid of him, because Math could get under her skin. She must have sensed that from the beginning. Known even before he touched her that his touch must be avoided. Suppose she had let herself go, in the fortress? Suppose she had let him undress her.... It was like the shower all over again. She went cold and hot at once. Cold with fear, hot with desire.

What a risk she was running, staying here.

Oh, but look at the time! And her hair was still soaking wet. She'd better get a move on. She ran to the dresser and pulled out her portable hair-dryer, unravelling the cord as she looked around for a socket. There was none showing on any of the walls. The lamp by the bed must be plugged into the only socket in the room.

She crawled under the bed, feeling blindly along the wall and finding nothing. The socket must be higher up, behind the springs. The bed was hard to shift and it would only go in one direction; that meant moving the bedside table. As she did that, the lamp came to the end of its cord and tilted gently off the table. Elain caught it just in time, barking her knee on the table as she did so.

The towel fell off her head and wet hair fell down over her face, blinding her, but she managed to get the lamp safely onto the bed.

There was a curious silver tinkle in the air, as though a bell laughed. Elain, absorbed, scarcely noticed it. She shoved her hair behind her ears, bent and heaved the heavy bedstead with all her strength. It moved two inches, and that would have to do. She knelt with the plug of the dryer in her hand, felt along the wall in the narrow space, and at last managed to align the three-pronged plug with the empty socket holes and force it in. With a sigh of achievement she stood up, dropped her hair forward and pushed the switch on the dryer.

There was a small popping sound from the socket and the dryer whined and died.

She went down to dinner wearing a cream-coloured sleeveless tunic dress in knitted silk, with her wet hair held back by a scarf. The dining room was lit by candles, and people were laughing and joking at several tables. Elain remembered suddenly that there were outside guests in tonight.

"How is Myfanwy at cooking by lamplight?" a woman was asking over the laughter.

"Myfanwy could cook blindfolded, I think," said a deep, amused voice. Math. Elain shivered with nerves and forced herself to step into the room.

"Hi, Elain," said Jan, appearing at her elbow in the gloom. "Where would you like to sit?"

One corner of the room was still lit by the rays of the setting sun, the light falling on an empty table for two tucked into the corner. "Over there?" Elain suggested.

"I'll just get a menu." Elain started moving towards the table, and suddenly Math was there in front of her, leading her to the table and pulling out the chair for her. She sank into it as Jan arrived, and he took the menu from her.

"Would you bring another, Jan?" he asked. Then he pulled out the chair opposite her and calmly, as if it were the habit of years, sat down. He opened the menu and offered it to Elain. "Myfanwy's garlic mushrooms are on offer tonight," he said, smiling. "I can recommend them."

She looked at him in the half-light, saying nothing as Jan returned with another menu and lit the candle on the table. As soon as the young woman had walked away, Elain, her head bent, said, "I'm sorry."

She was clutching her hands tightly on the menu, but when he reached out, she had to give him one. He held it between both of his, his elbows propped on the table, and bent and kissed her fingertips. Then he looked into her eyes, the flame of the candle deep in his own. "Don't apologize to me," he said roughly. He released her hand with a controlled urgency that betokened great restraint, and she felt an unexpected thrill at the thought that he wanted to be touching her.

He picked up the menu and opened it. It was very limited—two or three choices for each course, and all listed on one page. "Do you like the sound of the garlic mushrooms?" he asked. His voice was easy now; no trace remained of the tension that had roughened it a moment ago. She nodded mutely, and he grinned. "Good. Are you a steak eater? If not, the vegetarian omelette is excellent."

"The steak, please." He had put up a hand, and Jan came over to take their order. She wrote in quick code as she questioned them about their choices.

"And a bottle of Mouton Cadet," Math told her as he passed her back the menu.

"Would you like to drive with me into Aberystwyth tomorrow?" he asked, when Jan had gone.

"Are you going?" she asked stupidly. Math nodded. "Would the library be open?"

He nodded again. "That's where I'm going."

She was surely safe in a car with him, and she wanted to find out about her ancestors if she could. "All right, yes, please," she said.

"I see our ghost is at it again," Rosemary said loudly, entering the dining room with Davina in her wake. "Most unpleasant timing!"

Math turned in his chair. "Jess never messes with electricity, Rosemary," he said.

Elain smiled. "Why doesn't she?"

Math moved his head, grinning. "She doesn't understand it. After her time."

"I'm not so sure," Rosemary said, striding to a table but remaining standing to deliver as, behind her, Jan lit the little candle. "I was just walking across the room and nearly tripped on the edge of the carpet when the lights went out! Just her sort of trick, I thought."

"Believe me, the electricity in this house has all the temperament necessary for a thing like this. It's just a simple short somewhere, and as soon as Evan finds it, we'll be fine," Math said.

Elain started guiltily. "Oh! I never thought! I—I was just turning on my hair-dryer when it blew. I was in such a hurry I never thought—do you think—?"

Math burst out laughing. "Jan," he called. "Go and tell Evan it's the wall socket in Llewelyn's Room." He turned to Rosemary and shrugged good-humouredly. "You see?" he said. "Candles are more Jess's style. When you get a problem with a candle, you can count on its being her."

"I don't think you understand your own ghost," Rosemary said, and sat down. In front of her, the candle flame slowly weakened and then died altogether.

The room burst into laughter, and several people called out things like, "Hi, Jess! Nice to see you again!" into the air.

Elain was laughing, too, but abruptly she stopped, frowned and tilted her head. "What's that?" she asked Math. She turned to the other side, trying to hear. "What *is* it? I heard it awhile ago, too. Up in my room."

"What?"

"It—a funny kind of tinkling, like a—I don't know, a little bell or something. I can't describe it. There! Can you hear that?"

"Usually. Not everybody can. They say it's Jess laughing. According to tradition, she had laughter like a silver bell."

The corners of Elain's mouth went up in spite of herself. "It *is* like infectious laughter, isn't it? It makes me feel like laughing."

"Ah." Math lifted his hands. "Jess welcomes you to the White Lady Hotel."

The next hour was difficult and nerve-racking, with Math sitting across the small table from her. His attention was always on her, gently, lightly, but there, and it was magnetic.

She mistrusted the magnetism, even as it drew her, feeling that he stood on the other side of a chasm, and if she allowed him to draw her to him, she would fall into the chasm.

Other men had paid her attention in the past, of course, but with other men she had had no difficulty disengaging. Their attempts to attract her had seemed crude and obvious, and their own self-interest had always been so clear that sometimes she had been hard-pushed not to laugh.

But Math was different, drawing her out gently, letting her talk about things that mattered to her and seeming actually interested. There was an air about him of acceptance, as though he knew all about her and accepted everything. He was like a farmer, sniffing the rich earth of her character and finding it good—embracing the truth, as the farmer does, that in fertile ground there is always rot and decay.

It was this that unsettled her, though probably she could not have put her feelings into words. To her, it was as though he were painting her; and by that she meant the feeling she sometimes had of loving her subject, whatever it was, with all its warts and flaws.

It was a wordless invitation to lower her guard, and it naturally frightened Elain, who had lowered her guard once in the past twenty years, and had then been utterly defenceless when the boots came in.

Suddenly she was remembering what lines this conversation should have taken this evening. She glanced down at the evening bag in her lap. Inside, her tape recorder lay unused.

Math was saying, "There's plenty of time to visit the library on a wet day. If it's sunny tomorrow, perhaps you'd rather go up Cadair Idris."

She had a feeling of being trapped. How close would he get before she found it impossible to get away from him, before she was sucked into a vortex of trusting him, needing him? She was already nearly defenceless, as she had been with...

"I'm not sure I'm going to be here long enough to do everything I ought to do," she said with a smile.

"We must try to keep you here," he said. That sounded offhand, as if he didn't much care, so why was her heart beating as though it had been a threat?

Elain opened her bag and took out a tissue. She pushed the Record button, closed the bag and laid it casually on the table. She felt better suddenly, more in control. She had a job to do, after all.

"It's certainly a wonderful place," she said truthfully. "I think I could spend years here, painting. But I suppose the peace is going to be shattered soon."

He raised his eyebrows. "Is it? Why?"

"Well, when you start renovating, because of the fire. You'll be doing that soon, won't you?"

He shrugged. "I can't afford to do much till the insurance pays up. It doesn't look as though that's going to be soon."

"Oh, why not?" She wondered if the question sounded as false to his ears as to her own. But he didn't seem to notice.

"I imagine they're looking for proof of arson. That's the usual excuse for delay."

"Oh! Do you think they'll find any? I mean, do you think it was arson?"

He shrugged again. "The circumstances are unusual. Nobody remembers ever seeing those petrol cans in the cellar. Yet they are certainly fifty years old. But I can't see who would have wanted to do it, or why."

Elain frowned. "But who do they think could benefit, except you? The Welsh Nationalists?"

"Certainly not me," he said matter-of-factly. "The Welsh Nationalists do a certain amount of firing, but never, so far, of Welsh-owned property. It would be little short of amazing if they had decided to torch this property, three years after the English owner had sold up. And I've had to let half a dozen people go since the fire, all of them Welsh, and all from this community. They wouldn't have wanted that."

Elain grunted. "Is there no one else?"

"If anyone wants me out, they've been extremely reti-cent about saying so. There have been no expressions of in-terest in the place since I bought it, and Vinnie says there was none at all before I came along. The place hasn't been ren-ovated since just after the war, and the plumbing, as you've probably noticed, dates from the Victorian era. Nowadays, tourists want bathrooms *en suite* and central heating. Even in peak season it was rarely fully booked, and until I brought in Myfanwy, few non-residents came to the restau-rant." He spoke as though he was still trying to work it out, as though something about it bothered him.

"Why did you buy it, then? Are you planning major conversions?" That was what the company suspected, Raymond had said, that he had torched it so that he could rebuild from scratch on the insurance money.

"I am planning restoration," said Math.

Elain blinked. "What?"

"I don't want a hotel. I plan to remove most of the Vic-torian and all of the postwar additions and restore it to something closer to the original. Llewelyn's Room, where you're staying, is restored."

"And what then?"

As if absent-mindedly, he picked up her hand and held it between both of his, turning it over and looking at the palm. "Then live here, of course. What else?"

"And won't you be able to do that now?"

He traced her lifeline with one long finger, and she felt the whisper of its passing along her scalp and spine. She closed her fingers and took her hand away.

"I can, of course. And I will. But some very beautiful seventeenth-century woodwork has been destroyed by the fire, and there was a fifteenth-century tapestry hanging in the back sitting room that was a museum piece. It will be impossible to replace, even if the insurance pays its anti-quarian value." She could hear the regret in his tone.

"What was the subject?"

"It was a scene from the *Mabinogion*. 'The Dream of Rhonabwy.' Do you know it?"

Elain had heard of the collection of ancient tales that made up the Welsh national epic, but that was all. She shook her head. "I've never read any of those stories."

"'The Dream of Rhonabwy' tells of a game of *gwyddbwyll* played between Owein ap Uryen and King Arthur. The tapestry showed them at the game in the centre of a host of tents and pavilions and the troops of the various leaders—Rhuvawn the Radiant of Deorthach, Caradawg Strong Arm, March ap Meirchyawn and Cadwr, Earl of Cornwall—who have come to do battle with Arthur against Osla Big Knife."

"Oh! I wish I could have seen it!" Elain exclaimed spontaneously, her imagination abruptly falling under the spell of his voice and the romance of the names.

"Yes, the woman who did it was certainly an artist of the needle. The story describes the colours of the horses and troops, and they were faithfully reproduced in the tapestry."

"Do you have a picture of it? There are people who—"

Math shook his head. "I had Sotheby's due to come in October, when the season was over."

"I'm so sorry," she said.

"I am, too. Even more so because—" He broke off.

"What?"

Math let out a deep breath. "It was irreplaceable. It was unforgivable of me not to have taken better precautions. A piece of history that probably took a lifetime to produce and had lasted centuries went up in five minutes of smoke." He shrugged. "I had been told it ought to go into storage or to a museum, but I liked living with it."

"How much was it actually worth?"

"Somewhere over fifty thousand pounds, perhaps."

"Really," Elain said. If that was what was bothering the insurance company, it seemed like a lot of fuss over a relatively small amount. After all, one oil tanker could cost them hundreds of millions.

"At auction, one never knows," Math was saying. "Traditionally, needlepoint tapestries haven't the same value as woven tapestries, which might be worth half a million, but this one was rare and in very good condition. And of course, there is an increasing interest in Welsh traditions and history."

"Still, it's a fair bit of money."

He grinned at her. "It wasn't valued at that sum. The last valuation was done twenty years ago, at about five thousand pounds. It will be the devil's own work, trying to prove a higher value." His look was rueful. "No, it was a complete loss. There's no silver lining to this story."

Chapter 6

Elain sat on her bed with the tiny cassette tape in her hand. He hadn't done it. They could scarcely think him guilty of arson when he was so badly underinsured. Pulling out a pen and the folder of labels, she wrote the date and marked it with a star, to remind herself of the importance of the conversation, then fixed it to the tape.

She supposed her job was over now. She would phone Raymond from the village tomorrow, and no doubt he would tell her to return.

Idly she slipped the tape into the machine. Maybe she should make notes so that she could give Raymond exact quotes tomorrow.

The machine played both sides of a tape automatically, an hour and a half's running time altogether. In addition, the mike was voice sensitive, so that in periods of silence it simply shut itself off. Elain wound it back to the beginning of Side One, put her headphones on, lay back and pressed Play.

"Yr wyf i yn dy garu di," she heard Math say again, and shot up to a sitting position as if she had been scalded. What on earth was this! *"Fy nghalon i."*

And then there was her own voice crying, "Math, Math," and sounding nothing like her.

Her heart beating wildly, Elain chopped her hand down onto the controls and stopped the tape. How on earth had this happened? She must have... When he picked her up, perhaps, or when he laid her down, somehow the machine had been turned on.

She wouldn't listen to it. She couldn't bear to hear all that—her panic, her... She would just wipe it. Raymond was going to want the tape, and she wasn't letting anyone hear this!

But slowly, impossibly, her finger reached out and pressed the machine into play. "So beautiful," he said in that deep, hypnotic voice. "How beautiful you are."

That was what had brought her to her senses, because she wasn't beautiful. If he hadn't said that, would she...? No. It was when he'd touched her breast that she had really panicked. When he had begun unbuttoning her shirt. Elain glanced up into the full-length mirror standing across the room. She saw deep auburn hair and delicate eyebrows curving exotically out over grey eyes, skin the colour of rich cream, a small but full-lipped mouth.

Was she beautiful? She had heard other men say those words, too, but none of them had ever affected her the way Math did. She had never before been tempted to believe what any of them said. Might she be beautiful, in spite of everything?

"So beautiful."

Slowly, as if mesmerized, she stood up and moved closer to the mirror, his voice in her ears, telling her how beautiful she was. Only the lamp was alight, and in its soft golden glow she felt a kind of courage and determination she had not known before. "Beautiful," said Math, and then he repeated those other words—the same thing in Welsh, perhaps. *"Yr wyf i yn dy garu di."*

She stopped the tape and gently set it down on the chair beside the mirror. She pulled off the scarf tied around her head and dropped it to the floor. Then she bent and caught the hem of her tunic, and pulled it up over her head, tossing it onto the chair. She stood for a moment in bra and pants, and then she lifted her arms up behind and unhooked the bra clasp.

It fell down her arms, and her full, rounded breasts sprang willingly from confinement. For the first time in years, Elain looked at her own naked breasts.

Her face had not needed grafts, thanks to her father's speed in putting out the fire in her hair. Her ear had been damaged, and a small section of her scalp behind, but her face, mercifully, would heal, given time.

It had healed, but it had taken nearly two years for the redness to fade, and in that two years she had looked very strange, the left half of her forehead and cheek bright red, the right half creamy white, as though she were perpetually blushing with only one half of her face.

Even adults had made remarks. Friends her own age had been unbearably cruel. Some had simply burst into laughter when they saw her, and she had smouldered in her inarticulate pain and fury, making the red skin burn even more brightly.

Until her hair grew, the bald patch behind her ear and the burn-damaged tip of her ear had been hideously obvious. "Hey, Redskin, was your father *half*-Indian?" "Someone tried to scalp her!" "Musta been that half-redskin dad."

Even teachers had been staggeringly ignorant sometimes, showing no understanding of what had caused the behavioural changes they could see, and beginning to respond to the once-bright child's sullen, bewildered despair with sarcasm, or worse. "You used to know the answer to this, Elain. Please try harder or we'll be thinking you were brain-damaged."

After two years, it had seemed it was all over. Her hair had grown over the empty patch and was long enough to

hide her ear, which had healed well; the angry red of her facial skin had disappeared entirely. People simply forgot that
she had ever been disfigured, and even Elain was slowly beginning to forget how she had become ugly and unlovable
overnight.

She had scarcely noticed the square on her chest, once the
pain had faded. Grandmother always bought her halter-top
swimsuits, and people didn't seem to notice the patch of
darker skin that had come from her thigh.

But then her breasts began to grow. And her junior high
school had a swimming pool, and the girls' changing room
was communal. One day, she heard, "My God, Elain, one
of your nipples is higher than the other!" And she had
looked in the mirror and it was true.

All the humiliation and crippling embarrassment and
sense of her own physical disfigurement came roaring back
into her heart. Desperate to be normal, she went to the doc-
tor. Nothing could be done. It was a common story: the skin
from the thigh wasn't quite as flexible as normal breast skin.
It would probably never relax to the point where both
breasts would look the same. They would be the same size,
because the skin at the bottom of her breast would compensate. But the nipple on her left breast, drawn up by the
tighter skin of the graft, would always ride high, and the
oblong patch of skin would always be a slightly different
colour, worse if she tanned. She should consider herself
lucky. It would not prevent her breast-feeding her children.
She had escaped with a very minor disfigurement, when she
might have died.

Slowly she had learned to accept it, and although she
never stopped feeling deformed, when girls asked her about
the patch, she said calmly, "I was in a fire. I was very
lucky," and found that her own acceptance prevented the
violent reactions she so hated.

But that was before she met Greg. Elain turned from the
mirror, impatiently snatched up her pyjama top, and slipped
it on. She climbed into bed and put out the light. Greg had
thought she was beautiful, too, she reminded herself, until

he undressed her. And she wasn't risking going through that again as long as she lived.

She met Math at breakfast. "I won't come with you into Aberystwyth," she said. "I think I'd rather paint."

"It'll be clear all day," Math said. "It's a good day for the mountains. How about a picnic on Cadair Idris?"

"Thank you, I want to paint," Elain repeated firmly.

"Myfanwy's picnic lunches are the envy of non-residents everywhere."

She couldn't help laughing. But she knew this temptation had to be resisted. The water there was deeper than she could cope with. "Another time." But there would be no other time. With a little luck, she'd be leaving today.

He smiled at her, a slow, knowing smile that was balm to her sore, empty heart. God, she couldn't get out of here too quickly.

Math left a few minutes later for Aberystwyth. Elain, feeling let down, sat alone over her coffee until Vinnie and Jeremy arrived. "Painting again today?" asked Vinnie.

"Probably, but first I need a little exercise. I thought I'd go for a walk down to the village. How long will that take, do you think?" Yesterday she had driven.

"By the road, half an hour. But it's a very nice walk if you go by the public footpath. That runs by the fortress on the other side of the hill, about twenty yards down from the wall. If you take that to the right, it'll take you down through the forest, and Pontdewi is only about twenty minutes away."

She climbed over the wall, and scrambled through the heather, and then used the stile over the stone fence that protected the hotel grounds from grazing sheep. Upset by her presence, half a dozen of them set off running down the hillside. "Trust me," Elain called after them. But they took no notice.

The footpath ran beside the stone wall and then dropped down the slope and into the forest. It was a cool, pleasant

walk, and soon she was standing in the old-fashioned red
telephone box, fishing in her pocket for coins.

"Fast work," Raymond said approvingly, when she had
reported. "I'll check in with the client. Call me again in a
couple of days."

She wailed faintly. "Can't I come home now?"

"Whatsa matter, Red? You getting antsy for the big city
already?" he asked in a mock-American accent.

"Well . . ."

"Sorry, I wouldn't want to do anything rash here. My
clients aren't being totally frank with me on this one, and I
want you there till they give me the all-clear."

So much for the quick escape. Elain hung up and stood
for a moment in the village street, the sun pouring down on
her head. One pub, the George. One tiny little shop-cum-
post office. Nothing else. But the George was offering
morning coffees and afternoon teas in the garden, according to the blackboard stand. Elain crossed the road.

"You're staying at the White Lady, are you?" the waitress remarked, as she brought a tray of coffee and cookies.
"Terrible pity that was, the fire. My sister-in-law used to
work for Math, you know, but he hasn't the guests now, has
he?"

"Only a handful," agreed Elain.

"Terrible pity." She seemed inclined to gossip, Elain being her only customer so early in the morning.

"I wonder how the fire started?" she said.

"Well, it wasn't Jess, the way those women are saying,"
replied the waitress, with some heat.

Almost as a matter of habit, Elain's finger found the
button on her Walkman. "You don't believe that ghosts
turn?"

"I don't know about other ghosts," the waitress said. "I
never heard of it before, but I suppose as they're professional what-do-you-call-its and all, they must know. But we
know Jess. Jess would never have started that fire. She just
laughs, does Jess."

"Yes, I heard her."

The waitress smiled. "Did you now? Well, that's a sign that she likes you. Did you know that?"

Elain shook her head.

"People lie about it, but you can always tell who has really heard it, and who hasn't."

"Would you have another cup going spare, Gwen?" asked a voice, and Elain whirled so sharply she spilled her coffee.

"I thought you were going to Aberystwyth," she said accusingly.

"So did I," Math agreed. "But the closer I got to the sea, the more it seemed like a waste to spend such a day inside a library. We don't always have good weather in Wales, by a long way. So I came back to see if you'd like to go swimming in the sea. Thank you," he said to the waitress as she brought another cup. "They said you'd come to the village. I thought *you* were going to paint."

He regarded her with a grin, as if he had caught her out. She blushed. "Well, I am. But I wanted a little exercise first."

"Swimming is very good exercise. The sea is only a few minutes away." Math poured his coffee and stirred sugar into it, then looked up at her with a smile. Before she could answer that, he said, "You've been talking to Gwen about Jess?"

Thank God he hadn't come in time to hear her asking about the fire. "That's right. It's kind of unusual, isn't it?"

"Is it? After awhile, she just seems a part of life here, like the sheep and the bad plumbing."

"Will you tell me about her sometime?" Strange words from a girl who thought she'd be leaving tomorrow, but Elain hardly noticed.

"I will," said Math. He finished his coffee, stood up and dropped a couple of pound coins on the table. "Come on."

"What?"

"I'll tell you about Jess at the seaside," he said.

* * *

She had a green halter-top swimsuit, the fabric of the straps so loosely pleated that almost all evidence of the graft was hidden. Math wore black cotton boxer trunks, not in the least figure-hugging, but very sexy nonetheless. The sun glinted blindingly from the sea, and the air was so fresh her London-bred lungs could scarcely cope with it.

They swam and then lazed on a blanket, and then the inevitable moment came.

"Your skin is very fair. Where's your sun cream?" he asked.

He had put up an umbrella, but she was so hungry for the sunshine that she hadn't stayed in the shade. But he was right. She burned easily. "I've got it here," she said. He held out a hand, and like a hypnotized rabbit, she dug into her bag and brought out a large tube of sunblock gel and gave it to him.

And then Math calmly untied the knot at her neck and dropped the straps down.

The straps were entirely decorative; the suit itself had a boned stay-up bra, and the straps were designed to be tied around the neck or under the breasts in a floppy bow. But Elain had never before bared her shoulders in public, and she gasped as if he had left her naked. Her hands flew to her breasts, and then she blushed, feeling stupid. She bent forward over her knees as he squirted the cool gel on her back.

She had bought her suit at a specialty shop for women who had had mastectomy, but had not lost all sense of style along with their breast. The suit was cut high at the thighs, and low in the back, where a large triangle was cut out over the small of the back to compensate for the coverage in front. As Math's hands moved over her, she realized just how deep the V of the cut went—all the way to the cleft of her buttocks.

He covered every bare inch of shoulders, neck and back, and then some. She felt his fingers slide just under the edge of the fabric, around the top of the band across her shoulder blades, and then around the V cut-out. This touch of hands inside her clothing was so deeply and unfamiliarly sensuous that she bit her lip against a cry.

It was like electricity running over her as her starved body leaped to respond to the touch it needed. She could say nothing, do nothing, hypnotized by the stroking, like a cat. She knew she should stop him, but if she allowed herself to move a muscle, it would not be to get away from him. If she stood up, her legs would not support her.

"Lie back," he commanded, and the sound of his voice was like another touch, making her shiver in the heat. She lay back, her hands still holding the green straps to her chest. He delicately rubbed the gel onto the skin of her face, over her nose, under her eyes, around and across her mouth with a stroke of his thumb that was all the more erotic for being completely undeliberate.

Gently he drew her hands away from her chest and lifted the soft folds of the fabric. She kept her eyes shut tight, biting her lip as, inevitably, his fingers found the edge of the discoloured patch of skin showing over the bra top. She felt no check in his movement, nothing to signify that he had seen it, yet in the bright sunlight she knew he must.

"I was burned," she whispered, as his hands stroked across the top of her breasts from left to right.

"Were you? I'm sorry." She felt the lightest of touches then, indescribably gentle, above her left breast, and something was tickling her chin. Elain opened her eyes, and the breath rasped in her throat as if she were dying of oxygen starvation.

The soft touch was his lips, the tickling his black hair as he bent over her. "What are you *doing?*" she whispered, hoarse with fear or fury, she could not have said which.

He lifted his head and looked down at her. "I'm kissing you."

"Don't," she said. *"Don't."*

He took that in with a small frown of puzzlement. "Why not?"

"I was burned there," she said, as foolishly inarticulate as a child. "It's a skin graft."

"Does it still hurt to be touched?" he asked in surprise. "It looks very well healed."

"No," said Elain. "But—"

"Good," he said, and he smiled at her with an expression she couldn't read in his eyes before bending to kiss her again, with a mouth that was suddenly electric.

After that he covered her arms and legs with the cooling gel, while she lay all but trembling under his ministrations. His touch was never overtly sexual, but when his hands were high on the inside of her thighs, it did not need to be. Nor when he stroked the inside of her elbow, nor the soles of her feet. Nor anywhere. Her body translated it all, and if he had decided to make love to her there on the beach, she could scarcely have resisted.

At last he was finished, and she felt cooling shadow over her and knew he had pulled the umbrella to shade her. She sensed him settle by her side. She could no longer feel the blanket or the sand under her. Her body was so full of electricity she must be levitating. She lay feeling drunk on sheer physical sensation. A fly landed briefly on her arm and she felt every inch of skin shiver into goose bumps.

"Are you asleep?" he asked softly.

Was he kidding? Asleep? She had never been so awake in her life. Elain licked her lips and tasted the strange flavour of mint and eucalyptus in a chemical base. "No."

"Are you ready for your ghost story?"

She had no idea what he was talking about. Ghost story? In the middle of the day on a sunny beach when she was levitating from sensual excitement?

"Okay," she said, because any protest was beyond her.

"Her name was Jessica," Math began.

Oh, *that* ghost story!

"She was a descendant of the original builder of the house, they say, and she was her father's only child. Or some say he had a son who had bad blood, whom he could never love. Jess was a pretty child and grew into a beautiful young woman cherished by her father. When she was seventeen he chose a husband for her—an excellent marriage. But she had already fallen in love with the son of one of his own tenants down in the village. No one knows for sure that he was a farmer, but he probably was.''

''Who did her father want her to marry?'' Elain asked, getting interested in spite of her physical state.

''The son of his sister, who was married to a neighbouring lord. Our Jess refused. Her lover came up to the big house to see her father and claim her hand, saying that as he already had her heart, it belonged to him and no other.''

''Oh! Wasn't that pretty brave of him?''

''It was quite a statement for its time. He was horsewhipped for his pains. He sent a message to her father that, if he did not get his permission, he would take her away and the old man would never see his grandchildren.''

''He said that to the lord of the manor? That sounds a little rash.'' Elain opened her eyes and looked up, because she was going to have to look at him sometime. He was lying on one elbow beside her. She seemed to see him through a sensual haze, as if he had an aura of warm sunlight. ''What if her father locked her up?''

Math smiled, his mouth wide and generous, his teeth strong and white. Elain shivered and closed her eyes again.

''They say the lover must have been a master of the dark arts, for he had a way of getting right inside the house without being seen. They say, too, that he often spent the night in Jess's bed with no one knowing, slipping away before dawn broke. It was said that he had hypnotized her, and it doesn't take a strong imagination to see that they were saying he had a sexual hold over her.''

Well, Elain could understand that. So far no one had ever had a sexual hold over her, but today she could see how it might happen.

''Whether it was because he used the dark arts on Jess or not, she agreed to elope with her lover.'' She wished he would stop saying "lover" like that, the word dark in his mouth, and so full of meaning and promise. "But on the night that they planned their flight, they were discovered. Her maid betrayed her, and he was caught in the house with a horse at the door."

"Oh." She breathed a moment. "Did they kill him?"

"No one knows. He disappeared when they had him surrounded. The men said he had turned into a bird and so escaped." Absently he rubbed her arm where there were a few beads of the gel. She could feel her sweat as a slippery bond between the palm of his hand and her skin. She wished he would touch her lips again. "A stonemason was called up from the village, and afterwards it was said that he had been forced to wall up a door."

"Oh, my God!" Elain started and sat up. She had been wishing he would kiss her, but if he did . . . "Do you mean she was immured and starved to death or something?"

Math shook his head. "Not then, anyway. Jess was pregnant by her lover, and a few months later she was delivered of a healthy son, whom she named for him. But she did die soon afterwards. The grandson she had given her father was the only grandchild he would ever have, the only chance he had of leaving the land to one of his own blood." He lifted the tube of sunblock, one eyebrow raised quizzically. "Will you do my back?"

Ah. "Yeah, sure." She took the tube and stared at it uncertainly. Why did it suddenly seem to be a rattlesnake in her hands? He turned and lay on his stomach, and she scrambled to her knees beside him. How strong his neck and shoulder muscles looked. She squirted, and the gel came out in a long, liquid spray all across his shoulders and down his side. Nervously she dropped the tube and began to rub.

His skin was so *hot.* He was sweating, too, and the sweat mixed erotically with the gel under her palms. Idly she found herself wondering if his sweat-soaked skin would taste of salt . . . if he would be as warm to her lips as he was to her hands . . . how lovers held each other when they were so sweaty and slippery. . . .

"Otherwise it would go to the children of his sister's son. It seems the old man didn't want that."

"Do you mean that he wanted to leave it to the child of his tenant's son, the man he wouldn't let marry his daughter?"

Her thighs were wet with sweat; the day was getting very hot. Did people sweat all over when they made love? Did it matter?

He had a mole high on one shoulder, but his back was otherwise without a blemish, his skin smooth under her touch. She rubbed his shoulders and deltoids, and as he sighed and eased his neck, watched the play of muscles under his skin. "Ah, that's good," he said as though he liked the feel of her hands on him.

She had strong hands; painting developed the muscles. She began to massage his neck, feeling his energy, his vitality flow upwards from his blood to hers, and thence to her heart. She felt they were cocooned in a glow of heat. His thighs were beaded with water, too, sweat or the sea, and his calves were covered in fine black hair and caked with a thin layer of sand. No doubt it would feel gritty against her skin if she touched him there.

"He clearly did."

She blinked, roused from her sensuous reverie. "Did what?"

"Want the child to inherit his kingdom. Perhaps he felt remorse."

"But—he was illegitimate. Surely—"

His face on his arms, eyes closed, Math grinned. "Probably, but we'll never know for sure. A few months after the baby's birth, a record was discovered in the village register of a marriage between Jess and her lover, performed by the village priest almost a year before. So the old man was able to declare the child legitimate and his heir."

"They had been married all along? Why didn't they just tell him so? What could he have done?"

Math rolled over in mute invitation for her to do his chest. That, like his legs, was covered with curling black hair and beaded with liquid. She looked down at the dark purple nipples, the flatly muscled stomach and the whorls of his navel as if this were a foreign country, dangerous for the uninitiated. Then she squirted cool gel into her hand and slowly laid her hand on his stomach.

He was silent for a moment, taking one deep breath that made his stomach slowly rise and fall under her touch. "There has always been the suspicion that the marriage register was forged, at the behest of Jessica's father. The priest lived very well to the end of his days, it's said, and so long as he was alive, whenever you needed a favour from the big house, if you could get the priest on your side, you'd won the battle."

"And the boy inherited the estate?"

"In the fullness of time, he did."

"So why does Jess stay around? Waiting for her lo . . . for him to come and get her? And later, perhaps, to watch her son grow up, and then . . . she just got used to being here," Elain said, talking half to herself. His nipples grew taut under her touch, but he didn't seem to take any notice. She grew bolder. It was a new experience, touching a naked—a nearly naked man, and without any risk. It was so public, and so ordinary, she lied firmly to herself. It was what anyone would do. . . .

"Is that what you would have done? Waited for him even after death?" The curve of his thick black eyelashes was very attractive from this angle. Elain sighed. How could she possibly know what she would have done, with no experience of her own of love? Yet she could almost imagine staying around as a ghost if she were waiting for . . . Math, perhaps. Her hand stroked over his stomach, just at the edge of his trunks. She felt his muscles tense under her hands.

"I don't know. Maybe I'd have tried to get out of the house before telling my father I refused to marry my rich, well-connected cousin. Especially if I were already pregnant." His bathing suit was cold and wet against the side of her finger. She moved down and squirted gel onto his thighs.

"They say there was a very strong attachment between father and daughter. She might have believed that she would convince him in time." Math grunted softly as she began to massage the flesh just below the cuffs of his trunks. There was a bit of sandy grit now between her hand and his skin. She enjoyed the contradictory mix of creaminess and abrasiveness against her palm.

"I wonder where he went, the lover? Do you think he was killed that night?"

How muscled his thighs were. Hard and thick and firm. Nothing like her own skin at all. The boxer legs of his trunks weren't very long, so there wasn't much of his thighs covered, but she spread the gel a little under the hem, in case the sun caught him...

"It seems unlikely that a murder could have been so completely covered up. There would have been some whisper, if only from a deathbed confession later." Math sat up and lifted her hands from his thighs, though she hadn't finished.

"But he must have disappeared from the village afterwards, mustn't he?" He grunted as if her guess was as good as any, and dusted sand from his legs. Elain screwed the lid back onto the tube and tucked it out of the sun against her bag. She didn't want to ask, but she couldn't prevent her mouth from opening, nor her tongue from forming the words. "What would you have done?"

When he looked at her, it seemed as if his black eyes absorbed all the light of the sun. He smiled. "I'd have come back and got her," he said. He spoke lightly, without emphasis, but suddenly her heart was beating as if she were the one he had come for, and he would not take no for an answer.

Chapter 7

"What I need now is a strong, hot shower." Elain pulled her skirt away from her legs and gently lifted her sticky thigh from the leather seat of the ancient Land Rover. She laughed. "But I guess I'll have to settle for a shower."

"It'll be hot, won't it?" Math glanced at her as he drove. The sun was low in the sky behind them. They had swum and eaten the delicious picnic Myfanwy had made for them, and now she had the beginnings of a tan and was full of the sensuous lassitude that a day by the sea induces. And her skin was sticky with several alternating layers of salt and sand and sunblock. She hadn't felt so alive for years. "We do at least have constant hot water."

"True," she said. "I'll settle for a hot shower."

"How important is strong?" he asked with a grin.

"Trade my eye-teeth," Elain responded instantly, and he laughed, showing his own strong white teeth.

"All right, I'll tell you a secret. I've got a 'power shower' upstairs. You can use that if you promise not to brag about it."

"What's a power shower?"

"An electric motor that increases the pressure. The hotel water system doesn't come directly off the mains, but down from a tank. That's why there's no water pressure."

"And you have one of those? Where?"

"In my flat. I live on the top floor."

"And for the small price of my eye-teeth, I can have this incredible luxury today?"

"The price goes up as the shower becomes a necessity. We work on the same principle as drug pushers here."

She laughed much more than the joke deserved. She couldn't recall having laughed so much, or so light-heartedly, as she had been laughing today. It was because she saw a light in the darkness, perhaps. Elain marvelled at the ease of it. A man had kissed a patch of skin twice, and her heart was a soaring bird.

The flat was a beautiful mix of modernization with restoration. The high sloping ceilings, with reproduction decorative wooden rafters, had skylights that filled the huge rooms with light without altering the building's silhouette. The dark, worn wooden floors were polished and gleaming under the scatter of area rugs. The huge fireplace in the sitting room had been restored to its ancient glory of massive grey stone, and the windows were the leaded glass of former times, with ivy fluttering around the edges. There was a mix of stone and plaster walls and wood panelling.

The bathroom was a dream. Rough black stone tiled the walls and floor, including the floor of the walk-in shower, and around the basin. It looked basic and primitive, a bathroom Owen Glendower might have felt comfortable in.

The shower pounded into her, a luxury she hadn't had since leaving home five years ago. She stood under it without moving for five minutes, as if she had been rescued from a desert, sighing as it massaged her scalp, face, body, the soles of her feet.

A huge full-length mirror was set into the stone wall opposite the shower. When she came out at last, it was fogged with steam, and her reflection was scarcely more than a ghost behind. She pushed a switch and a fan came on, and a heater began to glow. She dried herself, watching her reflection as the mirror cleared.

It cleared from top and bottom first. For a moment, while the mirror was still fogged towards the centre, she could look at herself and see a perfectly normal woman. A woman a man might want to touch, to make love to: long, elegant legs, gracefully curving arms, a neat, curling patch of auburn pubic hair, slightly rounded abdomen, slender waist... long, slender neck, neatly placed head, thick, healthy auburn hair, creamy skin with a light tan showing on face and legs and arms...

Then the fog cleared entirely. Elain's jaw clenched, and she forced herself to watch, to see. Full, rounded breasts. One creamy white, perfect, with the dark-aureoled nipple, erect now from the shower, just where it ought to be, the other with an oblong patch of darker, coarser skin implanted across the top of the breast and around the side to just under the arm. The nipple riding too high on the curve of the breast, the erect nipple angled up, destroying the symmetry and any hope of beauty.

"Holy Hell! What's that?" His voice was so clear in the ears of memory it seemed to echo in this room of stone. *"What's the matter with your tits?"*

Her hand crept up now, as it had then, to shield her breast from his eyes. *"It's—it's a skin graft. I got burned."*

His nervous laughter rang loud against the stone. *"Jeez, I'll say you did! Jeez, Elain, you might have warned a guy!"* Laughing.

"I'm sorry."

"Yeah, well, I can see why you wouldn't want to. Gotta get some fun out of life, I guess. I guess I'm the sucker this time, eh?"

She never looked at it; she hated seeing her deformity. But now she kept her eyes open, dry, her gaze fixed. *Nothing's changed,* she told herself. *A man kissed you twice, but nothing's really changed.*

* * *

"Shall we eat up here, away from the crowd?" Math asked, when she emerged into the sitting room ten minutes later. "I can ask Myfanwy to send up a tray."

She looked around the cool, shadowed room, at the purple-and-golden sunlight angling in through the leaded panes, at the flickering shadows of leaves on the floor, moving in the breeze. Dust motes danced in the light, and her body and mind were tired with the effects of the day. The last thing she felt like facing was the company of strangers. But worse still would be facing what was in Math's eyes now. Because she knew how that look of desire would change, and she couldn't bear to watch that. Not from Math. She didn't ask herself why it would be worse from him than from another man, but it would.

She would probably be leaving tomorrow. Suppose she risked it, just this once? No matter what the humiliation, she wouldn't have to see him again....

"No, thanks," said Elain. "I'll go down."

"They want you to stay on awhile," said Raymond.

"What?" Elain's heart thumped uncomfortably, as if she were being asked to stay in the lion's den. "Why? He didn't do it! It's not possible!"

"Look, they're very pleased at the way you've managed to get on the spot, and they don't want to give up that advantage just yet. Stay on the spot, pick up what you can, and they may have something specific for you to do later."

Elain swore.

"What's the problem, love? Painting not going well?" Raymond asked unsympathetically.

"No," she said. No way was she going to start explaining to Raymond that she was looking straight at another kick in the guts and knew she couldn't stop herself walking into it if she stayed around.

"Tough," said Raymond. "Read a book. That's supposed to help pass the time. And get whatever you can on tape. You never know."

"Never know what?"

"Maybe he's lying, Elain. But at least he's talking to you. Who knows, he might tell you a different story another day. The tapestry wasn't valued at its current worth. Get him talking about it."

If she were taping their conversations, she'd be less likely to let them get off the rails. Elain sighed. "He didn't do it, you know. He's not the type."

Raymond said, "Elain, my dear, this is a big client, and they are paying both you and me for every day you spend on this thing. Now, there's a recession on. I need the money, if you don't. Let's not rock the boat."

She sighed again. "Raymond, there's nothing in it. It's stupid for me to stay here. They're paying good money for nothing."

"Look, love, this is an insurance company. They are rolling in lard up to their snouts, and they want things to stay that way." Rolling in lard? "I see no reason not to skim a little of that nice fat into my own trough. If you stayed there a month, they wouldn't even notice the bill."

"A month?" Elain shrieked. "I'm not staying here a *month!*"

"You sound like a Victorian maiden whose virtue is being threatened. Look, whatever you think, they have their suspicions and they'd rather pay us our pittance than that insurance. Now, get your little nose to the grindstone and produce something that looks as though you're working. It does my heart good to talk about my agent in the field. Reminds me of the good old days."

The countryside was more beautiful than she would ever have imagined. Deep, moss-covered hillsides covered in trees that seemed as old as the earth itself, and full of magic. High promontories and wide vistas. The sea blue as the Caribbean, the beaches wide and smooth. The houses old, nestled into the earth, surrounded by centuries-old drystone walls. Numerous lakes and rivers and streams, and green fields where black cattle and white sheep and handsome horses grazed more picturesquely than she could have dreamed. The stone circles, the rustling waterfalls, all the places that had not changed since her great-grandfather had left this land.

Elain drove and walked around the countryside, dragging her easel and paints, recording the beauty she saw; and it was like a homecoming. The myth, the history, the magic—this was the land of her ancestors, and she would never be the same again. This was where she belonged.

"Wales does have a very wet climate," Vinnie was saying as Elain stood looking out at the rain. She hadn't taken her paints out for two days. "That's why it's so green."

They were sitting alone together over a late lunch, and had seen no reason to move from the table. Rosemary and Davina had gone out early in the day, covered with macs and with their lunch in a rucksack; Jeremy had gone to London to see a publisher about his poetry; Math had gone upstairs an hour ago. But Vinnie and Elain had nothing to do save share another pot of coffee and chat.

She hadn't been running her tape because the talk had been all about the past. The loss of a husband when you were twenty-two and pregnant, losing the child, never marrying again, and learning to run a hotel when you had been raised never to lift a finger even for your own needs. Then a violent gust of rain had drawn Elain moodily to the window. The fortress was completely obscured by rain and mist, so thick it might never clear.

Now, as much from a desire to be doing something as anything else, she started the tape and returned to the table. "I've been thinking I'd like to paint the scene that was on the tapestry lost in the fire," she said. "Especially if this weather keeps up. Do you remember it well enough to describe it to me?"

Vinnie set down her cup. "What a very lovely idea, my dear! I'm sure Math would be delighted. He did admire the tapestry so much. Is he going to commission it from you?"

"Oh—I haven't mentioned it to him. I was thinking of a small canvas. Perhaps if he liked I could do something larger. But of course it would never be as valuable as the tapestry itself."

"Math didn't care very much about its sterling value, I think. He intended to make it a showpiece when he restored the house."

"Where did he get it from?"

"It has always been in this house, as far as we know. I found it in a store cupboard in 1956, but it wasn't until my father died in 1970 that I took it out and had it hung. My father had never admired it the way I did."

"Is that when you had it valued for the insurance?"

Vinnie sighed. "I'm afraid so. I never thought of its having increased in value. The estate agent who advised me during the sale simply passed over it."

"Quite a coup for Math," Elain observed drily.

"Yes, no one was more surprised than Math. He'd not done more than glance into that room, you know, when he was looking the place over. He was delighted when he finally saw the tapestry. He's very keen on Welsh myth. We agreed then that he would pay me half the price if he ever sold it, but of course he never meant to."

"It was the depiction of 'The Dream of Rhonabwy,' wasn't it? Do you know the story?"

"My dear, I have read it long ago, but I don't remember it at all, I'm afraid. Math has an English translation of the *Mabinogion*. You might borrow it."

"But you could describe the scene to me?" Elain pressed. She felt torn. She had never before in an investigation got so close to people she was spying on, and she hated what she was doing. On the other hand, she was genuinely interested in delving into her own ancestral background. She wasn't lying about what she planned: she did want to paint 'The Dream of Rhonabwy.'

The original artist had been a woman, she knew, working in the only medium available to her. Had her artistic soul been frustrated by the slow progress of her needle? And now all those years of work were lost. But perhaps Elain could make it live again.

"If you like, I can try," said Vinnie. "Perhaps if you were to draw it as we talked, it might come to me. It was done in a rather primitive style, I know. The colours had originally been very bold. And the perspective was—"

She broke off because the dog was barking loudly in the hall, and there were voices. The long inactivity of the afternoon made both Elain and Vinnie get up to investigate.

Rosemary and Davina had come in from the storm and were standing just inside the door, calling for Jan. The sight of them, covered in large macs and hats and mud-caked wellies, and dripping with water, had apparently set off Bill. He was barking ferociously at them, as if they were strangers.

"Oh, Elain! Vinnie! There you are!" said Rosemary gratefully. "I wonder if you could just find Jan and ask her to bring us something to wipe off the worst of this? We don't want to be tracking mud all over her floors."

"What a day! We got caught in a dreadful squall. Invigorating, of course, but we're rather wet," Davina explained. "And then Rosemary fell."

Bill was barking loudly over all this, beside himself with excitement. "Quiet, Bill!" Elain commanded, but without much hope of being obeyed, and she wasn't.

"He hasn't much sense of smell any more," Vinnie said apologetically. "And you look rather strange."

Rosemary's yellow mac was covered with black mud; Elain could see why the sisters didn't want to move inside. "I'll find Jan," she said.

Jan was in the kitchen, and she and Elain returned with a bucket and mop and a few old towels. Math had come downstairs. "Impossible to eat our picnic, of course," Rosemary was saying. "There hasn't been a dry moment since we left the house."

Bill could not be silenced, even when the macs had been wiped down and the women had taken off all their outer gear. He was a dog who had seen the Enemy, and his tri-

umph in having driven the enemy away and leaving Rosemary and Davina in its place knew no bounds. In the end,
they all stopped trying to shout him down. He was getting
more excited the more he was told to be quiet.

Vinnie shook her head sadly at Math. "I suppose he's
approaching senility."

Rosemary was dirtier and wetter than Davina. She stood
looking damp and limp in her socks and sweatpants, wisps
of her hair plastered to her head as she continued to wipe her
muddy hands. "Well!" she said. "I think next time—"

She got no further. Bill, his excitement at a peak, dashed
against her legs in an excess of friendliness, and then suddenly his excitement was too much for his control, and he
emptied his bladder all over Rosemary's foot.

Rosemary was, much as she tried to disguise it, a rigid
person at heart, with too much self-consequence to allow
room for a true sense of humour. She was not capable of
laughing at herself in this predicament, and the fact that
Elain had let out an involuntary cackle of amusement did
not help.

"Good God!" she cried, lifting her left foot, encased in
its newly sodden sock, and regarding it with astonished
outrage. "What on earth—!"

Vinnie and Math both had better self-control than Elain.
Math dived on the hapless dog, grabbed him by the scruff
of the neck, opened the nearest door, which happened to be
to the lounge, and thrust him inside, ruthlessly shutting the
door on him. Bill, who had momentarily stopped barking,
now began again, quite hysterically.

"Well, I'm sorry, Rosemary," Math began. "I don't
know what—"

Vinnie clutched his arm. "Math," she said urgently.

Elain caught the smell in the same moment. "Smoke,"
she said, frowning. "Something's burning." And then, as
the smell triggered that old memory, she turned, sniffing.
"Oh, my God, fire!"

Bill was throwing himself against the door of the sitting
room, barking and whining as if he'd been locked up with

a ghost. Math whirled and opened the door, and the odour of smoke wafted out into the hall. They all dashed wildly into the room, including Bill, who had clearly not been leaping at the door in a desire to get out, but to bring them in.

In the centre of the carpet that lay just in front of the fireplace, a cloud of smoke was rising from a sullen blue-and-red flame. "My bucket!" cried Jan, whirling for the door. But her bucket wasn't necessary. Bill, leaping and barking, suddenly squatted down, his hind legs spread, and sniffed at the burning carpet. Then, as if making up his mind what sort of object this thing was, he straightened up, lifted his leg and peed again.

His aim was extremely good; the small burning area was extinguished before Jan had returned. A high, pungent odour spiralled up from the burn—a mixture of smouldering wool, burning dust and cooked dog's urine.

They were all laughing in hysterical relief. Davina, who had moved close to the scene, got a lungful of the damp smoke, coughed and backed away hastily.

"Well, Bill!" said Vinnie admiringly. The black dog sat on the other side of the mess looking at them, quiet now, his tail thumping the floor and his mouth open in a broad grin.

"Woof!" he remarked happily.

Math was looking at him, one eyebrow raised. "We won't be calling *you* senile again, will we, boy?" he said with a grin.

"No, indeed!" Vinnie agreed. "And to think we thought he'd lost his sense of smell!"

"But what happened?" Elain asked. "How did it start? Was somebody smoking?"

But only Jeremy smoked, and Jeremy was in London. Math crouched down over the burnt carpet, waving the acrid smoke away with one hand. There was a blackened patch about a foot in diameter. At its epicentre there was a small, ashy lump. Math raised his eyes to Jan.

"When did you lay the fire in here, Jan?"

"About an hour ago. Just after lunch. You told me to do it when you went upstairs, because it was such a wet day, didn't you? I did it right after that." She bridled. "And I didn't drop any burning coal on the carpet."

Math shook his head. "No, this hasn't been burning for more than fifteen minutes, I'd say. Anybody been in and out of this room in the last hour?"

Elain shook her head. "Vinnie and I have been sitting over our coffee in the dining room. We'd have noticed anybody, I think." Because they had been only three at lunch, Jan hadn't set the residents' usual table in the niche, but a small table for four by the window overlooking the valley. There was a clear view into the hall and the doorway of the sitting room.

Vinnie nodded. "It's all been so quiet. Jan came out of here and along the hall to offer us more coffee—about an hour ago, so I suppose that was when you lit the fire, my dear—and there's been no one since."

Davina closed her eyes. "I feel the Presence," she said in soft, thrilling tones. She opened her eyes and looked at Math. "I'm afraid this is—Jess's work."

Math grinned and got to his feet. He eyed the fire in the fireplace, well burnt down now, its glowing coals giving off a very pleasant warmth. "Much more likely that a coal leaped from the fire," he said calmly. As if in confirmation, the fire suddenly shifted, and several small glowing coals fell off the grate.

"Yes, I expect you're right," Vinnie agreed.

Rosemary shook her head. "You would do well to heed my sister's warnings," she said.

Elain said suddenly, "Don't forget Bill."

"What has Bill got to—" Rosemary began.

"What set him off?" Elain demanded. "You've always said he's lost his sense of smell, and it wasn't the sitting-room door he was barking at, was it?"

"Well, perhaps..." Vinnie began.

"No, don't you see? Something excited the dog, but it wasn't the fire, was it? He was just generally—spooked.

And if he hadn't peed on Rosemary—'' Elain choked, coughed and continued ''—Math wouldn't have opened this door, would he? Maybe no one would have come in here for another hour.''

"What are you saying?" asked Math.

"Well, just that—'' She broke off as her train of thought died. "I don't know," said Elain, shrugging.

But there was something. She would have to think.

Chapter 8

The mist nestled between the hills like a smoky sea. It shrouded the valley, giving the rounded green-covered slopes that rose above it an air of mystery and enchantment, even under the bright summer morning sun.

I might sail to Avalon across that sea, Elain thought dreamily. *Or if I stare long enough, the sword Excalibur will appear.*

It did appear, white and grey and shrouded in mist, slowly forming itself under the delicate strokes of her brush, another reality imposing itself on the image of the world beneath, for those who dared to see. There was a smile on Elain's face as she worked, though she was unaware of it, the smile that meant the painting had taken over from the painter and would be what it wished to be. She had not meant to put Excalibur in the simple landscape, but then she had not *meant* most of her best paintings. To resist such inspiration as intrusion would be to kill the painting.

Excalibur had apparently had a gleaming emerald embedded in its hilt, engraved with runic letters. She realized this as it took shape under her hand and, slipping her tongue between her lips, she bent to the task of making the emerald glitter. The inspiration came from elsewhere. The technical delivery was all up to her.

A little white underneath a facet or two added lustre...and there was something within the emerald, too... some image.... Her hand picked up a number one brush and trailed it in carmine...a rose, perhaps...a rose, or a pair of ruby lips...or something that was both...and behind...

"Oh, I say! How extremely interesting! I should imagine that's Excalibur, isn't it?"

Elain's hand jerked, sending a red thread across the grey-blue sky. The vision shattered and fell into the mists and the world returned with the curious sense of loss that always accompanied such a rupture. She turned to look over her shoulder, blinking. A woman was standing there, and for a moment, still between two worlds, Elain saw a complete stranger.

"Oh, Rosemary...hello," she said at last.

"Oh, I am so dreadfully sorry!" said Rosemary. "I had no idea I would startle you! I thought you'd heard me coming!"

"I don't hear much when I'm painting," Elain said. She laid her brush down. She might recapture the image, but not just at this moment.

"And I've spoiled your painting! But I just didn't think, you see. In fact, I thought you were chatting."

Elain frowned in puzzlement, then felt the belated prickle along her spine that should have told her long ago that she was not alone. She turned on her seat, and he was there, lying loosely propped on one elbow in the long grass, chewing on a stem of it, the sun burning on his black head, and another light altogether burning in his dark eyes.

She had been avoiding him for days, but if she had hoped to reduce the impact of his presence on her, that had not been the way to do it.

Math smiled and shrugged, saying nothing. For a moment, her flesh going hot and cold at once, she could not

break the look between them. Then she lowered her eyes and
bent to lock her palette onto the little hooks inside her
paintbox.

Rosemary's laughter trilled in light remorse. "Oh, I've
stopped you working! I am so sorry. Oh, I do hope you will
be able to fix it." Undeterred by what she had already done,
she came closer and bent to examine the painting and the
thin red line. "Do say you'll be able to fix that!"

"Yes, of course," Elain said softly. She was glad of the
diversion, taking her mind off those eyes taking in the thin
cotton of her summer dress, the curve of the sweat-damp
flesh of her shoulders and arms, the tendrils of escaped hair
on forehead and neck, her paint-smudged, capable hands.
"It won't be difficult."

It was true: painting out the carmine was a simple technical matter. What had been in the emerald, however, might
be a more serious loss.

In the silence that fell then, Elain lifted a cloth from the
depths of her box and idly wiped the brushes she had been
using. "How long have you been watching me?" she asked
over her shoulder, looking down at her task.

"Since a few minutes before the birth of Excalibur," he
said. Curious that he should put it that way, as though he
had an intuitive understanding of the creative process.
"Where do you get your ideas?" was more the kind of thing
she was used to hearing, as though she went off and bought
them at a market. As if *ideas* were a commodity instead of
the richness of the universe. Elain couldn't help smiling at
this, and turned to look at him. Once her gaze met his, he
held it so that she could not break away. Held it with a look
so full of unconscious promise and intent she could scarcely
breathe.

Rosemary was staring out over the scene, where the mist
was lifting under the increasing heat of the sun and the valley was again becoming visible down between the hills. Elain
had come out early to catch the mist several mornings running, scrambling with all her paraphernalia over the wall,

where she was hidden from view from the hotel and might hope for an uninterrupted couple of hours.

"I might have looked at that scene forever and never thought of hanging a sword in the sky!" she said brightly. "Where *do* you get your ideas?"

There was the faintest sound of disapproval in the voice, reminding Elain of an art teacher she had had as a teenager, who had been one of the natural enemies of art. She tried to suppress a grin, but what she saw in those dark eyes when she glanced irresistibly towards Math again made her laugh, as though the air were champagne.

"It just came to me," she said, because there was no way to explain. Idly she found herself entertaining the thought that the sword had apparently "come to her" not long after Math had come up behind her. Was there something Freudian in that? Had she unconsciously felt his presence and painted not a mystical, but a plainly phallic symbol over the breastlike hills?

But of course to the ancients it wouldn't have been a cold and shallow question of "phallic symbol" at all, but the deep mystery of sexuality. So perhaps the answer was one and the same, only that modern theory robbed sexuality, as it robbed the world, of mystery.

With a twinkling wave, Rosemary climbed over the stile to the path and wandered off down the hillside towards Pontdewi, leaving Elain in silence with the dark man behind her. She busied herself packing away her painting and easel, and he lay there in the sun against the green grass, waiting. At last she was forced to turn and look at him again.

He looked as though he understood all that she had not said, smiling at her with a lazy smile and a tenderness that brought a lump to her throat. Leaning on one elbow in the summer-scented grass, he lifted his other hand to her. He did it casually, simply, as though they both knew she belonged beside him, and she would come to him because he asked.

She stood for a moment, gazing at him, resisting the pull of his eyes, his presence, and that extended hand. At last she mutely shook her head, and he dropped his hand. "No takers?" he asked softly.

Elain shook her head again and turned back to look over the valley. "The mist's gone," she said. "It'll have to wait for another day." She bent to pick up her equipment, and Math got lazily to his feet and came to help her. At the wall he took everything from her and leaned over to set it down beside the ruined tower. Then he caught Elain by the waist and lifted her to sit on the wall before climbing over himself.

Balch was tethered outside the fortress, where he munched grass. "Have you been riding? I didn't hear you!" Elain exclaimed.

"No, you were completely immersed," Math agreed. He took the horse's reins. "You've been keeping out of sight."

She felt her cheeks grow hot. "I've been working," she said. It was true enough, but it was also true that for the past couple of days she had been hiding from Math. She had even eaten at the pub twice.

"So have I. Feel like a break? It's market day in a village not too far away—Machynlleth—and I've got a long list from Myfanwy."

The sun was already hot, and she couldn't go on forever ignoring Raymond's instructions. "All right," Elain said. After a moment, she added guiltily, "Thank you."

Math laughed.

The country market was beautiful in the summer sun. They strolled along the village street between the stalls, where the vegetables lay, bright red and green and yellow and brown, sometimes coated with a crust of rich earth, reminding one that all this was the bounty of the Earth Mother. There were stalls of eggs and Welsh butter, of the local cheeses and imported ones; stalls where silver-coloured pots and pans glittered, where brightly coloured shirts and skirts hung in the breeze; stalls that sold farm equipment and hardware, teacups and long knives.

"This is quite a market," she observed. She had been in London street markets, but there was something about this one—perhaps the number of people selling their own produce—that made it somehow more real. "Is it always here?"

"Machynlleth market has been running every Wednesday for eight hundred years," he said.

She smiled up at him in astonishment, the sun blinding her. "Are you kidding me?" She put her hand up to shade her eyes, trying to see his face.

Math shook his head. "I am not. The charter was granted by King Edward in December, 1291. There's a copy of it just down the road, in Owen Glendower's parliament."

"Every Wednesday? Without fail?"

"So far as we know. The cattle used to be down there where the clock is."

"I'm Canadian," she said. "I don't think I'm equipped to cope with the concept of an eight-hundred-year-old tradition."

"Ah, but your blood is Welsh," he reminded her, and then she looked down the street, with its market stalls lining both sides, and wondered if some ancestress had come here to buy food for her family centuries ago....

She trailed after Math as he shopped, pausing when something caught her eye, and then looking around wildly for him in the crowd. She stopped at a stall selling little framed prints and watercolour originals. Most of them were not very good, overdone portrayals of unnaturally cute animals with big eyes, or precociously saintly children, or poorly executed landscapes, but one water-colourist whose hand Elain recognized in half a dozen of the offerings had a good eye and a delicate way with a brush. And at least as important, a mind not devoted to cuteness. Elain asked the prices and made a face. Awful. Too low for original watercolours. The artist was selling herself short. Offered beside better work, they should command a better price.

Behind her, Math said, "This is mostly for people to hang in their kitchens. There's a shop selling the work of local artists to the tourist trade just across the road. Would you like to look? I'll be through in a minute."

So she followed him to the next stall, where he bought a supply of ruled-paper notebooks and a box of typing paper. These weren't on Myfanwy's list. "Are you working on something at the moment?" she asked.

"Yes," he said absently.

"What's it about this time? Or wouldn't I understand?"

He paused. "I'm writing about the *Mabinogion*."

"The Welsh epic," she remembered, as he led her across the street.

"That's right."

"Is it true, Math?"

"What do you mean by true?"

"Is it based on real history?"

He laughed. "That depends on what you call history. Here's the shop."

It was the sort of shop you might see wherever there was a vibrant artistic community. A group of artists and crafts-people whose work did not compete, Math told her, rented the shop and ran it as a joint venture. Two potters of very different styles, a jeweller who worked in silver and polished local stone among others, a water-colourist, a weaver and a wood carver.

Elain wandered among the displays, wondering why she hadn't had the courage to try something like this after graduation. Why stay in London, where costs were so high, working for Raymond, when this avenue had always been open to her?

She had sometimes sold a few things from a friend's stall by the Embankment, but she had always put that down to simple luck. Perhaps Wales had brought out an individual vision which made her more confident. For the first time, she felt an inner conviction that she might actually make a living through selling her art to people, rather than through commercial commissions.

"No oils," she observed, half to herself.

"That's right," Math said, and then, "John, how's it going?" to the man sitting behind the cash desk.

"*Bore da,* Math. Bit slow last week. But pretty good overall."

"Elain, this is John Llewellyn. He's the weaver whose work you see displayed. John, my friend Elain Owen. She paints in oil."

"Do you now?" said John, shaking her hand with a very firm grasp. "Are you staying around here?"

"I'm spending a few weeks at the White Lady."

The weaver's eyebrows went up, and he tilted his head at Math. "How's that going? Have they paid up yet?"

Math shook his head. "Still delaying."

Elain took one of the shop's business cards from the counter and slipped it into her shoulder bag, where her Walkman lay on top of her cotton jacket.

"What's the problem?"

"They aren't saying. Or they're saying it's a question of getting the estimate together. But I don't think that's the whole story."

John raised his bushy brows again. "Hasn't the fire officer made a decision?"

"He has. Petrol cans both at least fifty years old. Grime on the cans matches that of the basement. He's satisfied it was an accident."

"But they don't want to pay." Math inclined his head. "And until they do..." John clicked his tongue. "They'll put you out of business at this rate! You could be booking those undamaged rooms if you got the place cleaned up."

"I may have to start without them."

"Olwen was saying the tapestry went. I didn't know that. That's a real tragedy, that is." Math only nodded, and the weaver suddenly remembered Elain's existence. "So you're a painter? Are you Welsh?"

She grinned. "Welsh extraction."

"Painting the local scenery, are you?"

"In a manner of speaking."

"Well, if you're planning on staying around, bring in something to show us. We might display a few, see how they go."

That was a pretty generous offer, considering he knew nothing about her. "Thank you," she said.

Then they were back in the heat and noise of the market. "Lunch, I think," said Math.

They spent the afternoon driving and sightseeing, and then went to the sea. They had no swimsuits with them, but they paddled barefoot along the shore late in the afternoon, getting back to the hotel long after tea had been served.

"Do you want a shower?" asked Math as they pulled up, and when Elain laughed and nodded, he handed her a ring of keys. "I'll drop this stuff with Myfanwy. You go on up. Make tea or pour yourself a drink if you like."

She stopped at her room for a change of clothes. He hadn't returned when she had showered, and she poured herself a dry sherry. Reluctant to leave without knowing why, she wandered around the flat, towelling her hair dry.

One of the rooms was his study. The walls were full of books, there were a couple of maps and prints, a typewriter and desk with a large black chair in front of a narrow, leaded window...and a brown cat lying on the desk among piles of open books and papers, in the last rays of the sun, watching her.

"Well, hello," said Elain. "Are you the watchcat?"

The brown cat yawned, stretched out one hind leg, and carefully licked a tuft of fur into place. Then it settled down to ignore her. Drawn as much by the presence of the cat as by the window, Elain walked over and looked out.

It was the view up to the fortress, rather restricted because the window was so narrow. She had the curious sensation that she was looking through a magic window to a land of enchantment. It was that sort of window. Elain laughed and decided to ask Math if she could paint the view from here. Who knew what she might see?

Absently she stroked the cat's head. He was an odd colour for a cat, his pelt deep brown and thick, like a bear's. Idly her gaze fell onto the page in the typewriter.

"Lord," said Caradoc, "your messengers can do no more. Will you not set out yourself on the path that you saw in your dream? For if you lead us..."

She broke off guiltily. She was as bad as Rosemary! She turned and left the room, the cat following her. Back in the sitting room, she told herself she should go, but didn't.

There were books here, too, on a set of low shelves against one wall. She crouched down, browsing through the titles without any real intention. This was a very mixed collection of old and modern—fiction, poetry, history, myth, religion. She wasn't a great reader, but she did like some modern fiction.

Some modern authors were in a cluster: D. M. Thomas, Robertson Davies, Taliesin... were they Math's favourites? She didn't read much, but of course everybody knew these names. Elain settled down cross-legged, dropping the towel and setting her sherry on the floor beside her. *The White Hotel.* She'd read that. She had found it compelling; it had been as powerful for her as a painting. There were few writers who did that for her, but then she wasn't much of a reader. She ought to read more.

Bred in the Bone. "Booker Prize Nominee." She'd always meant to read that, someone had told her it was about artists. Maybe she would ask Math to lend it to her....

Taliesin she'd never read, she was pretty sure. That curious one-word name. Hadn't someone been mentioning him the other day? *Atmospheric Changes. The Goddess Letters.* She'd heard the name recently. *Wounds Which Bleed Profusely.* Yes, somebody had mentioned that one. She pulled it out. "A powerfully erotic exploration of myth and reality."

The cat came over, sniffed her sherry and settled itself in her lap, making it impossible for her to move. So she idly paged through the book where she sat, unable to concentrate, feeling restless. What was she doing here? Why was she waiting for Math anyway?

A woman was riding a black horse, whispering into its ear, urging it to gallop faster....

She took a sip of sherry and stroked the cat, frowning at nothing. Why *was* she waiting for Math? The cat rolled over and presented its tummy with a sensuous chirrup, inviting her touch. Absently she obliged, smiling as she was rewarded with a growl and the offering of another angle of approach.

Elain bent down and rubbed her face in the cat's fur. "I understand how you feel," she told the cat softly. "Just the way I do when—"

She broke off, for she did not want to know that the end of that sentence was the answer to her question, and returned to the book.

The horse had no reins, no saddle; he was controlled only by the pressure of the girl's thighs and hands, and her voice. Elain got the feeling there might come a time when he would not be controlled at all. She read slowly, not noticing the glide into eroticism until it was fiercely evident, until it was clear that between the horse and the girl on his back there was some kind of passionate union of the senses that was no less physical for being unconventional.

Of course she had read sexy writing before; these days how could anyone fail to? But those clinical descriptions of the sexual act had not moved her the way this tangential, poetic passion did. Elain was unprepared for the shiver of sensuality that coursed through her as the horse took flight into the night sky, the sudden, unbidden thought of Math's hands stroking her...and the abrupt confrontation with the truth she had looked away from.

"Just the way I feel when Math touches me," she had nearly said a minute ago to the cat. And that was what she was waiting for: for Math to come and touch her, stroke her....

She clapped the book closed with a whack that made the cat leap from her lap, thrust it anyhow onto the shelf, scrambled to her feet and snatched up the sherry glass. She must get out before he came. She had no power to resist any more, only the frailest of surface defences and an inner being already gone over to the enemy. And what had happened to her when Greg turned away in disgust was nothing compared to... That look in Math's eyes would kill her.

She whirled and set the glass down on the nearest surface, bent to pick up the towel and started for the door. The cat ran beside and in front of her, slowing her up, but she'd have been too late anyway. Halfway across the room she stopped, immobile as salt. She heard the sound of the door opening with a heart as thunderous as if a tumbrel were waiting to take her to her death.

Chapter 9

"Hi," said Math, with a slow smile that curled her toes. "Nice shower?"

"Yes," she said, snatching wildly at the first excuse that presented itself. "I—I didn't bring my comb." Her hair was wildly tousled over head and shoulders, and she had the towel in her hand. He had stopped directly in her path to the door. She smiled nervously as she walked towards him.

He reached out an arm and gently put it around her, turning her back into the room in the process. "That's all right, I've got one. Stay and keep me company for a bit."

He took the towel from her helpless fingers and dropped it onto a small wooden stool that sat in the inglenook fireplace. "Are you drinking something?"

"Sherry," she said. Her blood was thundering around her system so powerfully that she felt faint, and yet instead of being warmed by it, her skin was a rush of shivers. Nor did the extra oxygen it must be delivering to her brain help the functioning of her mind.

He was unbuttoning his shirt. "Will you pour me a whisky? I'll find you a comb."

He disappeared into the room she knew was the bedroom. She had glanced in and then quickly closed the door, but she probably could have painted the room exactly: for some reason, that one glance had imprinted it on her mind's eye. After a minute she stepped to the drinks table. No ice in the ice bucket. She moved to the fridge and took out the ice cubes. Then she paused, her brain clearing a little. She didn't have to wait just because he'd said so. She could leave right now.

He came out of the bedroom wearing nothing but a worn terry bathrobe, black, full-length, voluminous. The kind of thing a grateful lover might have bought for his birthday. She froze, the ice-cube tray in her hand.

"Math..." she began hesitantly.

"Yes." No question mark, as though he were answering a question, not asking one. And the way he looked, Elain thought crazily, a woman could be seduced into believing he was the answer to any question she might have.

"Ice? In your whisky?" she asked weakly.

"Yes, thanks." He disappeared into the bathroom, and after a minute she heard the motor of the power shower start. Standing there with the bottle in her hand, pouring whisky over the ice cubes in the glass, she was assailed by a vision of Math in the shower, his hair dark, his skin pale against the wet black stone of the walls, the water plastering his hair to his head, his eyes squeezed shut as he held his face to the spray, his neck arched...his body compact, firmly muscled, his hands running over neck, chest, armpits...thighs...the soapy water streaming down his chest, his hips, his abdomen—

The cat made a mewing noise of satisfaction and pressed between her feet to lick the floor, and Elain came to with a jerk. Bloody hell! She'd just poured out most of a bottle of whisky! The glass was overflowing, the drinks table was awash, and the brown cat had decided to experiment with what was on the floor. Elain set down the nearly empty bottle with a crash and looked around wildly for a cloth.

There was a small towel on top of the ice bucket, and she began to wipe the table with that, wringing it out into the bucket. Lord, what a mess! She dropped the wet cloth into the ice bucket and carried it to the kitchen, where she set it in the sink, picked up the sponge hanging over the tap and located a small pail under the sink.

By the time she got back, the cat had disposed of most of what was on the floor and had sat in the remainder to lick its paw. Elain rolled her eyes. How on earth was she going to explain a whisky-sodden cat? "You smell like a brewery," she accused it. The cat blinked myopically but lovingly at her and flung itself down to offer its tummy again.

"Meow," it said encouragingly.

"Meow yourself." She carefully scooped the ice cubes out of the glass and, the whisky at a more manageable level, set herself to the task of pouring some of it back into the bottle. Scotch double malted. Aged 15 years, she noted. Oh, great. The cat alone had probably drunk ten pounds' worth of the stuff. Elain swallowed some of her sherry and felt its warmth comfort her.

She had got about half the glass back into the bottle, another half ounce dribbling down over the label and onto the table, when the shower stopped. She started guiltily, set down the glass and began to wipe the new spills. Then she dropped the ice back into the glass.

When Math came out of the bathroom in a cloud of steam, wrapped in his bathrobe and still rubbing a towel over his head, she was sitting in an armchair by the empty fireplace with her second sherry. His whisky was on a square wooden table between her chair and the arm of the leather sofa.

He stood by the table, uncomfortably close to where she was sitting, picked up the glass, looked at it and then turned to smile quizzically down at her. "Are you trying to get me drunk?" he asked, and the laughter that threaded his tone was at least as intoxicating to her senses as the whisky had been to the cat.

She bit her lip, dropped her eyes and shook her head. "Is it too much?"

Before he could answer, the cat chased wildly across the room, collided with his ankles, rolled over and began biting and clawing at the hem of his robe like a kitten with a catnip mouse. "Ow," Math said mildly, as one of the claws found his ankle. He eased his feet away, and the cat lay pressed against the floor, ears back, eyes wild. "What's the matter with you, Mudpie?" Math asked, bending over and offering to rub the cat's head. Mudpie took off again in a mad dash for parts unknown, kicking up a small area rug in its passing.

"What the hell," observed Math.

"Mudpie, is that his name?"

"Mudpie's a very female cat."

"Mudpie is also a rather drunken cat," Elain informed him.

She could see his mouth twitch. "I see. You know that, do you?"

She nodded gravely. "I do."

"When did she start hitting the bottle?"

"About ten minutes ago. While you were in the shower. She had what you might call an uncontrollable urge for some of your best whisky."

He had strolled over to the drinks table, and now he picked up the nearly empty bottle of Scotch. "Ouch," he said. He looked around in the direction the cat had gone. "Will she survive?"

"I think so. She didn't drink all of it. Some of it she sat in."

"Very sensible." Math crossed back to the sofa and sank down into it, laughing with her, and somehow all the joking had only served to increase her awareness of him.

Nervously she got out of the chair and walked over to where her towel still lay on the stool in the inglenook. She picked it up, bent forward and ran her fingers through the fall of hair. Behind her a soft light went on.

"Come here."

It was softly said, even gently, hardly a command at all. Yet something in the tone made her go still, and the nerves just under her skin began chasing each other up and down her back. She turned because she was incapable of resisting the impulse, and looked over her shoulder at him.

He smiled. His eyes were warm in the lamplight, the lids drooping a little as he watched her. "Come and sit here," he said, indicating the sofa beside him. He held up a silver comb. "I'll comb the tangles out."

If she sat beside him she was a goner. She came over, turned and settled down in a lotus position in front of his knees. His hands on her shoulders gently drew her farther back, his knees opening as he tucked her between his legs. Oh, great. Out of the frying pan, straight into the inferno. His hands were on her scalp now, threading through her hair, drawing it down onto her shoulders.

She was surprised it wasn't standing on end, so electric were his fingers. Even her eyelashes felt the charge as his touch radiated down her face and neck, over back and arms, across her breasts and stomach and legs. Nervously she shifted and extended her legs.

She was wearing soft brown cotton leggings under her cream-coloured cotton sweater, and her feet were bare. As Math began to run the comb through her wet hair, she wiggled her toes. The glow of lamplight was a cocoon around them, for the room was in shadow now as the sun set behind the mountains.

His feet were on either side of her, strong, muscled, with curling black hair around the ankles. In the clasp of his legs she felt small and secure, as she hadn't felt since . . . oh, for years. She wondered absently if his toes were as sensitive as her scalp seemed to be.

Too late, she realized he would probably notice her still slightly damaged ear and the little bald patch. He paused to take a drink, and then he leaned forward behind her and a second later was handing down her sherry glass. She took it gratefully, glad to give her restless hands something to do, hungry for the false courage alcohol would give her.

When he had finished, he set down the comb and dropped his hands lightly onto her shoulders and began a slow massage of her neck. Elain closed her eyes and dropped her head forward while his touch tingled through her. She knew where this was leading, and she should get up and go, but somehow she couldn't. She was starving for his touch, and it was impossible to force herself away from the feast.

When he had massaged her neck and shoulders and upper arms into melted honey, she turned and knelt in the embrace of his knees, putting her arms around his waist and dropping her head into his black-robed lap.

She put her cheek straight onto his aroused flesh, and sat back with a gasp. It was mostly sheer surprise, but Math's hands grasped her upper arms and held her. "It's all right," he said steadily. "Elain, it's all right."

Maybe, but she was shaking like a frangipani in a hurricane. How far she had come without realizing it! She'd thought she was dabbling in the shallows, sensually aroused herself perhaps, but Math physically unmoved. How wrong could you be? Yet he'd only touched her shoulders! And she hadn't touched him at all! And yet—

He drew her up against his chest and bent and kissed her, his mouth soft and delicate against hers. "Where the bee sucks," he whispered, kissing her again, "there suck I," and though she wasn't at all literary, she understood that he meant her mouth was a flower.

Everything affected her physically now—his touch, his voice, his words, his intent, even the wet weight of her own hair against her scalp and neck. When his mouth pressed hers again, she moaned.

"Nothing you don't want," he whispered. "Nothing you're not ready for." Oh, God, what had she got herself into? When he saw her...

Somehow she was lying on the sofa, and he was sitting between her open legs, her left leg behind his back, her right across his lap, and he was stroking her, not gently at all, her thighs and her midriff and her shoulders and arms, and she was arching and crying out for more. He ran his hands up her thighs, slowly, waiting for a protest, but she wasn't capable of it. His thumbs met at her centre, and he stroked up, then over her abdomen, under her sweater, up to her breasts, around to her sides and down again. Over and over, until she was drunk on sensation.

She knew what was coming, but she could not push him off, could not stop him by a word, a look, a touch, as his arms slipped under her back, lifted her up and began to slide the sweater over her head.

He dropped the cream cotton to the floor, paused and looked into her sleepy, half-lidded, desirous eyes. *Jeez, Elain, you might have warned a guy!* She heard the echo distantly in her head. But she could do nothing, say nothing; she could only wait to be touched and taken if that was what he wanted.

He bent down, and his mouth pressed the racing pulse at her throat and slowly, slowly, followed the line of her breastbone down to the centre of the plain, serviceable bra she always wore. Then she felt his hands meet between her shoulder-blades, and took in a gasp of air between her parted lips.

"Math," she whispered, and he went still. She saw his jaw muscles clench as he swallowed and found control.

"Too much?" he asked softly. "Stop?"

She closed her eyes, unable to speak, then opened them again. His gaze was so dark, something to drown in, oh, and she wanted to drown! "Math," she breathed again, and he carefully undid the clasp of her bra and gently drew it away from her body.

A little chill slithered down her spine, fear counteracting desire as nothing else could have done, and she watched as he looked at her bared breasts, and she saw nothing in that black gaze but desire.

She moaned helplessly and bit her lip, and then he bent his head and kissed her breast, and the next thing she felt was the heat of his hand encircling her damaged breast and the damp of his mouth enclosing her nipple.

"What are you *doing?*" she cried, wildly, for while she had imagined he might be able to ignore it, this was beyond understanding. "What are you doing?"

He raised his head and smiled at her. "What is it, my love?" he whispered. "Can't I kiss your breasts?"

"Not that one!" she cried like a child.

He lifted his hand in surprise, glancing down and then back up at her face. "Not this one? Why?"

"Because it's ugly. It's deformed. I'm ugly," she said, choking on the truth but knowing she must face it.

He leaned up over her, in that one second losing control, and kissed her passionately and deeply on the lips, as if to crush the words into nothing. Then he lifted his face and looked at her, almost angry. "You are not ugly," he said hoarsely. "You are the most beautiful woman I have ever seen. Your breasts are beautiful and your body is beautiful and your face is like a flower. And I want you."

"Still?" she asked, her voice high and unnatural.

"Always," he said roughly. "What do you mean, still?"

Her eyes fell before the blaze of passion in his. "I was afraid—I thought—when you saw this..." Her voice cracked as she fought for control in a whirlwind of feeling. "I was burned. It's a skin graft."

He went still. "And what did you think I would do when I saw it?" he asked, and there was a look in his eyes that almost frightened her now. She swallowed, and did not answer him.

His eyes on her, his hand slipped up her ribcage and firmly embraced her breast again. Then he dropped his head and once more she felt the heat of his mouth around the nipple. But this time there was no fear between that touch and her body, so that when his tongue moved on her flesh it was transformed into pure sensation. She shuddered with the knowledge of her new-found freedom. Her back arched then, and she cried out, and he heard surrender in her cry.

His left hand grasped her arm so tightly it hurt, and he held her till she opened her eyes and looked at him. "That's it?" he asked. "That's all of it?"

"All of what?" She could hardly speak, so drowned in the newness of sensation was she.

"There's nothing else you're afraid of?"

"No...what do you mean?" What was he talking about? Why didn't he make love to her, if...

"No man has hurt you? You aren't afraid of making love with me?" She was too far gone to understand any of this.

"I was afraid you wouldn't...want to, once you saw..." she tried to explain again, but no other word got past her lips. As though what she said had cut through a cord of superhuman control in him, his arms were suddenly around her, rough with uncontainable passion, and his mouth smothered hers as he pulled her against him.

"Elain," he whispered. "Elain, I thought—" Then his mouth was against her neck, her breasts, his arms pressing and stroking her as he drew her body up to the caress of his lips.

Her leggings came down her legs in one wild sweep, and then his hands and his mouth enclosed her centre, and she cried a high, hoarse cry of passionate surprise at the newness and strangeness of the world she had entered.

She lost track of time, of everything except sensation. Then he was naked above her, naked in a glowing, staggering beauty that rocked her to the core, and he lifted her and set her on himself. She cried out with the pain of the newness of what happened then, and heard his voice break on her name as if it were a precious, secret word.

There was nothing in her experience to guide her. He was her only guide, and surely and certainly he led her and drove her through a savage, uncharted world, where she found the wildest, most unimaginable pleasure. He lifted her and kissed her and moulded her and pushed her until his hands and his mouth and his driving, pulsing body were the whole world, wild and sweet and drowning her in pleasure.

At last he drew her up against him, her arms around his neck, and the passion in his eyes burned her till she was almost unconscious with her own passion. "Kiss me," he commanded then. "Kiss me, Elain."

She pressed her mouth to his, kissing and sucking his lips, licking him with her greedy tongue, her hands pulling his hair, her mouth running along his cheek to his ear. "Math," she whispered, and then, "Oh, Math!" Because he was powerful and thrusting inside her and calling her name.

She put her mouth over his, and the sound of her name on his lips burst inside her in another flowering eruption of sensation, deep within—as deep as the flooding of his own uncontrollable pleasure, as rich as the forest at the dawn of the world.

Chapter 10

Later she lay in his arms on the sofa, enclosed and safe. She snuggled against his chest, slightly awkward. "I've never done that before," she said softly.

"I know you haven't," said Math in a tone that said he had been surprised. "How did you manage that?"

"I—I thought no one would..."

"You thought no one would...?" He waited, but she did not continue. "Would what? *Want you?*" he asked incredulously.

Elain nodded mutely.

He leaned back and gazed down at her. "How could you imagine that no one would want such a beautiful, sexy woman as you are? And how is it no one has managed to convince you otherwise?"

She smiled disbelievingly. "Do you think other men are like you, or like—" She broke off. "Do you think other men are like you?" she repeated, not knowing how to explain.

"If you mean do I think other men find you unbearably desirable, the answer is, unquestionably. But don't let that go to your head." His arm tightened around her. "Because none of them can have you."

"Greg said . . . Greg didn't want me when—" Elain took a deep breath. "After he saw me naked," she finished. And suddenly Greg was nothing but a stupid memory. She saw how foolish she had been to allow one ugly moment to poison her life. She snorted on a laugh. "Mind you, he was a high school football hero. He went off to some American college on a football scholarship and graduated in push-ups or something."

"I rest my case," said Math. His arms around her, her back against his chest, he cupped his hand possessively over her breast. Suddenly she felt tears burn her eyes. To have felt cold for so long, and now to feel so safe!

"Thank you," she said, and he heard the tears in her voice and tilted her head up. Then he bent and kissed her wet cheek. His own eyes were suspiciously wet, and she said, "Why are you crying?"

"Am I crying, my darling? I suppose it's because of the vast plain of difference between what I imagined and the truth."

"What did you imagine?"

"You trembled so desperately that morning when I wanted to make love to you in the fortress. I thought someone had done something to make you hate sex."

"You thought I'd been raped?"

"Something like that."

"What were you going to do?"

"Take as long as it took."

She remembered the control she had sensed in him, and knew that he spoke the truth. She would have been safe with him. He would not have lost patience, he would have waited.

"I'm glad it wasn't that way," he said.

In the night she awoke beside him. A full moon poured liquid light over the big bed through the skylight in the peaked roof, but she felt that the light came from her own eyes, as if she were seeing in the dark. The world was magical, new-made, and she was wide awake in it, a creature who had been born with the world.

She slipped from under the duvet and padded softly from the room. She had never slept naked, not once in her life, but she was naked now, and as she glided through moonlight and moonshadow, beautifully insubstantial, she felt that the moon had accepted her as one of her own.

The sitting room was awash with light, and the full moon was perfectly framed in the skylight. Elain lifted her arms above her head and pirouetted, raising her face to the moonglow, dancing to the subtle night music she heard within.

An owl hooted, and she knew why. She understood the creatures of the night, fellow worshippers of the moon goddess. The night was alive around her. She crept to the window and looked out at the dark, mysterious colours, the softly moving shadows. Up on the hill, the tower of the fortress was starkly white and black, half in its own shadow, glimmering with an unreality that made it seem alive. She was still for a moment, unbreathing, watching, and wished she could be out in the night with the owl's hoot and the fox's cry, the dew-dampened grass and the insect song.

Poets talked about the first day, the first morning of Creation, of light arising from darkness. Yet what mystery there was now, in this night like the first night. Surely the Great Mover who had decreed Light had also decreed Darkness. Surely this beauty had never been, even at the first, merely the absence of day, the failure of the Light?

She moved to the fireplace and stood looking down at the sofa. A shiver of memory brushed up her back, and she saw Math's face, felt his dark, passionate gaze, and then she melted again within. Gently, lightly, her hand brushed the soft, worn leather of the sofa back, and as tendrils of sensation trembled along her nerves from her fingertips, she closed her eyes.

The owl hooted again. "Thank you," she whispered in her own night cry. "Oh, *thank you.*"

It was as she was turning away from the sofa that her gaze fell on the bookcase where she had knelt a few hours ago, another woman in another lifetime. She stepped closer, smiling, only vaguely remembering that woman she had once been, untransformed by love. Moonlight played on the books, and she saw a shadow where she had replaced a book hurriedly on the shelf...in the moment when Math had come in and she had turned to meet life.

The dust jacket of the book had come half-adrift; that was what was causing the shadow. She stepped over to the case and pulled the book out again. *Wounds Which Bleed Profusely*, by Taliesin. She opened the back cover and tucked the dust jacket straight, then frowned down at it. What curious tricks moonlight could play....

Elain straightened and flicked on the lamp that stood on the bookcase. But it was not a trick of moonlight. Over the name of the author, Taliesin, was a photo of Math.

The moonlight had moved by the time she returned to the bed. As she slipped in under the duvet, Math's body heat made her feel how chilled she had become even in the warm night, and she gently slithered closer to him.

"Mmm?" he murmured drowsily, his arm warmly encompassing her as he drew her close against him.

"Nothing," she whispered.

"Mmm."

What luxury there was in the warm body of another self. She snuggled against him, smiling. He stirred then, as if her cool flesh had brought him to consciousness. "Trouble sleeping?" he murmured.

"No...Math?"

"Mmm?"

"Are you Taliesin? The writer?"

"Mmm." He yawned and snuggled against her neck.

"Why didn't you tell me?"

Another yawn suffused him. "I'd have got around to it, I guess."

"You're famous, aren't you?"

He opened his eyes, and his hand tightened against her waist. "Not really. Is it a problem?"

"Of course not."

"I'd have got around to telling you about it tomorrow, as it happens. There's something I've been thinking about."

"Oh, tell me now!"

He yawned again. "No. Go to sleep," he said heartlessly.

Elain turned in his arms till she was facing him, her nose buried against his neck. She breathed in his sleepy male scent with pleasure and pushed at his shoulder. "*What* have you been thinking about?"

His eyes were half-lidded in the moonlight, and a slow smile curled the corners of his lips. "What?"

"What are you thinking?"

"Now?"

"Now."

"Right now I'm thinking how much I'd like to make love to you again, and wondering if your body is too sore for me to make the attempt. What do you think?" He had lifted his head and was stroking her shoulder and arm.

"I am sore," she admitted in some surprise. "Making love hurts, doesn't it?"

"Only at the beginning, my darling."

"Ah." He was still massaging her, and in spite of the utterly new sensitiveness she felt in her body, it was responding to the touch with little shivers of demand.

"I'm sorry you're uncomfortable." Math shifted up on one elbow and looked down at her, stroking her tangled hair out of her face. She closed her eyes languidly, and he smiled. "Shall I kiss it and make it better?"

Body and mind leaped to attention at the implied promise in his voice. She bit her lip. "I—but—"

He was already sliding down against the sheet, his hands on her thighs. She felt the gentle pressure of his hands parting her legs, and then another, featherlike touch that struck every nerve in her body into singing awareness. She grunted, and gasped, and then was silent with the overwhelming joy of having to do nothing but accept the pleasure he gave her.

* * *

"Why do you write under a pseudonym?" she asked in the morning.

They were up early, taking the public footpath down to Pontdewi for breakfast. They had both missed dinner in the restaurant last night, and now, by missing breakfast, would confirm any suspicions that they had raised then, but Elain was too light-hearted to care what anyone knew.

"So that I can be anonymous when I want to be."

"Have you ever published under your own name?"

"Never."

"Didn't you ever regret not using your own name?"

Math turned on the forest path to grin up at her. "For a few years in my twenties, I imagined I'd have had better success with women if they'd recognized my name." He was laughing at himself, and at her a little, and she couldn't help joining in. Yet she had the feeling there was something behind the joking tone, something that he couldn't laugh at.

It seemed strange to her; Elain could never have signed a painting with some other name. For her, mortality was too close, and whatever contribution she made to the world of art, she wanted her own name on it. But the sun was glinting through the trees, and the patterns of sun and shadow on the forest floor were too beautiful and forever to be thinking of transient things like fame and immortality.

"Why did you choose that name? Just one word?"

"There was a sixth-century Welsh bard of that name. It was presumptuous of me, but I was only twenty-six."

In the pub garden they ordered a full English breakfast: eggs, bacon, sausages, fried tomatoes, fried mushrooms and toast. Elain usually had a pretty good appetite, but not for fried foods in the morning. This morning she was ravenous.

"You sure know how to make a girl hungry!" she said, when she had gobbled the lot in record time and was surveying the table for new pastures. Her eyes fell on Math's toast. "Are you going to eat that?"

He laughed. "Help yourself." He called to the waitress for another cup of coffee, leaned back in his chair and said, "Mind if I put a proposition to you while you eat?"

Elain looked up, startled. "Oh, right! You said last night—what's it about?"

"Have you read the *Mabinogion?*"

"No, not yet." She made a face. She had borrowed a copy of the national epic from him, but she hadn't read it so far. Except for "The Dream of Rhonabwy." She had read that.

"I'd like you to read it, tell me how it appeals to you."

"All right. But why?"

Math smiled at her, a long, slow smile that melted her where she sat. "I'd like you to see if it interests you enough to paint it. Scenes from each of the tales of the *Mabinogion*," he said. "I'm planning on producing a coffee-table book of it. I thought we might collaborate on it, Elain. What do you think?"

Elain took a deep breath of excitement. It would be a fascinating project, if "The Dream of Rhonabwy" was anything to go by. Something in her had been stirred by the simple story, the descriptions of costumes.... And it would be the biggest thing she had yet worked on, a chance to develop a theme over a series of paintings.

"I'd love to do it," she said. "Would anybody be interested? Would we get published?"

Math laughed, showing his teeth, picked up her hand and kissed the palm. "I think I can promise you that we would," he said.

Early in the afternoon, after a walk along the public footpath to visit an old Roman mine and a twelfth-century church, they returned to the hotel. Olwen came out of the office, where she had been watching television.

"You've had a phone call," she told Elain.

"Sally?" Elain hazarded. She was the only one of her friends to whom Elain had given the number of the White Lady.

Olwen glanced at Math, then hastily away. "No," she said. "A man, it was. Raymond. He wants you to call him."

Elain opened her mouth in surprise as reality intruded into her magical dream. How on earth had she managed to forget Raymond, her job, and the reason she was here, so thoroughly? Yet she had; for twenty-four hours—more!—it had been as if none of them existed. She could feel herself blushing, and she knew what Olwen was thinking. She was thinking Elain had left a lover behind and had taken up with Math in a holiday fling, and now her life was going to come and get her. But it was harder to guess what Math was thinking. He had stopped just behind her and was saying nothing.

"Thank you." Elain hoped she managed to sound casual. "What time did he call?"

"Nine o'clock this morning. Jan went up to your room, but you weren't there."

"No." She might as well have taken out a full-page ad in the paper. MATH AND ELAIN SPENT LAST NIGHT TOGETHER. "Well, thank you. I'll call him." What on earth did Raymond want? It was rare for him to ring her on a job.

"You can use the phone here in the office, if you like." Nothing like underlining the fact that she felt Elain would want to be private with Raymond.

Olwen was far too interested in what she believed was a complication in Elain's love life for Elain to risk using any phone on the premises now. She would have to get down to Pontdewi. "Thanks," said Elain. "I'll probably ring later. It's not urgent."

"What the hell's going on, Red? You should have reported in yesterday. What's the matter?"

Should she? Had she so lost track of time? "Sorry, I just forgot. Nothing much to go on here, Raymond. I mean, he just didn't do it. I don't think anybody did. Unless it was the ghost, it was an accident."

"Oh, I'm likely to tell my clients that," Raymond said drily. "Look, whoever you've found to fancy there, don't

lose sight of the fox, will you? The clients are awfully
damned determined that this is arson by the owner. If you
fail to prove that, I'm going to have to work hard to justify
your time. So do something that makes you look worth it,
dear, during the days, whatever you're doing at night.''

Was she an open bloody book? How on earth did everybody know? "Don't be stupid, Raymond," she said repressively. She hoped. Maybe she just sounded guilty. Or happy.
Or as though she'd just lost a tiresome virginity that had
lasted long past its sell-by date, and felt like flying. "All
right, I'll try to think of something. Maybe we should look
at some of the guests. After all, all but the psychics are permanent residents and were here when the fire started. And
the staff are all Welsh. You might pretend we think there are
connections to the Nationalists.''

"They won't buy that. Has he got a girlfriend?''

"What?'' Elain said blankly.

"Is he screwing any of the guests?''

"I don't know,'' she replied hesitantly. "I mean, no.''

"Someone in the village? Check him out from all angles.
Get the brain working again, love. Right. Get back to me
tomorrow.''

She spent the afternoon painting and saw Math again just
before dinner. He didn't mention her phone call, didn't ask
if she'd made it. He ordered what was clearly a special wine,
if Jan's face was anything to go by, and then engaged her in
the lightest of conversations. But the look in his eyes was not
light. The blackest flame burned there, watching her, ab-
sorbing her own light....

She knew nothing about how affairs were run, but she
knew this: Math was planning on her spending the night
with him again, and making love to her. The knowledge
melted her, so that she spent the meal with her nerves singing and her stomach churning. She drowned in his eyes,
trembled at the sure, firm way his hands moved on his
wineglass, shivered as his voice called up her blood. A bell
rang in her ears, summoning her body to awareness.

Math smiled ruefully and shook his head, and Elain came to with a start. Jeremy was tapping his glass with a spoon, asking for silence. All the residents were in the restaurant, and a number of outside guests. Most people had finished their main course. Conversation all around the room died.

"You are going to read us another poem, Jeremy?" someone called.

Jeremy got to his feet. He was holding a sheet of paper.

He bowed. "'Five Years Before the Eclipse,'" he announced, and then began.

"'Five years before the eclipse—
My father
Waking in his bed
Saw the shadow of its coming against the mottled
Wardrobe of life.
Five years before the eclipse
He saw the sunshadow of earth
And its fragility
Made him weep
For the full moon he would never see again
For the brightness.
Five years before the eclipse
My father knew
That life would not wait for him again.'"

There were congratulations and applause as he sat down. Elain didn't understand the poem, but she applauded politely along with the others when it was over.

"I don't know much about poetry," she said to Math.

He leaned across the table. "You're in good company. Neither does Jeremy," he whispered.

She choked on laughter. "Really? Is it bad?"

"You might call it turgid," Math said.

Elain grinned. "No, I wouldn't. I don't even know what that means."

He laughed, but not at her. "Think of cold porridge."

She let out a crack of laughter that caused heads to turn. "Does it get published?"

"He says so. I imagine in one of the more pretentious literary magazines."

Jan arrived with their dessert and a pot of coffee. "I shouldn't drink coffee," Elain said when she had gone. "It'll keep me awake."

"If the coffee doesn't, I will," Math promised softly.

She simply wasn't capable of disguising the effect this had on her. The electricity of his words hit her in the stomach, depriving her of breath, and then spiralled out all through her body. She looked at him, opened her mouth two or three times and closed it again. And all the time Math was looking into her eyes, and that made it worse. "Will you?" she managed at last.

Math smiled.

Elain sipped her coffee. "This place is unusual, isn't it?" she said, a bit desperately.

"Is it?"

"Well, it's not every day you go to a restaurant and one of the patrons gets up and…" She shrugged, smiling. "Does he do it often?"

Math shrugged. "Every now and then."

"I call that strange."

"Perhaps it's the Welsh love of poetry and minstrelsy," Math suggested. "The tradition of the eisteddfod is still very much alive here."

She had a brochure in her room describing the public contests of poetry and singing that still went on all over Wales. "But those are only in the Welsh language, aren't they?"

"Well, we let the Sassenachs take part from time to time." Math grinned. "Would you like to see one?"

"An eisteddfod? Is there one nearby?"

He nodded. "The week after next. I'll take you."

The other world of which she was part abruptly impinged on her. She couldn't afford to stay once the job was over. "Oh, I—I don't know if I'll still be here," she said awkwardly.

Math looked at her, opened his mouth and then paused. He shrugged. "Well, if you are." He said it casually, as though he didn't much mind, but Elain had the uncomfortable feeling that he hadn't said what he had meant to say.

Chapter 11

Elain closed and locked the door to her bedroom awkwardly, her paintbox in her hand, one foot keeping her easel and canvas case propped against the wall. Then she picked these up and started down the back stairs.

Usually she used the main staircase beside the lift. But there was a narrow flight of old service stairs right beside her room, which ran from Math's apartment on the floor above down into the kitchens two flights below; and this morning, for no good reason, she took that. On the next floor she would have to go along the hall to the main staircase if she didn't want to end up in the kitchens. The house was a rabbit warren, with some parts not accessible from others, and several different staircases. She was still unsure of its geography.

She was singing just under her breath as she awkwardly manoeuvred her equipment down the narrow stairway. Math had done just what he promised last night; they hadn't settled to sleep until the dawn chorus had started. Elain had slept late after that, and had awakened feeling worn but wonderful to find Math already working in his study.

She would start a new picture this morning—the light wouldn't be right now for the Excalibur one, even though her mood probably was. Perhaps she might try...

Elain gasped with dismay as, two steps from the next floor, her paintbox lid simply opened. Tubes, bottles, brushes, cloths—the entire contents burst from the box like escaping prisoners and leaped down the last two steps to the floor, skittering and sliding. The convulsive grab she made, of course, didn't help, and her big bottle of turps, thus encouraged, flew wildly through the air, landed on the polished floor right up against a bedroom door, and broke neatly into three pieces.

The smell of turpentine billowed up from the spreading puddle, and Elain groaned when she saw that most of it was seeping in under the door. Turpentine would eat the polish of the floor alive. Quickly she set down all her paraphernalia and rushed over to hammer on the door.

"Hello, hello!" she called, but there was no answer. The door was locked. She put her ear against it and banged again. She could hear something, a whispering movement, or perhaps a small motor, but no one answered. Elain turned and rushed to the service stairs and down into the kitchens. "Jan!" she cried. "Jan!"

It was after eleven o'clock. The kitchen was spotless, and Jan and Myfanwy had their feet up, drinking a cup of tea before continuing the morning's work. Both of them jumped up. "Elain, what is it?"

She explained, and Jan grabbed up a bucket and mop and her keys and started up the stairs after Elain. "Pooh!" she said, wrinkling her nose as her head came level with the floor above and the stink reached her. "That's Davina and Rosemary's room," she said, fishing for the right key. "I've just cleaned it. They went out early. They won't be back till this evening, they said."

She knocked as she unlocked the door, but as a ritual only, then pushed the door wide. They looked at the little pool of turpentine for a second, then into the room. The room was empty, but now the whispering noise Elain had heard earlier was much louder, and Jan gasped and gave a smothered shriek. Elain pushed her head farther into the room.

A fountain of water was shooting up from one of the taps on the sink in one corner of the room. The wallpaper was already dripping, and a corner of the carpet was sodden, but there was no serious damage yet. A blanket was lying on top of a small wooden chest, and Jan leaped on it, snatching it up and pressing it over the broken tap to absorb the flow. "Go and get Evan!" she yelled at Elain. "Tell him to shut off the mains!" As Elain whirled to obey, she added, "And to bring his tools!"

Elain lost no time, and within five minutes the hotel handyman had shut off the mains and the lead from the water tank, and had settled down to mend the broken tap as Jan, Olwen and Elain tackled the mess.

They stuffed the sodden blanket into a green garbage bag to carry down to the kitchens. Then Elain and Olwen rolled up the carpet as Jan and Evan lifted the beds off it.

"Oops!" Elain exclaimed as the carpet came out from under the bed and she spied two paperback books, both a little the worse for the damp. They were open and lying face down, as though someone reading at night had pushed them just under the bed before going to sleep. Elain reached for them and tossed them onto the bed.

When the carpet had been carried out, and the floor wiped clean of both water and turpentine, she picked up the books and carried them to the open window. The sun was shining brightly, and there was a breeze coming down from the hill. The books might have slightly thickened pages, but they would still be readable when they had dried out.

Ghosts of Britain and *The Dictionary of Ghosts*. Elain grinned. No doubt this was Davina's research reading for her own book. She didn't think much of the cover illustration, and the other illustrations were pretty lurid for a serious work. Amateurish. If she'd been doing the artwork...

"'A Ghostly Explosion! In the pretty village of Cheslyn Slade, Wiltshire, an explosion took place that has never yet been explained in scientific terms! On the night of June 13th, 1944..."'"

Elain giggled. This was written for children! It couldn't possibly be serious research material for a psychic. That was why the illustrations were so bad. What on earth did Davina want with a book like this? Elain opened the other one. It was written in a similar style, with very little technical language. It had fewer illustrations, but the cover illustration had been done by the same artist as the other book's.

Elain frowned for a moment, and then began to grin irrepressibly. The author of both books was Diane Middleton. It seemed this was Elain's time for discovering the pseudonyms of authors! So Davina, the "serious psychic," the woman who was insulted by the term "medium" and by any implied association with Madame Arcati, wrote cheap books about ghosts for the credulous!

She turned, but both Olwen and Jan had gone out with the bedding. Maybe it was just as well. She shouldn't tell them Davina's secret.

But she could tell Math. It was the sort of joke he'd appreciate.

By twelve they were all in the kitchen having another cup of tea and laughing the quiet laughter of those who have shared a disaster. "Do you know—thank God your paintbox broke," Olwen said, pouring Elain a refill. "In those few minutes there wasn't much damage done, but suppose we hadn't noticed anything for an hour or two."

"Or even all day," Jan chimed in. "I'd just cleaned the room. Davina and Rosemary took a picnic lunch today, so they wouldn't have been up there. And the water would only have leaked down into the sitting room, and that's not much used on a fine day." She took a breath, shaking her head. "It might have been dreadful. Their clothes ruined and the mattresses and carpets soaked... Thank God for your paintbox, Elain!" she said.

Elain only smiled and nodded. But she was remembering that if she had not taken the back stairs down that one flight, her paintbox would have come apart on the main stairs, and the burst tap wouldn't have been found.

She frowned in thought. She never took the back stairs, yet this morning, something had made her do so. Even as she was doing it, she had thought her own behaviour curious.

The day was beautiful all day. Elain went up to the fortress and worked on the painting she had begun over a week ago, of the watcher and the valley. It was an odd painting, very different from her usual work. It was the sort of thing she had sometimes painted for Stephen, her tutor.

"You get behind the surface of things, all right," he had said to her once. "I want to see you also get behind the surface of yourself."

She had been uncomfortable working with him, too uncomfortable to admit that what the principal said might be true—she did her best work for Stephen. All she had known then was that she was afraid of him without knowing why. When she insisted on being assigned another tutor, everyone was thunderstruck, and she knew now that they had been right. Her work during her last year at the college, under another tutor, had not lived up to her early promise.

She had never understood herself why she felt so threatened by Stephen, why she had so desperately wanted to get away from him. But she could see it now. It was the same reason she had been afraid of Math, had imagined him dangerous. She had been sexually attracted to him, an attraction too strong to ignore, almost too strong to disguise. That was what had made her uncomfortable, though if anyone had suggested at the time that her problem was that she "fancied" Stephen, as they put it here, she'd probably have hit them.

She was more than sexually attracted to Math. From the beginning, she had felt that strange sense of a deeper knowledge of him than time would ever give. He, too, was someone who would, by his presence, encourage her to look beneath her surface. Still, if she hadn't been fixed here by her job, she might have run away from him, too, and gone on through her life in the same way—protecting herself from rejection by never wanting a man, never loving. By hating and fearing any man she was attracted to.

And never being artist enough to get under her own surface. Being mediocre, when she might have been a real artist. Waking up one morning to discover that she was doing the illustrations for a book like *Ghosts of Britain*.

Elain picked up another canvas and set it on her easel—an unfinished view of the hotel and the valley. There was something else that she had not had the courage to look at. Quickly she squeezed out orange and red and yellow onto her palette, blue and brown and black. With swift, urgent strokes, she began to paint the hotel in flames, a bright, terrible, all-consuming blaze, of the kind her nightmares were composed of.

Through an upper window, in a few strong strokes, a man took shape, turning away from the window into the flaming room as the roof above began to fall.

Below, outside, a child in a pink-flowered nightgown, caught in the hold of a large man, stretched her arms longingly to the window above, her tiny mouth open on a desperate cry.

I knew then, Elain realized sadly as she painted. *I knew when I heard that roar that they would never come back. All the rest was just pretending.*

She was just opening the door of her room when she heard Davina and Rosemary's arrival at their own door on the floor below.

"That's strange," she heard Rosemary say as the key turned in the lock. "The—"

"Rosemary!" Davina interrupted, her voice shocked. Elain bit her lip. Somehow the two sisters had managed to return without anyone waylaying them to tell them what had happened, although she knew Olwen had meant to be on the lookout for them.

"What?" Rosemary demanded, prepared to be horrified. "What is it, Davina?" Her voice was loud with shock, so Davina's face must be something to behold. Though there wasn't that much to see. Just a carpet missing and the beds stripped. "Good God!" she exclaimed after a moment.

"Something happened!" Davina said.

"Yes, indeed. I wonder what?" Rosemary returned.

Elain shoved all her stuff inside her room, closed the door and started down the stairs. Olwen had just arrived, and all three women were inside the room, the door open.

"I'm so sorry. I meant to catch you before you came upstairs. Fortunately there was little harm done."

"Jessica again," said Davina flatly. "She certainly *meant* harm, I know. Did our things get spoiled?"

"No, only the carpet and some of the bedding suffered. A tap burst. The water was shooting up, but we caught it almost as soon as it began. We've moved you into a room on the other side of the hall. The Nursery. It has a view over the valley."

There was a stony silence. "But we always have The Chapel," Davina said, horrified. "Every time we've been. We always book this room!"

"Yes, but Math thought—"

"We must go and check out the other room, Davina," Rosemary spoke over Olwen.

"But—" The sisters exchanged a look, then Rosemary turned calmly to Olwen.

"My sister is rather restricted at times as to the places where she feels comfortable. This room, of course, was the old chapel, and there are rooms in this hotel she simply cannot be expected to stay in, the more especially now that the ghost is in transition. If the other room is satisfactory of course we will be happy to move. Come, Davina."

But Davina wasn't to be soothed out of her negative vibrations. As soon as the door of the other room was opened she shuddered and turned away. "No," she wailed, looking pitifully at Rosemary. "Please, Rosemary."

Rosemary bit her lip. "Perhaps for one night, Davina. If you're still of the same mind in the morning..." She turned to Olwen. "I expect The Chapel can be made habitable again in the morning."

Olwen glanced at Elain, her face expressionless. "Yes, of course," she said.

"I won't get a wink of sleep," Davina promised herself heavily.

"Why the hell didn't you tell me this before?" Raymond demanded. Elain had just told him about the incident of the burning coal on the carpet.

"Because I didn't think it was significant. But now something else has happened, and it's starting to look a little weird, to say the least." She told him about yesterday's burst tap. "Now that was serious, Raymond. No one would have got hurt, but there would have been maximum damage and another insurance claim."

"Mmm," she heard down the wire. "I see your point."

"It can't be him. No one would be so stupid. It might make the insurance company even more suspicious, mightn't it? And less likely to pay."

"You think there's somebody sabotaging this guy?"

"I don't know. If you believe the psychic, the ghost in the house is turning, or something. Did I tell you that? Becoming sinister and dangerous after centuries of humorous tricks." When the sisters had recovered from the shock, Davina had explained to Math how she felt "the hand of Jessica in this."

"I don't believe the psychic," Raymond said succinctly. "All right, you've sold me. We'll investigate the others in the place."

She felt like a traitor, giving him the names and what she had learned of the other guests and the staff. Never before had she got so close to those she was investigating. She told him everything she had gleaned over the past two weeks, including the fact that Vinnie's husband had died at Arnhem; that Jeremy, cousin of a noble house, was also a poet who might be published in a small, pretentious magazine; that Davina might be the author of popular ghost books under the pseudonym Diane Middleton; that Jan was married to a local farmer; that Gwen from the pub had a cousin who used to work for Math, and numerous other little facts.

She was a traitor, and yet…what else could she do? If she quit the job, the insurance company would probably just send someone else in, someone who might be more dedicated to the theory that Math was an arsonist. What good would that do Math? If someone else *had* committed arson, Elain was more likely than anyone else to find the proof of it—she at least was looking for it.

And if she quit, she would have to leave and go back to London. Elain knew she couldn't bear that. She didn't ask herself why; she didn't want to examine it too closely. She wanted to stay, that was all, and why shouldn't she want to? Wales was absolutely beautiful; it was the home of her ancestors. She was painting well. There were lots of reasons for staying.

"Look," she said.

They were at dinner in the hotel restaurant. Math obediently reached out and took the thick sheet of artist's paper from her hand. He looked at it, and his eyebrows went up. He picked up the candle on the table and held it to get a better light. "How on earth did you manage this?" he asked in surprise.

It was a watercolour reproduction of the tapestry "Dream of Rhonabwy." "It's the tapestry," she said, like a child.

"I see it is. I'm—"

"Is it good?" she demanded.

"If it's not a perfect copy, it must be very close," he said. He gazed at it again. She could see that the sight of it pleased him. "You found a photo of it?" he asked. He glanced over to the table where Vinnie and Rosemary and Davina were eating. "Or are the psychic capacities contagious?"

Elain giggled. "Vinnie found an old black and white—not of the tapestry, but of somebody standing in front of it. She'd forgotten she had it. Most of the detail showed. She only had to remember the colours, and of course the descriptions in the story helped a lot."

Math smiled, turned and set the sketch on the edge of the wainscot just above the table. He propped the salt and pepper shakers in front of it, leaned back and looked at it again. Then he reached for her hand and dropped a kiss on it. "I don't suppose copying is very satisfying to an artist. But I would like a mural-size copy of this in oils. Would you be interested in the commission?"

"I'd be interested, but if I do it, it won't end up a perfect copy. There'll be too much of me in it, and you'd notice the difference."

"All the more reason," said Math.

They climbed through the sun-speckled forest to the top of the ridge. They had left the public footpath some time ago, Math promising to take her to see something special. The last few hundred feet were steep enough to make Elain pant, and then suddenly they were there, and she drew in an enchanted breath and gazed around.

It was a magical place—a small sunlit glade with a huge oak at the centre, and the ancient trees of Wales sprinkled over a thick bed of grass and moss and wildflowers.

Near the tree, rough, splotched with white lichen, was a standing stone. It was no more than four feet high, a couple of feet square. Yet somehow it had power. Standing stones always had that—the ability to capture the attention—but this one had more of whatever quality it was than most. It drew her gaze immediately.

"This is magical," Elain breathed. "How long has this place been here?"

Math shook his head.

"They must have worshipped here. You can feel it! Do you think they worshipped the tree, too?"

"The White Goddess was certainly associated with trees in pre-Christian times," Math said.

Elain crept across the grass and under the spreading canopy of branches to touch the stone, unsurprised to feel the thunder of the Earth's power under her hand. "Do you come here?" she asked. She felt the curious compulsion to speak quietly, as if she were in a church.

Math nodded.

She was still receiving timeless messages from the stone. "What do you do?"

He shrugged. "Read, or write, or just sit and think."

"Are we going to eat our picnic here?"

"If you like."

"As long as it wouldn't be sacrilegious."

"I suppose they might have feasted here on the holy days. Hard to say."

So they spread their blanket and their meal in the sunshine and shadow at the edge of the oak's spread, and ate the Earth Mother's bounty in her holy place. When the edge was taken off their hunger, Elain refilled their wineglasses from the frosted bottle of delicate white wine and lay back against a knotted root that thrust up out of the earth. "I think you should tell me a story from the *Mabinogion*," she said.

"Very fitting," Math agreed.

"One that you want me to paint."

"There's the story of Math ap Mathonwy, or the story of Elen of the Hosts. Any preference?"

She hesitated, charmed into indecision. "We're both in the *Mabinogion*?"

"That's one way of looking at it. Shall I tell you about Maxen's dream? That has Elen in it."

"Yes, please."

"Maxen the ruler," Math began in a deep, mellow voice, as she lay looking up at the tree and the perfect sky, "was Emperor of Rome. He was handsome and wise and well fitted to his rule. One day, Maxen called together all the kings of his realm, and with them he went hunting into a river valley near Rome. When the sun was high overhead, and it was very hot, Maxen grew sleepy and lay down to rest.

"In his sleep, he had a dream. He dreamt he travelled across mountains and plains, following a great river, until he came to the sea. There he boarded a magnificent ship and sailed to an island, and crossed the island to the farther sea. Here he came upon a great fortress. The fortress had a roof and doors of gold, and the walls were studded with jewels. Inside, on a golden chair, was the most beautiful woman Maxen had ever seen. He embraced the woman and lay down with her, but just then the stamping of the horses and the clanging of shields in the wind awakened him."

"Ah."

Math laughed. "So in love with this woman was Maxen, and so unhappy to find her not with him when he awoke, that he soon fell into a melancholy. He would neither go hunting with his men, nor listen to songs and entertainments, nor drink. He only slept, in order to dream of his mistress.

"At last his chamberlain came to him and told him that his men were unhappy, for he gave them nothing to do and never spoke to them. He urged the emperor to action. So Maxen summoned his wise men and told them what case he was in, in love with a woman he had seen in a dream and unable to take any interest in anything else.

"The wise men advised him to send out couriers to try to find the woman of his dream, for then at least he could live in hope. Maxen sent messengers to roam the world, but at the end of a year they returned having found nothing.

"Then one of his subject kings advised Maxen to try to find the place of his dream himself. Maxen journeyed until he had found the river of his dream, and then sent his messengers along that river. They travelled and found all as he had described it, coming at last to the distant island and the fortress. They entered the fortress and found Elen, daughter of Eudav, with her father and her brothers, Kynan and Avaon, sitting in a golden chair. They knelt before her and called her Empress of Rome and told her they were to take her to Maxen. But Elen would not go with them. She said that Maxen must come to her.

"So the messengers returned to Rome and delivered their news, and Maxen set out with his army. He conquered the island of Britain as he went, and then arrived at Eudav's fortress. Here he went in and saw Elen, as she had been in the dream.

"That night they slept together, and in the morning she asked for the gift that was her due, as he had found her a virgin. When Maxen told her to name her own gift, she asked for the island of Britain for her father, and the three offshore islands for her own, and for three strongholds to be built at Arvon, Caerleon and Carmarthen. Later she had these three fortresses linked by roads.

"Maxen stayed with Elen seven years, and then word came to him that a new emperor had been elected in Rome in his place. He set out to reconquer Rome, but after a year of laying siege to the city, he still had not succeeded.

"Then, in Britain, Elen's two brothers rallied a host to Elen's name and came to Maxen's aid, and when they had conquered Rome, they gave it to Maxen. Maxen accepted his throne and gave the two brothers the freedom to conquer whatever territory they wished.

"The brothers went and conquered castles and cities, and then Avaon and his men went home to Britain, while Kynan and his men stayed in Brittany, the land they had conquered. To preserve their British language, they cut out the tongues of the women, and that, the story says, is why they still speak the Celtic language in Brittany.

"The three roads linking the three fortresses of Elen were always called the Roads of Elen of the Hosts. She was given that name because the men of Britain would not have assembled for anyone but her."

Elain had been almost dozing while his voice had conjured up pictures in her mind. Now it stopped, and the only sound was the wind in the leaves above her. She opened her eyes and shielded them from the sun. "Is that the end?"

"I'm afraid so," Math said apologetically. "They were sometimes a little short on plot. In the old days, the importance was in the singing and the poetry."

"I see," said Elain. "And you want to make up for the deficiency with pictures?"

He smiled, glad to find her so quick. "That's it," he said.

"Well, there are quite a few pictures in the story. The river, the fortress, the woman in the golden chair. And the armies. Is it a true story?"

"It's based on some historical facts. There was a Spaniard named Magnus Maximus who served with the Roman army in Britain in the fourth century. His troops proclaimed him emperor, and he crossed the channel, conquered the Roman armies in Gaul, Spain and Northern Italy, but was then defeated by the Emperor Theodosius and beheaded in 388. It's not impossible he took up with a high-ranking Welsh woman."

"It seems funny to have the Romans in the Welsh national epic," Elain said.

"The Romans ruled here for three centuries. They certainly left their impact," said Math. "I like this story because I think it suggests that when the Romans conquered Wales, it was a matriarchal society, and that under the influence of the Romans, that largely changed."

"Really?" Elain had seen none of that. "What do you mean?"

"It's Elen who is sitting in the golden chair, isn't it, even though her father and brothers are there? What we might call a throne, perhaps. And although her father is alive, the Romans don't make the request for Elen's hand to the father, as is the way in patriarchal societies. They approach Elen direct. And she refuses to go when the Emperor of Rome summons her to be his wife. She demands that he come to her, and she makes that stick."

Elain blinked in the sunshine as these elements of the story struck her. "That's right."

"When she is asked to name a gift, she doesn't ask a favour, as women in such stories so often do. She demands dominion over the territory that Maxen has conquered. And she builds castles and links them with roads that are afterwards called after her. Like any ruler getting the best for her people out of the skills the conquerors have brought." Math picked up a bright green apple and polished it absently against his thigh. "Avaon and Kynan, her brothers, can only raise their army in her name, not their own nor their father's."

"Yes, I see."

"And then what happens? Maxen gives power to the brothers to conquer as they wish. Suddenly Kynan and Avaon have direct power, where before it was derived from their sister. That is, they have taken the concept of male superiority from the Romans. And what's the first thing they do after they take their power?"

"What?"

"They cut out the tongues of women. Women's voices have been stilled, as must always be the case if the patriarchy is to endure." He leaned down and touched her cheek. "I think the Romans brought the idea of masculine supremacy to Wales. I'd like you to paint Elen as a Celtic queen of real power, Elain. Real female power."

Chapter 12

The sun was so warm, and the story had lulled her into a lazy, languorous mood. She fell lightly asleep and dreamed in bright images of blue rivers and glittering towers.

She awoke to find Math asleep on his back beside her, his arms folded under his head. She sat up lazily and looked down at him, drinking her fill of the masculine planes and hollows, lines and curves. It was a new pleasure. Elain had never before allowed herself to look so directly at a man, and now she knew why. Because to look might have been to desire.

He was wearing a faded cotton shirt loose over shorts. As carefully as she could, she lifted the cloth away from his skin and unbuttoned it, laying the two sides apart so that his chest was exposed to her sight. She moved slowly in the heat, feeling no sense of urgency, nothing but the honeyed movement of the senses in her.

Black hair curled over the expanse of his chest and down over his stomach, inviting her touch; but she did not want to awaken him. He was neither fat nor thin, and though he was nicely muscled, there was a cushion of fat between the muscles and his skin, his body's velvet glove. This was no weightlifter's body, but that of a man who rode horses and walked for his exercise, and who ate what he liked.

His legs were more obviously muscled, his thighs thick and strong, his calf muscles rounded and curving down to lean, strong ankles and neat, bony feet.

Perhaps she would paint him like this, a god fallen in the forest, asleep after the hunt or some adventure with a daughter of the trees or the river.

But not clothed; she would not paint him clothed. Elain reached out and slipped the waist button on his loose cotton shorts, and then, half-hypnotized, three more buttons. Softly she opened the fabric and folded it back.

With a faintly audible breath, she saw that he was naked underneath, and that he was aroused. She glanced at his face, but he still slept. Perhaps, like Maxen, he was dreaming of a Welsh princess on a golden throne.

The sight of that powerful flesh drew her gaze, drew her body. Yes, this was how she would paint him, a dark god on a bed of grass, naked and aroused. Elain bent closer over him and then, because it followed naturally, she dropped the most delicate of kisses on that compelling flesh.

It stirred under the touch, and she smiled and kissed him there again. Then she remembered the pleasure his mouth had given her, the dampness, the heat, and she opened her lips and softly embraced the tip.

At this touch, his flesh leaped like a live thing in her mouth, stirring her into sudden arousal, and she pressed her lips tight against him, and felt her own heart's slow thunder in her back and abdomen and thighs.

She moved by instinct then, half trying to remember what he had done that had given her such pleasure, half simply doing what gave her pleasure. It gave her pleasure to move her tongue over his flesh, she discovered, to enclose him deep in her mouth, to kiss him and trail her lips over all the flesh of his thighs and abdomen.

A hand stroked her from the back of her head down to the curve of her bottom as she knelt over him, and she looked to see that Math was watching her, his eyes dark and narrowed with the pleasure she gave him. She smiled lazily at him, and he drew her up and kissed her mouth, at the same time lifting the flower-patterned skirt of her dress.

He drew her leg over him so that she knelt up, her centre pressed against his aroused flesh, and then she felt his hands as he drew the cotton briefs aside and opened her to the thrust of his body. He pushed once, deep into her, and then, holding her there, lay smiling up at her.

Kneeling over him, her full skirt spread out around them like a bed of flowers, she was still; and they looked into each other's eyes and smiled at the truth that they were one flesh. He felt the enclosing warmth of her body, she the hard pressure of his; and somewhere the ancient gods awoke and smiled their approval at the old rite of worship being performed again under the sacred tree, at the sacred stone.

Then the girl bent forward, her hands resting on the shoulders of her lover, and raised and lowered herself on the tree that was his share of divinity, her long hair falling forward to veil their faces in the small cocoon where they became each other's world. Her lover's hands grasped her hips, and he helped the lifting and the downward thrust.

Slowly, slowly, with that rise and fall, they moved towards the central rhythm of creation. Slowly, and then more quickly, until they found it, the heartbeat of the Great Earth Mother and her lover, the Sky. The Sky became aroused, and gathered his blessings together over the worshippers, and the Mother held them cupped against her breast. Then that great rhythm caught them, and moved them, and they were writhing and powerless in its terrible, wonderful hold, crying out their nearness to the deepest mystery of the world. The pulse thundered through them, and the girl's skin glowed with the exertion, and her face moved and writhed until she was as beautiful as the Goddess herself, until, as was right, in the mysterious way such things happened, she became the Goddess, taking her pleasure from her earthly lover.

The Sky opened his coffers then, and poured down his anointing on them, and on the grass, and the trees; and the Great Goddess the Earth accepted it, for this was the ritual designed to call up Her fertility, and His favour, and they were pleased to answer.

Then the girl called out loudly, the keening cry of worship, and together the two cried out to Creation their oneness with it, and with each other. And because they were human and could not for long sustain the Oneness, the rhythm broke, and their bodies shuddered with the knowledge of what they had known, and what they lost.

His arms encircled her, in tribute and in memory of the Great Mother, and she, human again, fell down into his embrace and lay unmoving.

The gods were well pleased. They smiled and applauded. They liked the old ways.

"Is that *thunder?* My God, it's absolutely pouring!"

Math's chest trembled with his laughter. "Is this the first you've noticed?"

"No, of course not." She had turned her face up to the downpour as they made love, drinking in the rain as another contribution to their sensual feast. "But I didn't realize it was so heavy! We're drenched."

"It's hotting up. If we get under the tree, we'll have protection from the worst of it."

So they dragged their knapsack and the blanket under the spreading arms of the oak and finished off the last of the wine as they waited for the storm to abate. There was lightning over the valley, and loud thunder, but at last the heavenly show was over, and the sky cleared and showed a burning sun.

"Elain, this is Theresa Kouloudos, my agent. Theresa, this is Elain Owen, who'll be doing the artwork."

"Nice to meet you." Elain shook hands with a thin, very smartly dressed blonde who looked as though she would be comfortable feeding with sharks.

"How do you do?" Theresa returned, seating herself. They were in Math's flat. "You're what—Canadian? Not Welsh, in spite of the name?"

"Ah—well, sort of. My great-grandfather was born here."

Theresa nodded, accepting a whisky on the rocks from Math and taking a swallow that would have had Elain seeing double. "Mmm," she nodded thoughtfully. "Yes, that'll work. Returning to your roots and all that. Anything you can dig up for me on your ancestors?"

Everything seemed to be moving very quickly. "Well, I've meant to look him up in the library at Aberystwyth, but I've never got round—"

"Right. We can put someone on that, if it looks necessary. Do a tree for you. Meanwhile, will you put your c.v., including all the details you know about your Welsh origins, on paper for me?"

It was a half hour before she asked to see any of Elain's work, and in that time the project had been discussed from a variety of angles. Theresa was intelligent and it was clear she knew her job, but she was also hard. Elain got more and more nervous as the time passed, increasingly convinced that her work would not suit the commercially minded agent and dreading the look that would tell her the agent was going to be doing this as a favour to Math.

"Right," Theresa said at last. "Have you got anything you can show me in the style of what you intend to do for the book?"

Nervously Elain opened her portfolio. She had a number of completed pictures now, and she brought them out one by one: the fortress with the population of the valley coming up the hill; Excalibur in the sky over the valley; Arthur's men and the car in the forest; a few others. From the *Mabinogion* she also had one completed painting—the beautiful Elen in her golden chair—and two sketches of other stories, as well as the tapestry. At the last moment, to make up the numbers but not without a great deal of doubt, she had included the watcher over the valley. But the fire picture wasn't finished yet.

Theresa looked at each one closely, then spread them out around her, standing them up against the empty fireplace and various stools and chairs before returning to her seat to gaze at them again.

"Mmm," she grunted after an agonizing delay. She glanced up at Math. "Yes, I see. Very lush, very detailed." She nodded at Elain. "Right. Well, I'll have no trouble placing this, not with this to offer. We'll go for very high production values, all full-colour illustrations. Cost a bomb to produce, but worth it in the end. I know one or two editors who have got some money to play with. I'll talk to them this week."

She looked around at the pictures again. "May I take a few of these with me?" she asked Elain. She still hadn't smiled. It was as though she was so firmly brain-driven, she had forgotten there was such a function of the facial muscles.

Elain nodded. "Take whatever you like."

Theresa moved quickly and unerringly to pick up three of the paintings, one after the other, paused over and then chose a fourth. These she set on the sofa beside her. "I'll bring these back, of course." She picked up several more and handed them back to Elain, in the end leaving one painting still leaning against the fireplace.

The painting of the watcher, the woman whose world was empty. It was different from the others, fundamentally different, and as Theresa sat staring at it, her chin resting against her fingers, Elain waited nervously to be told not to paint anything like this for the book.

At last Theresa moved. She turned to Elain, and her hand dropped away from her chin in a firm arc to point at the painting. "Would you sell me this one? I'd like to hang it in my flat."

* * *

"He's not what?" Elain asked. The line wasn't very good, and she was having trouble hearing Raymond's voice.

"Not related to Althorpe," Raymond repeated. "Sorry, I mean to Spencer."

"Bill? Bill's a dog!" Elain said in amazement.

"Wilkes!" Raymond shouted. "Dammit, Elain!"

"Oh, sorry, I couldn't hear you! Oh, right! Jeremy who's a cousin of an earl isn't a cousin after all? Who is he then?"

"A failed actor of lower middle-class origins," Raymond said brutally.

Elain plugged one ear as a tractor trundled past the phone box. "But Raymond, that's impossible! Where does he get his money? He has an income he says is from a family trust."

"He is lying, my dear. His income is simple building society interest on money he inherited."

"But from whom?"

The tractor moved on up the road. She could hear paper being moved. "From a partner who died of AIDS two years ago. He's also eroding the principal. At the rate he's spending, he'll be without funds in three or four years."

"Has he been published at all? Does he have an agent?"

"If he has an agent, we haven't found him. If he's been published, we haven't found where."

"He goes to London to see his agent, he says."

"Yes, I have the note I made when you told me that before. Let me know next time he leaves for London. I may put a tail on him."

"Anything on anyone else?"

"Your friend, Vinnie Daniels, is straight up and down, as far as we can see. Hasn't told you anything not substantially the truth, except that there's no record she and her fella got married before he died at Arnhem. She took his name when she moved to Wales."

Elain felt sick suddenly. What right had she to root into Vinnie's past, discovering things Vinnie didn't know she knew? When she got out of this job, she'd quit Raymond's employment for good.

"That Welsh waitress, the same," Raymond continued over her silence. "Jan. Straight up and down. If there are connections to the firebrand nationalists, she's covering them very well. There's nothing on anyone else yet. The psychic sisters are proving difficult. Try and get me a bit more information. What area they come from, where they were born."

She wished Vinnie had been more difficult, and Davina easier. She wouldn't mind exposing Davina as a charlatan. "Anyway, they weren't here when the fire happened," she said. "But I wish you'd find out something about the author of those books."

"The books were published twenty years ago and are out of print. The publisher is having a comb through the records, but that'll take time."

"You let me know."

"I'll do that. Now, what have you got for me?"

Precious little, Elain thought guiltily. "Not very much. Math has decided to start the clean-up without the insurance money. He says they'll pay it or they won't, and he's tired of waiting."

"Ah," said Raymond. "Has he had the company's approval?"

"I don't know. But their loss assessor was here weeks ago and hasn't said he'd be returning. Even if there had been evidence overlooked, it's been raining. I mean, he's got the place covered with tarps, but there wouldn't be any evidence left now, would there?"

"I wonder. Keep me posted. All right, what else?"

There was nothing else, and she promised to do better and hung up. She left the phone box with relief, shucking it off like a dead skin. She didn't like what she was doing for Raymond, so she thought about it as little as possible. Elain was two people now, one who lived her "real" life with her painting and with Math, and the other who came into exis-

tence only at odd moments—when she asked people inno-
cent-seeming questions, or as now, when she entered the red
phone box.

Math came out of his study to where Elain was sitting on
the sofa, her legs stretched out, surrounded by the prelimi-
nary sketches of the *Mabinogion.* "Lunch?" he asked.

Elain nodded, dropped her pad and sat up, flexing her
right hand. "Yes, please." She held up a sketch. "What's
that?" she demanded. She had no worries about trusting
Math with something unfinished.

Math came over, bent to kiss her and took the sketch from
her. A rider galloped into a river, sending a wall of water
over a group of men sitting on a small islet in the river. One
of these had his sword drawn, one wore religious clothing,
one wore a great ring. They were surrounded by tents and
pavilions.

"Avaon, son of Talyessin, splashing water over Arthur
and his bishop," he said. "Very nice, too."

"Right!" she carolled, kneeling up to rest her hands on
the back of the sofa and raising her face for another kiss.
Math obliged.

"Now, what about lunch?"

"Is it too hot for soup?"

"Salad might be better."

"All right, and sandwiches?"

They were in the middle of the meal when the knock came
on the door. Math opened it to a heavy-set man whose face
and hands and clothes were blackened with soot.

"Math," he said. "It's about that area we're clearing."

Elain was still sitting at the table, but it seemed to her that
she felt Math tense. "Yes?" he prompted.

"We've found something I think you'll be wanting to
have a look at. Maybe you'd better come."

* * *

The cellar was in an L shape, like the house, though smaller in extent. Under the main part of the building, the floor had been dug deeper at some time, and the walls lined and electricity installed. Here were the laundry room and the storage rooms of the hotel.

But the space under the longer wing, in which the fire had occurred, was low and dark and narrow, and had never been modernized. Where this section met the other, through a door space in a thick stone wall, two steps led up to a higher floor level, while the ceiling height remained the same. The men had to stoop, it was black and dirty, and there was no light. George pulled out a flashlight. The stone walls were original, and the long narrow space was nearly empty. Ahead, where fire had destroyed half the wing, sunlight filtered down through the burnt ceiling, giving the scene the curious unreality of a war photograph.

Elain had never returned to the house where her parents had died. She shuddered a little, wondering if it had looked like this, desolate with destruction and loss.

Everywhere there was the evidence of the work going on: stacks of burnt timber, tarpaulins, props, jacks and other equipment. As well as the workmen, all of the hotel guests were standing around, turning to look in their direction as Math, Elain and George arrived.

Math shook his head wearily when he saw them. "Are you all crazy? What the hell are you doing down here? This stuff could come down on your heads!"

"Oh, but, Math!" Davina cried faintly. "I believe you should stop them! They mustn't go in there! Please listen!"

Math looked at George. "They weren't here when I left to find you, I swear, Math." He turned on his young assistant. "Somebody must have been spreading the news."

The alarmed underling began to stammer a denial, but Davina overrode him. "No, no! No one told us! I was *drawn*, Math! I scented danger. Please listen!"

Math snorted. "If it had kept you away, I'd understand better. Now, I want everybody not part of the work crew out of this area immediately, please. If you must stay around, you'll have to stand well away from the fire area." He spoke quietly, but there was no doubt he meant it. Vinnie, Davina, Rosemary and Jeremy filed carefully through the debris and into the unburnt portion of the basement, where they stood, as expectant as children, watching. Math turned to Elain. "You're staying here?"

She nodded firmly. The smell of fire was strong here. If there was any danger she wasn't leaving Math in it. Her father was all the men she intended to lose to fire.

He seemed to understand. "All right," he said. "Stick close to me. I want you where I can grab you if anything goes wrong. George. How much danger is there of any of this coming down?"

George shook his head. "Not much. We've been and cleared out the loose stuff above. What's left is solid. Today we've been in here checking the foundations. This looked pretty bad, you see."

Light splayed onto a portion of the right-hand wall, where it had buckled into a concavity. Math frowned. "What the hell caused that?" he asked.

"Well, it's right where the petrol cans were, Math, so the explosion would have been pretty concentrated there."

"Not concentrated enough to blast a stone wall into solid earth!"

George nodded. "That's what I thought. We went very carefully in case we were wrong, but there's no doubt about it. It's not solid earth behind, you see. It's a hidden room, or a passage."

Chapter 13

"Math!" The voice came from the darkness behind them. "Math, it's dangerous, I feel it! There's evil coming from a very long time ago. Don't go in."

"Thank you, Davina. I'll use my own judgement. First I'll find out what it is."

George was leading him along the wall, back up towards the unburnt section, where a large cupboard, charred with heat, leaned drunkenly against the stone. "We tried to move this, you see." He slapped the wood, and the blow produced only a dull thud. It was a very solid piece of furniture. "It doesn't move, not with four of us lifting."

"What's it fixed to?" asked Math. "A door, you think?"

"There would be bolts if it were fixed to the stone. If it's a door, it may be the heat has melted the hinges. The only way through is with an axe."

"All right," said Math.

"Math!" Davina pleaded. She had crept close behind him to stare at the cupboard. Math turned and put a hand on her elbow.

"What exactly do you feel?" he asked.

Put on the spot like this, the psychic became nervously uncertain. She shuddered. "Something evil locked up in there."

"You may well be right," he said. "It's possible that what we are going to find is a body that was immured. But it'll be several centuries old—a skeleton—and I'm not worried about that." Elain suddenly remembered the story of Jessica. So Math was thinking she might, after all, have been walked up with death in this tomb. She shuddered. "If you find the prospect unpleasant," Math was saying, "perhaps you should leave."

"No, you don't understand. A deeper—a spiritual evil!"

"If there's a spiritual evil in the cellar of my house," Math said flatly, "I want to know about it."

Behind him, in a crack like doom, a workman's axe came thundering down to splinter the ancient wood.

The shattered wood was cleared away, exposing a doorway about four feet high and two feet wide cut into the stone. Beyond was darkness. There was no keeping anyone back now. They all drew close, residents and workers, crowding around the strange secret entrance with murmurs of amazement. The bright light of the flash pierced the dark and fell on a stone wall two feet behind.

"That'll be the true foundation wall," George said matter-of-factly.

Math took another flashlight from the hands of one of the workmen. "Let's see if there are any bones," he said, stooping down to step inside the dark space and flashing the light ahead of him. He went left, and George followed him.

Both men disappeared from sight. "Aha," they heard George say, and then they all pushed in behind.

It was dark and spooky, a narrow passage running the length of the burnt wing of the hotel behind the damaged wall, down towards the burnt-out end and in the direction of the hill. The lights of the two men played eerily over the stone walls, floor and ceiling and into the darkness ahead, casting their shadows blackly down the passage towards the others.

"A passage!" they were all murmuring in awe. "It's a secret passage!"

"Oh, I say!" Jeremy said, in the mock child's tone of excitement the English always seemed to use when there was adventure afoot. "Come on, Famous Five! I wonder where this leads!"

Math turned to look back at them, and shrugged. There was no point trying to keep them out, and his shrug seemed to say he knew it. They were like dogs who have the scent, even Vinnie.

As Elain moved to catch up with him, her foot struck something, and she smothered a shriek. "What's that?" she gasped. "Is there another light?"

Behind her, one of the young workers started guiltily. "Oh, yes, I have one in my belt." The light was not strong, but it enabled them to see what her foot had found. Over a small grey mound of what looked like earth, flapped the remnants of a cloth. Elain bent closer. "It's a sack of cement or something," she said.

Vinnie, whose eyes were excellent despite her age, eagerly bent over and examined the manufacturer's logo on the rotting cotton sacking. "Not cement," she said. "That's flour. A half-hundredweight sack of flour. I remember those from before the war."

Math and George had come back at Elain's call, but there wasn't much to see or say about a sack of flour, not when they had been half expecting human bones.

"There may be rats," Math warned.

But though there were shudders, they all continued, and soon everyone could feel a cold draft around their ankles. George and Math were muttering to each other. Suddenly under the beam of the torches the mortared stone walls changed into rough rock and earth, and the passage was a passage no longer, but a tunnel.

"We'll be under the end wall of the house now," George said.

"What is it, Famous Five?" Jeremy called, still in that excited but stalwart twelve-year-old voice. "Is it a gold mine?"

"Don't be ridiculous!" Rosemary said repressively. "Anyone can see it's a tunnel."

"Right." Math's flash futilely tried to pierce the gloom ahead. "I suppose it leads up to the fortress." He turned. "Everybody stay here for the moment, or go back." When there were mutinous sounds, he said, "There's not enough light. You might break a leg. And there may well be bats."

The women shrieked a little, and even the young workman with the light shifted uncomfortably. Jeremy merely said, "Golly, the Famous Five aren't afraid of a few bats!"

Math grinned, just visible in the darkness. "Nevertheless," he said. He squeezed Elain's hand as he left them.

He and George went slowly down the tunnel, and the rest were left in the small pool of their own light against a sea of blackness, watching those other lights get farther and farther away and the two shadows stretch longer and longer behind.

"Did you know this was here, Vinnie?" Elain asked.

"No, I don't think my father can have been told about it when he purchased. There would have been no reason for him to keep it secret from me."

"Perhaps it hasn't been used for centuries," Davina said.

"That sack of flour can't be that old," Vinnie pointed out. "It certainly was put there this century."

"It's terribly exciting," Jeremy said. "The Famous Five are going to be kept busy exploring this summer, aren't they?"

"It may be extremely dangerous," Rosemary said dampingly. "I am surprised that Math has allowed us even so far. He would be responsible, of course, if anything should happen to any of us."

"I warned him." Davina's voice rang hollowly, and abruptly the atmosphere seemed frightening, even hostile.

"Someday someone is going to have to tell me who the Famous Five are," Elain said. "I seem to be missing out."

"They were the protagonists in some rather unfortunate children's adventure stories. Enid Blyton," Rosemary informed her in a clinically disapproving tone. "Much condemned today for racism and snobbism, among other things."

"Gol-*lee*, Famous Five!" Jeremy exclaimed helplessly.

"But a world of delight, of course, when one was a child," Vinnie said. "I was too old for them, but my younger sisters adored them. And the writer was certainly not more racist or sexist than the times she lived in. It does seem hard to blame one person for the sins of an entire culture."

"Think of all the twentieth-century writers who will be condemned in the future for homophobia," Jeremy agreed. "But people don't notice it particularly now. It's just an expression of their own unconscious views."

Between the two of them, Rosemary was somehow silenced. Elain would have given something to see her face, because it was clear she didn't like it when her pronouncements were challenged.

Suddenly the distant light was reflected back from the darkness as it fell on stone. "They've reached the end of the tunnel," Rosemary guessed. Math and George stopped, and the murmur of their voices came back down the tunnel. Then they turned and retraced their steps. The others waited for them in silence.

"There's a rockfall," said Math. "It's impassible."

"You mean it goes on behind?" That was Davina.

"Do you think it originally led up to the fortress?" Elain asked.

Math shrugged. "Maybe. Hard to tell just when it was built." But he wasn't concentrating on what he was saying, Elain could see. He was thinking of something else, something that worried him. "Let's go," he said. His hand caught Elain's in passing. "All right?"

She murmured an affirmative, and he let her go. Math and George led them back up the passage, and as they all drew close to the grey-shadowed rectangle cut into the wall on the right, the lights fell on something beyond. The passage ran both ways from the door. Math and George had naturally taken the left when they entered, but they could, it appeared now, also have gone right.

The passage was shorter in this direction, running only a few yards to a stone wall, where this wing of the house met the other. But it wasn't the wall that interested them. In front of it, both sides of the passage were lined with boxes and sacks, all in an advanced state of rot. Rusted tins were falling out of broken cartons, and seeds and powders spilled from burst sacks.

"A forgotten cache, by the look of it," said Math, playing his light along the earth floor. "Somebody expecting a siege."

"From whom?" Jeremy demanded. "This looks interesting, Famous Five. This stuff is too modern for Owen Glendower!"

They were all silent a moment. It was left to Vinnie to answer. "From the Germans, of course," she said softly, in a tone of wonder. "This must have been here since the war. The last descendant of the old family died in 1942, and the place was boarded up. Nothing was done till after the war, when the estate sold the property to my father. I suppose these things had been put here before rationing came in, and when the owner died were simply forgotten."

They were all black with soot when they returned up the staircase and into the kitchen. Jan shrieked when she saw them. "You'll be tracking that all through the place!"

So they took their shoes off and carefully crept to their rooms like naughty children.

In Math's flat, Elain got the bathroom first. She caught sight of herself in the full-length mirror. Her clothes were smeared. She hoped biological detergent would get the dirt out.

She stripped off, showered and then, wrapped in a towel, came out to shove everything into the washing machine. Math had stripped in the kitchen, and his clothes were already in the machine. While he took his shower, she started the machine and slipped on a cotton dress.

By the time Math came out of the shower, Elain was bursting to talk about what they had found. "What do you think? Has it been there ever since the fortress was built? Who built it?" she demanded when they had settled down to the remains of the meal they had abandoned two hours ago.

"The passage must have been constructed either with that part of the house, or shortly afterwards, I suppose," Math said. "But I'd give something to know why. Was the tunnel already there?"

"Well, at least now we know how Jessica got into the house," Elain said.

Math's teeth tore into a bit of bread. He looked at her. "You're right. Of course."

"And maybe it was the secret passage that the stonemason had to wall up, and not Jessica at all."

"There's another problem solved, too," Math said softly.

"What?"

"Where the petrol came from that started the fire." He drank a sip of wine and smiled as Elain soundlessly opened her mouth. "But it leaves one question unanswered."

"But—"

"Who was it who moved the petrol cans from the passage? And why did they want to burn me down?"

"What?" shrieked Elain.

Raymond cursed. "You nearly deafened me, Red! This line's bad enough as it is. You heard me, but I'll repeat it. The forensic experts say the tapestry never burned."

"That's impossible! How would they know anyway?"

"A fair bit can be learned from charred cloth. There was cloth where the hanging had been, but the samples prove that it was not fifteenth century, and it was not a tapestry. Plain old twentieth-century cotton.''

"What are you saying—that it was rescued from the fire and Math is lying about it?"

"It seems more likely, my dear," Raymond said gently, "that it was removed before the arson."

That pointed unerringly to Math. Who else would have had the opportunity to remove the tapestry? "I don't believe it," she said. "Their loss assessor probably picked up the wrong fabric. Maybe there was a protective cloth hanging behind."

There was a short pause. Then Raymond cleared his throat. "Ah...you wouldn't be getting personally involved here, would you, Red?" he asked uncomfortably.

"Well, I'm living right here," Elain said hurriedly. "Naturally I've got friendly with them all." She coughed. "But that's not the point. It's not clouding my judgement, if that's what you mean."

"That's what I mean, Red."

"Anyway, if the tapestry wasn't burnt, why doesn't the company just say so? All they have to do is refuse to pay the claim for the tapestry. It doesn't prove arson. It doesn't prove the rest isn't a legitimate claim."

Raymond sighed. "It shows," he explained slowly, "that someone knew the fire was going to take place. And a fire that someone knows is going to take place, Red, is called arson."

Elain snorted. "Oh, come on! There might have been lots of reasons it was removed. For cleaning, for repair. To be valued. Because it was going to be hung somewhere else. Coincidences happen!"

But her heart sank, because any of those explanations meant Math was involved in fraud, even if not arson. It meant he was an opportunist and a liar.

And Raymond said wryly as she knew he would, "But he just claimed for it anyway, did he? Perhaps he forgot he'd sent it to the cleaners."

"There's another explanation," Elain said doggedly. "It must have burnt. They've made a mistake."

"Look," said her boss kindly. "This isn't the first thing that's made them suspicious. You can take it from me that both arson and fraud are involved, and that the owner is the guilty one."

Elain was silenced.

"Now, what have you got for me?"

"Rosemary and Davina come from a village outside of Godalming. That's all I could get."

"Right. What else?"

She paused. Should she tell him? She had made up her mind to say nothing of the discovery of the secret passage, letting Math tell them himself. She knew something was worrying him.

"Spill it, Red," Raymond said.

When she had made that decision, she had been convinced of Math's innocence, convinced that any day now the insurance company would have to bite the bullet and admit their mistake.

If she was wrong, if they were right, what did it mean? That she was in love with a cheat? Elain bit her lip, pushed open the door of the stifling red booth, and breathed deeply. She put the receiver down on her chest. "Sorry," she said to the air, "I'll be through in a minute." Then she spoke into the receiver again. "Sorry about that, Raymond. Somebody wanting to use the phone. I haven't got anything at the moment. I'll call you again tomorrow."

She hung up before he could complain and pushed her way out of the phone box. God, she was covered in sweat! She wiped her hand over her forehead and dried it on the seat of her shorts. Then she blindly headed towards the pub. Maybe what she needed was a drink.

Perhaps she had needed a shock like this to wake her up, make her face the truth: she was in love with Math.

And he might be involved in fraud. Or worse.

"Hello, again," said Gwen at the pub. "Made your phone call all right, have you?"

"Yeah," said Elain, hardly hearing. She had asked for it, hadn't she? Common sense should have told her not to fall in love with a suspect in a fraud case. In any kind of case.

"Coffee?"

"Yes, please." Arson. People had nearly died. It had been early in the season, so the hotel wasn't full, but Vinnie had told her two people had been lucky to get out. Was Math a man to risk people's lives for gain? What did she know about him? Nothing. Her heart had told her he was innocent, and she had looked no further. But first, she reminded herself, her heart had told her he was guilty. She had talked herself out of that theory with a lot of psychobabble, because she was so deeply attracted to him. In truth, what did she really know?

"There's your coffee. Bad news, was it?"

Elain blinked herself into consciousness. "Sorry, what?"

"Your phone call. Bad news this time?"

Dear God, Elain thought, suddenly hearing the whole conversation in her head. *Made your phone call all right?* Did the whole village know her business?

But of course it did. Common sense should have told her that, too. A hotel guest who came down nearly every day to make a call from the public call box was going to be noticed. And talked about.

She knew as clearly as if it were written on the wall in front of her that it was only a matter of time before Math learned something that made him suspect her. And seeing that, she saw something else, too: how what she was doing was going to look to him. No amount of explanation would disguise the fact that she had been leading a double life all the time that she was here.

Several times she had been tempted to confess, and now she wished she had. But it was no longer an option. If Math was the arsonist, she couldn't bear it if he started lying to her. . . .

Suddenly she was in a race against time. She had to find out whether Math was guilty of arson and fraud before he found out she was a cheat.

* * *

The stranger arrived at lunch-time the next day, with his bag and his excuse, and almost as soon as she saw him, Elain knew she should have expected something like this to happen. The residents and all the workmen were at the tables in the garden, having a lunch Vinnie and Jeremy had made, of salad, sandwiches and wine. The restaurant was closed for lunch to outside trade while repairs were going on. Myfanwy had taken the morning off.

Elain had seen them from her vantage point on the hill, where she was spending the sunny morning painting, and come down to join them. A few minutes later, Math arrived. Elain guessed he'd been at work in the study, but for once she didn't know—last night she'd slept alone in her room. She'd tossed and worried most of the night, but not to much purpose. There were two possibilities: he was either guilty or innocent. If he was innocent, she was the best person to find it out. If she quit her job now and left, the insurance company would send out someone else, and that someone would certainly now be biased against Math. And there were investigators who simply found what they were looking for.

With each minute she stayed, she increased the risk of being discovered. But she couldn't leave, and she couldn't quit. Because she couldn't afford what it would cost to stay without Raymond paying the bills.

Elain sat in a chair in the sun and picked up a sandwich. She smiled her hellos as Math came across the grass towards her. Guilty or innocent, he would be furious if he started to suspect her. But if he was innocent, and she found the proof, maybe she could mend her fences.

And if he was guilty, nothing mattered anyway.

"Hi," he said. "Feeling better?"

She'd pleaded a headache last night, a need to be alone. "Yes, thanks," she said. But there was a frown between her eyes and he didn't believe her.

"You need a hat when you're working in the sun."

That was when the car arrived, stopping in the drive opposite the tables. A man got out, nodded to them all and walked into the hotel. Math raised an eyebrow as he passed, but said nothing.

"Who can that be, I wonder?" Rosemary asked.

Math shook his head.

"A prospective guest, perhaps," Vinnie said.

Olwen appeared on the steps. "Math," she called, rather harassed, "could you come?"

"Uh-oh," said Jeremy.

Elain whirled. "What's the matter? Who do you think it is?"

Jeremy shrugged. "I've no idea."

"But you said, 'uh-oh.'"

"Well, it's obvious there's a problem, isn't there? You scarcely need eyes to see that. Probably something to do with the tunnel we found yesterday."

When Math returned, the man came with him. "It's quiet now," Math was saying, "but there will be construction noise all day long."

"That's all right," said the man.

Math led him to the tables. "This is Brian Arthur, everyone," he said.

"Surely not another guest?" said Vinnie with a smile, holding out an elegant hand.

Math shrugged. "Apparently we lost another reservation. Somehow we must have mislaid some after the fire. Vinnie Daniels, Brian."

Elain felt her throat close. "You're staying?" No one knew better than she that no reservations had got lost because of the fire. But clearly someone knew that the excuse had already been successfully used to get a room. And the man reminded her of someone....

"If you don't object," said the man jokingly, taking her hand. She couldn't place his accent.

Math finished the introductions, leaned against a table and bit unconcernedly into a tomato sandwich. "Brian is one of the railway volunteers, here for two weeks."

"Oh, really! The Talyllyn Railway?" asked Davina.

"That's right. Have you had a ride?"

Math poured him a glass of wine as Davina nodded. "What job do you have on the railway, Mr. Arthur?" she asked.

"This year I'm fireman."

"It's a sweet little railway," Jeremy said, and there were murmurs of agreement. "I haven't ridden it, but I've heard it's fabulous."

"Very nice indeed," said Brian Arthur. He turned to Elain. "How about you, Elain? Have you taken a ride on the Talyllyn?"

Elain shook her head. She'd seen the brochure, but hadn't read it. Something about a lot of volunteers restoring an old mining railway line.

"Oh, you must go, Elain!" Vinnie exclaimed. "It's a perfect little railway, and everyone has such fun. Railway lovers from all over Britain come to spend their holidays playing at engineers and conductors and ticket sellers."

Maybe they did, Elain thought. She smiled and made some response. Maybe they did. But the man who had just booked a room at the White Lady was not among their number.

The person he reminded Elain of, she realized suddenly, was Raymond Derby. Brian Arthur was another detective, or she'd eat the table as well as the sandwiches.

Chapter 14

"They've sent someone else in," Elain shouted. Rain was thudding against the phone box so she could scarcely hear. She was drenched, too. But she had wanted to talk to Raymond immediately, and if she'd taken the car, people would have seen her leave and be sure to ask her later where she'd been. She'd been caught in the downpour halfway to the village.

But this was the last call she could make from here.

"Who have?"

"Your clients, damn them!" Elain said accusingly. "Raymond, please don't tell me you don't know if you do. I want to know what's going on."

"They haven't made the smallest suggestion to me of any such plans."

"Well, then, they're double-crossing you," Elain said darkly.

Raymond sighed. "Red, you have unexpected shallows. But I think you told me that you were a fan of old movies."

Elain giggled self-consciously. "You're right. Sorry. But you know what I mean."

"How sure are you that the man is an investigator?"

She thought a moment. "Seventy per cent. Eighty."

"Mmm. And why now?"

"Isn't it obvious? Because of what you just told me. They don't think the tapestry burnt in the fire."

"I'm not convinced. They're happy you're there—even though you haven't come up with much yet," he added pointedly. "They're prepared to give you the time to build up a trust."

Elain's stomach heaved. Oh, yes, she was doing that all right. She was building up a trust. Thunder rumbled overhead and rain smashed the little phone box. The weather agreed with her stomach.

She said, "Raymond, he used the same excuse I used—he claimed he'd had a reservation and the hotel must have lost it. Now, who but you and me and your clients knew that excuse worked?"

"Everybody at the hotel, Red," he replied. "Now, don't get your knickers in a twist. There's something you're not telling me, something that's happened. That's why this guy's turned up. Now, tell me what it is that's happened, and then we can figure out who sent him in."

She was as good as dead anyway. It didn't make her position with Math any worse, and if she told Raymond and he figured something out...

"The fire exposed a secret passage in the basement. Someone had been hoarding goods during the war, and they're all still there. Math reckons that's where the petrol came from."

She could feel Raymond blink. The storm had settled into a steady downpour, and it streamed down the little panes of glass, enclosing her in her own world. The small, grubby world of betrayal.

"I'm sure he's right," he said.

"But it means somebody shifted it. Because it was on the other side of the passage wall when it went up, in the main part of the basement. Right under the room with the tapestry."

"Where does the passage lead?"

"Probably it used to lead to the fortress I told you about. But there's been a rockfall that's closed the passage off, and now it leads nowhere."

"Nah, Red, you're not thinking."

"What do you mean?"

"Nobody's going to risk setting a petrol fire and having to get out through the house, are they? That was the real problem with the arson theory. That tunnel leads somewhere. You find out where."

Outside in the village street, lightning struck a stationary car. For a second, she watched the glow envelop it, illuminating the ground underneath. Then came an almighty bang of thunder that threatened to flatten the world. "They're out to get me, Raymond," Elain said. "The elements, I mean."

But the line had gone dead.

"Do you ever think someone might be trying to force you out?" she asked Math as casually as she could over dinner that night. It was the one possibility she could think of that left Math innocent.

"Out of where? The house?"

"Yeah."

He grinned at her. "Why would anyone want to do that?"

"I don't know. Have you refused to sell to anyone lately?"

Math smiled. "Ask Vinnie how long the place was on the market before I bought it. She had despaired of finding a buyer. And the value has dropped since, along with other property values during the recession. I'm not looking to sell, which is just as well. If I were, I'd be in trouble."

"No one's offered?" she pressed.

"No one has suggested a hair of interest in the place. It needs far too much renovation before it'll be even a three-star hotel. Bathrooms have to be installed, the kitchens need modernizing.... The place was built on what's called the unit system, Elain. You must see yourself how various doors and stairs lead to different parts of the house, which don't interconnect. Where would an architect find space for all the bathrooms needed? You couldn't do it without spoiling the proportions. It's not the kind of hotel your average Japanese or American tourist would look twice at.''

''But you used to be full in the summer.''

''We have a small band of loyal but eccentric patrons who like Jessica, like the isolation, like the light and the wainscoting and the stone and even the antique plumbing. But that group is diminishing year by year. That's why Vinnie was selling up in the first place. That, and her age. She thought a hotel chain might want it, or someone might want to turn it into a conference centre. But it's too small to interest such people. It's really best being restored to residential housing.''

''Oh,'' she said limply. ''Math—do you have any enemies?''

''Not as far as I know.'' Math picked up her hand and kissed the tips of her fingers. ''Now tell me why you think I might have.''

She looked at him. Suppose she just told him, right now, the truth about who she was and what she was doing? Suppose she said she was convinced of his innocence and wanted to help him prove it? Elain took a deep breath, then paused. But what if he were not? What if he lied, and she believed him, and then one day she found out the truth?

''Hear you've found a secret passage under the house, Math,'' said a voice. It was one of his regular customers, an English travel-guide writer who lived nearby. Elain had met him in the pub one night. He nodded to her now.

''Word's got out already, has it?'' Math shrugged resignedly. ''Well, it was bound to. If anyone asks you, will you spread the idea it's not much of anything, Mel? A cache of rotting wartime supplies in a walled-up corner of the basement. All I need now is a couple of tourists falling into the basement and suing me.''

The man laughed and agreed, and after a few more minutes moved away.

Elain tried again. "Do you think Brian Arthur is who he says he is?"

Math was clearly taken aback. "I haven't thought about it. Why, who do you think he is?"

"For a guy who's supposed to be in love with trains, he sure hangs around the place a lot."

"It has been raining, Elain."

He wasn't making excuses for the man. He just wasn't interested. How would she ever succeed in putting him on his guard—and anyway, what did she want to put him on guard against? Math was right. There was nothing anybody wanted from him, and how likely was it he would have an enemy of this kind without knowing it?

She wished he would take her seriously. If he'd put his mind to it, he might have remembered something, some clue that would tell her why someone had torched the White Lady Hotel.

Math filled two brandy snifters with Armagnac, passed her one and lifted his own, absently watching how the soft light sparkled in the honey-coloured liquid.

She had come to his flat. It was beyond her to plead a headache again. Slowly the proportions of the hole she had dug for herself were being revealed: she was betraying Math with every breath she took; he might be a liar and a cheat; and yet she had not been able to find any way out of coming upstairs with him tonight.

Now getting away would be even more difficult. What excuse could she find that would not put her at risk of the exposure she was trying to avoid? Math would question her, try to find out what was wrong. And she had no idea how good she might be at that sort of cover-up. She had never been under serious pressure on a job for Raymond before.

And if she did stand up to his questioning, what was that but adding lies to lies? Even if Math were guilty, it was not Elain he was betraying, only his own honour. But she was guilty of terrible duplicity.

He sat on his haunches in front of her, his arms resting on her thighs, his hands nursing the glass. He tilted his head up, offering a kiss, and it took no more than that for her body to kick into awareness. Whatever her head thought, her heart and her blood were his. Her smile of languid desire was entirely involuntary, and she thought, as she leaned forward and her mouth so eagerly found the soft heat of his, *this is how women feel who love men who cheat, or who cheat men they love. I always wondered. Now I know.*

Ah, how sweet his lips were, moving so sensuously over hers, tasting, touching; how artful his tongue, flicking delicately across her sensitized lips; how electric his teeth, lightly biting her into shimmering awareness of her body's yearning.

His hand came up and caressed her cheek as the kiss went on and on, melting her senses into honey, her self-reproaches into mist.

"I've got my period," she lied against his lips, grasping at the slender strand of control that still connected her to reality.

Math drew his head back half an inch, and she saw the lazy, tender smile on his face and closed her eyes against what it did to her. "There are ways around that," he said.

He kissed her again, kneeling up now and pressing his mouth against hers, so that her head fell back against the high back of the sofa. Oh, the clamour in her blood! Oh, the drunken, wild awareness of the senses! How she loved him, this man who had every right to call her cheat! How he gripped her heart!

He set their glasses down on the little stool beside the hearth, then lay back on the rug, drawing her down on top of him. She rested on his chest, elbows bent, and smiled down at him as his fingers stroked her face, her cheeks, her hair.

He had let her out of her prison, and was she going to put him into one?

"I love you," he said.

Her heart thundered in her breasts, in her temples, her ears, deafening her to everything but the echo of the words. Her lips parted and she breathed in little pants.

"Do you?" she whispered.

His arms tightened around her. "You're everything I have ever wanted, Elain. You're my life, the breath in my body. I want you with me. God, how I love you!"

"I love you," she whispered. She could not stop herself saying it, though she could smell the burning, from the future, of her life consumed in hell's fire. "Oh, Math, I've never loved anyone like this!"

Her heart was tearing apart with love of him. Nothing had ever been like this. She whimpered as he pulled her down to meet his kiss, moaned as the pressure of his arms tried to pull her into his heart, sobbed as his kiss melted her, his hands remoulded her, his mouth devoured her.

Her back was against the rug, Math above her, wild, unleashed, uncontrolled. There was no gentleness now in his touch, as he kissed and kissed her. "I will never get enough of you," he said hoarsely, harshly. "God, how I love you. From the first moment I saw you, there could never be anyone, anything for me but you." The words came from his depths, and as he spoke his hands pressed and pulled her to him, shaping her, wanting her, the soul that has found its other half.

She was in a frenzy of love, passion and desire. There had been nothing like this since the dawn of the world. Her heart was breaking, her body was breaking, she was earth and water, fertility and storm, pouring over him, under him, through him; she was the bed he lay on, the sky that embraced him, the flood that swept him.

She cried and moaned as he pulled off her dress, tore her briefs out of the way of his wildly, fiercely seeking flesh. She spread her naked, sweat-glowing legs to embrace him, with a cry of passion and demand that even the universe must obey, and howled her acceptance of the powerful thrust of his body into hers.

"Elain!" he cried, wild with astonishment, stopping at the end of the thrust, deep inside her, his eyes burning down into hers. "Elain, my heart, my love, there's never been anything like this." He closed his eyes against sensation as his body involuntarily drew back and thrust home again, and his wild grunt of pleasure coursed along her nerves, driving her body's joy, flooding into her brain.

He pushed and pushed into her, thick and strong, all-encompassing, driving all before him, cramming golden, melting sensation into every nerve, every cell. She was moaning, crying, tearing, embracing, drowned.

He held her head between his two hands, his face close above hers as what they felt drummed and flooded through them, wave after wave of it, a sea of feeling smashing over and over against the lush shore of their bodies.

"I love you, Elain," he said hoarsely. "Tell me you love me."

It was true; nothing else in the universe was true, but that was true. "Math, I love you," she whispered. And then, as his body swelled in her in response, and pleasure took hold of them, driving him into her uncontrollably, she cried it aloud. "I love you, I love you!"

There was nothing between them now, only the raw flesh where their souls met and joined in a bond that was forever. The nightingale cried out the song of all the words of his yearning, and the rose drank them in, through petals and parched roots.

Later, by her lover's sleeping side, she remembered, and wept.

"Let's get your stuff up here this morning," Math said over breakfast.

She choked on her coffee. "What do you mean?"

"There's no point in your staying down there, is there?"

"Um, I—well, my painting—"

"Come with me."

He set down his cup and stood up, leading the way to a door in the sitting room. Then she was in a curiously cosy room with two windows that faced the fortress, and a skylight above. The outside wall was naked stone, the inside rough-carved wood. An antique table and chairs sat in the middle of the floor, and there were a couple of sideboards, but she and Math had never eaten here. Only the electric light showed what century they were in.

"It's north facing," he said. "What do you think of this for a studio?"

"Math," she said quietly, "I'm not ready for this."

It was a lie. There was nothing she wanted more. But the way things stood now, how could she move in with him? Her position would be intolerable.

He went still, as though he were listening to some distant sound. Then his head moved. "Ah," he said.

"I'm sorry, but it's ... it's moving too fast for me."

His face was expressionless. "Of course," he said. "What will you do then, stay where you are?"

"If you don't mind."

He grinned at that. "I mind like hell," he said. "But the decision has to be yours, doesn't it?"

She was walking on glass. She would never get through without breaking something.

She had to find out the truth, or she would be destroyed.

She found her chance next day at lunch-time. All the men broke at twelve-thirty, and the restaurant was so busy Olwen was helping. Elain slipped into the office and turned quickly to the guest file.

"Brian Arthur," she read. "Fifteen Branwen Close, Cardiff." She memorized the address and the car licence number. Then she went to the kitchen, meeting Jan on the way out, her arms full of plates.

"Do you mind if I get a glass of water?" she asked, and Jan just waved her through. Elain crossed to the large old-fashioned porcelain sink, said hello to a harassed Myfanwy and picked up a glass. She slowly filled the glass, then leaned against the wall to drink. Myfanwy was working with her back to the sink. It wasn't difficult to slip around the corner and down the stairs to the basement.

There were no lights on, and she didn't dare put them on. It took her five agonizing minutes to feel her stumbling way across the basement, and when she hit the steps unexpectedly she nearly fell flat.

But at least when she turned the corner there was some light, from the open roof at the far end. The plastic sheeting everywhere distorted images, but the light still came through, and in another minute Elain was picking up a large portable lamp. It was too heavy for her, but she'd rather strain a muscle than run into something in the darkness.

They'd boarded up the doorway with two crossbeams, but it was an easy matter, if a bit dirty, to crawl under them and into the passage. For a moment she stood there, playing the light around. The supplies were still there, no one had touched them. Could there be a clue here? Elain wondered. Was there anything in what had been hoarded?

But if so, why hadn't they simply taken it, whoever they were? If they had had access to the petrol, they had had access to whatever was in the passage.

Some scene from one of her favourite old movies vaguely tried to surface. Hadn't hoarding been illegal during the war? But surely no one would bother to prosecute such a crime now—or even care. And anyway, whoever had owned the house and done the hoarding had died before they could use their stash.

Like the man in the Bible. Storing everything up and then dying in the night. She flicked the light over the pathetic bundles that marked someone's fear of going without and shook her head. *Give us this day our daily bread,* but that wasn't usually enough for most people, Elain thought. We all want security.

Behind the hoarded stocks there was nothing but a stone wall to mark the end of the passage. She frowned. There was something she'd seen.... Elain lowered the light again, playing it over the dirt between two rotted sacks. Yes. There it was. Two deeply cut circles in the dirt of the floor, and a few chips of earth where whatever had made the circles had been shifted. The earth was too hard packed to show other marks, but fifty years of pressure would have driven the rim of the petrol cans down into it. Of course Math had seen this the other day. The question was, had he blocked off the passage because he was afraid someone else would figure it out? He had tried to keep everybody out at first, hadn't he, but had given up when he saw how determined they were.

Elain shrugged and turned the other way down the passage. Raymond was right. No one would have risked setting petrol alight when the house was their only escape route, and still less would they have dared to stay here in the passage—or even deep in the tunnel—while the house burned down above them. Anything might happen—the oxygen getting used up, the wall exploding....

It was heavy, but still the lamp's glare seemed feeble as Elain walked down the passage and into the dark tunnel beyond. At least she knew she was safe up to the rockfall. Math and George had been that far. But it seemed a long walk, and the uneven floor threw moving shadows that disturbed her vision and made her halting progress slow.

She felt the wind around her ankles. Of course. That meant that the tunnel was open somewhere. She wondered who else had realized that the other day, when they had felt the breeze. No one had said anything, but they might have guessed. Math must have realized.

The walls were roughly cut. For all she knew, they might have been made at any time. The wall and the roof had collapsed on the right and spilled rocks and earth right across the tunnel. It looked, at first glance, as though the fall had closed the tunnel completely. But there was still that breeze.

Elain tried to feel it with her face, her hand, tried to locate the direction it came from. Time must be passing. How long had she been down here? Would they need the lamp? Would they suspect what had happened and come after the thief?

Never let urgency get to you. That was one of Raymond's rules. One of the hardest to obey. Elain took a deep breath and tried again, playing the light over the fall of rock and around the walls.

It was a trick of shadow, and of assumption, that kept it hidden. She had been looking for a hole in the rockfall, a place where it did not quite meet wall or ceiling. It seemed to be flush everywhere around its perimeter. But up on the left, the wall was throwing a curious shadow on the rocks. The rockfall was flush with the line of the wall all right, but there was something not quite right. . . .

Elain scrambled up the long, slanted heap of stones closer to the junction, and saw that there was a hollow in the wall itself. Where the fallen rocks seemed to meet the wall, there was a niche. The rockfall had occurred just where there was a U-shape in the wall, and had not quite filled the space. And she could feel that it was here that the air came through.

It looked hardly big enough for a child, but someone must have been through here, someone not a child. Flattening herself, she pushed sideways into the niche, carefully leading with the lamp, though there was nothing to see. Then suddenly, there was space. Not a U-shape at all. Beyond that narrow passage, the left-hand wall simply disappeared.

So did the tunnel. Elain played the lamp into the darkness, but its beam fell on emptiness, so that in an atavistic impulse, she nearly screamed.

She stood perfectly still for a moment, trying to calm her panicked heartbeat, when what she really wanted to do was turn around, press her way back into the tunnel and run home. She was in a cavern, that was all. With enough light she would see the walls, and it would be simply a perfectly normal cavity in the rock. Even now she could see distant rocks glinting in the rays of her lamp.

Ever since her time in the burn ward, isolation of a certain kind frightened her. She had dreamt then of being swallowed up by empty darkness, and this was too much like her dream for comfort. Her lamp was so frail against the darkness, and what would she do if she fell, if she dropped it, if . . . ? The thought of dying of thirst in complete darkness where there might be rats made her chill.

At last she came out of her reverie and shook herself. An old nightmare it might be, but it was not irrational. People got lost in caves with horrible regularity. It would be foolhardy in the extreme to explore this space by herself. At the very least she should have left a letter in her room saying where she was, so that if she did not return, they would know where to look.

But her fear was abating with time. At last she decided to explore only within easy reach of the opening, only to the extent where her light still reached it. Slowly she crept and slid along the rocky slope to the solid floor, then turned and played the light over the way she had just come, memorizing that curve in the wall that led to the tiny cleft.

Broken rocks glinted in the light. The cavern itself wasn't as big as she had first imagined, but there were tunnels or caves leading off it, making it perhaps the hub of a wheel.

Without warning her ankle turned, and she fell, and the lamp went out. Elain screamed, panic flooding her brain as the utter darkness closed in. She lay still, winded and unable to catch her breath, and the horror was, her eyes did not accustom to the darkness. It was complete, and it would never get any lighter. Not even vague shapes became visible. She realized suddenly that she was cold.

She groped around her for the lamp, praying as hard as she had ever prayed in her life. When her fingers did not find it, she got to her knees and crawled a few inches, carefully feeling the ground before her, trying desperately to hold down the rising bile of sheer terror that gripped her throat.

Please, please, please. There! Her hand brushed something. Stifling the superstitious urge to snatch it back away from the touch, she reached out and felt the comforting shape of the flashlight. She rolled over into a sitting position and drew it onto her lap. *Please, please.* Her groping fingers found the switch and she pushed it.

Nothing. Tears of fear burnt her eyes. *Please!* she begged, and then suddenly there was another switch under her fingers, and she pushed that.

A flashing red glow came from the other end of the lamp, and her heart nearly burst with relief. Of course, this was the kind of lamp motorists carried to warn of danger if they were stranded on the highway. Elain laughed with the crazy joy that suffused her, and the sound of her own cackling mirth echoing from the empty walls sobered her. That was the sound of hysteria, and she must control herself.

She rose carefully to her feet. She could see almost nothing in the red glow, and she was no longer sure of her direction. She had kept her back to the rockfall as long as she was on her feet, but God alone knew where she was now.

She stood staring into the darkness that surrounded the intermittent red glow, trying to see her way. Then it seemed to her that she was not quite alone, as though something drew her, some knowledge both within and without. She didn't resist. She followed her sixth sense, her intuition, her guardian angel—whatever it was, and soon her feet struck the loose shale of the rockfall.

"Thank you," she breathed aloud. "Oh, thank you." And a minute later she had squeezed through the little opening and into the tunnel beyond.

She heard the thunder of sawing and hammering as she approached along the secret passage, but the men were all on the next floor up. Elain set down the lamp and moved as quickly as she could through the darkness and to the stairs.

"Where on *earth* have you been?" Rosemary demanded, staring at her in fastidious horror. Elain stopped where she stood, cursing her luck. She had come straight up the stairs from the kitchen, and what rotten luck to bump into Rosemary coming out of her room! Another second and she'd have been halfway up the next flight and home free.

"I fell," said Elain lamely.

"Into *what*, pray? A coal mine?"

It occurred to Elain that she didn't have to answer the question, and she just grinned and dashed up the stairs.

She was certainly filthy. She stood in front of the full-length mirror and admired the greasy black streaks that covered her jeans and shirt and arms. Also her face. She really did look as though she'd been down a mine.

She wrinkled her brow. The greasy dirt reminded her of something. For a moment she tried to remember, then shrugged it off. There was too much else to think about.

Chapter 15

Mudpie was sensuously rolling in a patch of sunlight, ruffling her head against the rug, offering her tummy to its warmth. When Elain tapped on the open door, the cat flung herself upright and glared reproachfully.

Math turned from his work and smiled, the lazy, loving smile of a strong man disarmed by the sight of his beloved. "Hello," he said. His eyes narrowed and his smile grew quizzical. "Have you been somewhere interesting?"

She had done no more than wash her face. She looked ruffled and very grubby. "Math, I've been down in the tunnel again."

He frowned. "Alone?" When she nodded, he said, "You shouldn't have done that. Dammit, it could be dangerous. What if you fell and broke a leg?"

"Yes, well, I did fall. I broke the flashlight. But not before—Math, the passage isn't closed by that rockfall. There's a way through."

"And you, of course, found it."

He wasn't at all surprised. "You found it, too," she said.

Math nodded. She came into the room and up to him. He reached up to rest his arms around her waist and dropped a kiss against her stomach.

"I broke the lamp before I'd seen it all. What is it? Is it a mine?"

"Probably. Not a recent one."

"What, then?"

"There are a few crumbling wooden artefacts, a couple of arrowheads. It probably hasn't been worked since Roman times."

"What—lead?"

He shrugged. "Maybe. Maybe gold. The Romans did mine both in Wales. Maybe tin. I don't know enough about the geology of this area."

"Where does it come up?"

"In the fortress. The shaft marked out of bounds." He stood up. "I haven't had lunch, have you?"

Shaking her head, she followed him out to the kitchen. "It's so exciting!" she said, as he poked in the fridge, looking for inspiration. "Aren't you excited by it?"

He came out with lettuce, cheese and eggs. "Well, it has its drawbacks. You're very excited."

"Of course I am. Don't you see it's the way they came in?"

"The way who came in?"

"The arsonists. Whoever st—" She coughed. She had almost said "Whoever stole the tapestry." "Whoever started the fire. They found the petrol in the passage and dragged it through into the cellar, and then escaped again via the tunnel. Can't you see that?"

He was beating eggs in a bowl. "Yes, I can see that. What I still can't see is why."

She looked at him. That was the question. Why. And who. And whether anyone but Math could have a motive.

"Hello, Elain, forgive me for disturbing you," Rosemary said.

"No, no, I wasn't working," Elain said. "Do come in."

It was true—she had been lying on her bed reading the *Mabinogion,* and had dozed off over it. Rosemary's knock had startled her awake, and she had jumped up without thinking and opened the door. Too late she remembered the painting of the hotel fire still on the easel, and the *Mabinogion* sketches scattered around the room. She had been trying to immerse herself in the epic. Elain didn't care who saw her work once it was completed, but an unfinished piece was vulnerable. Especially to someone like Rosemary.

"Have a seat," she said, and turned quickly to open her paint case. The four clamps that held a wet oil painting were empty, and she quickly reached for the picture she was calling *The Fire.*

"Have you recovered from your fall?"

"Oh, yes. It wasn't serious. I didn't turn an ankle or anything."

"I suppose you went down the tunnel again."

If she admitted that, she might start a trend of adventuring, and she didn't want everyone finding out about the way the tunnel continued. "No, I was out prospecting for new views, as it—"

"Oh, my!" Rosemary cried in a high voice.

At the sound of stifled panic in her voice, Elain turned. But Rosemary was merely gazing at the sketches from the *Mabinogion.*

"How very interesting!" she began, in a tone that was already sending cold chills down Elain's creative spine. "I wonder..." As quickly as she could, Elain piled them all up and turned the stack face down.

"I'm sorry. I don't like anyone to see an unfinished work," she said. It was rude, but she couldn't afford to be polite.

"But could I not just see—" Rosemary broke off. She looked at Elain oddly. "I quite understand." She clasped her hands together like a games mistress at a girls' school. "I came to enlist your cooking skills for tonight's meal. It's Monday again."

* * *

"What is it this time?" Elain demanded at the kitchen door. "The *Carry On* gang?"

Math was standing over the stove with Myfanwy's huge white apron wrapped around him and an egg lifter held up in his hand, watching a saucepan intently. Jeremy was standing, wringing his hands over a bowl of flour wrong way up on the floor. Vinnie, her face dusted with more flour, was energetically beating eggs. Mudpie and Bill were sniffing the flour, but without much hope of finding it edible.

At the sound of her voice, Math turned. "Are you suggesting we don't know what we're doing?" he asked with a grin.

"How do you get flour up off the floor?" Jeremy demanded, gingerly lifting the bowl. "Is there some way to save that lot?"

"Oh, no!" said Vinnie softly, just as Elain said drily, "Not if you're planning on feeding it to us after."

"But that was the last in the tin," Jeremy replied, still worriedly gazing at the mound of flour.

Mudpie was making scraping motions on the floor, trying to bury the offending mess. Bill sat on the floor, grinning up at Elain, while his friendly tail cut a swath through the pile of white stuff.

Jeremy shrugged. What he wouldn't accept from Elain and Vinnie by way of judgement, apparently, he was prepared to accept from the animals. "Do you think there's any more flour, Math?"

"Try the basement stores," Math said, and then they all thought of the same thing at the same time, looked at each other and laughed. "But not the secret stores," he added.

"Of course," Vinnie told them, "during the war, one *would* have picked that up and used it. Not once Bill and Mudpie had been at it, though, I suppose," she added doubtfully.

Jeremy wrung his hands. "It's a real mess now, isn't it?"

Elain said, "I'll look after the disaster if you like. You carry on cooking." He gratefully left her to it, and disap-

peared down the stairs. Elain found a broom and held Bill
still while she dusted off his backside and tail. "Your animals seem to have a thing about sitting in edible commodi-
ties," she observed to Math.

"With Bill it's just fair comment," Math said. "Mudpie
was operating on the feminine principle."

"Which is what?"

"A little attractive scent..."

Elain, efficiently clearing up the mess, snorted with
laughter and then, inhaling flour dust as a result, sneezed.
"Whisky for perfume?" she asked disbelievingly.

"That was no whisky. That was my Highland malt."

"What can I do now?" she asked when the floor was
clean.

"Sit and talk to us," said Math. "Three cooks are already enough to spoil the broth, as you see."

"Oh—Rosemary told me I was needed down here."

"Jeremy stepped in."

For no good reason, she was suddenly remembering what
Raymond had said about Jeremy. "He's also eroding his
principal. At the rate he's spending, he'll be without funds
in three or four years." Would Jeremy have the contacts to
sell the tapestry, no questions asked? she wondered idly.

And who else might need the money? It was a question
she ought to be looking at. Not Vinnie—her deal with Math
meant she was here for life. Even if she had stolen the tapestry, she'd have been unlikely to burn down her home to
disguise the fact.

She thought of Rosemary and the scene that had just
passed in her room. Something had surprised her, made her
suspicious of Elain. Suddenly Elain remembered that she
had been putting away the painting of the fire when Rosemary had had that odd, immediately suppressed reaction.
Yet why should that upset her? She must have known it was
painted from imagination.

"You're preoccupied tonight," Math said gently.

Elain came to with a blink to find him bent over the back
of her chair, smiling down at her. She smiled, because it was

impossible not to smile at Math. But though she wasn't really aware of it, the smile was shadowed by a frown deep in her eyes.

"What's up?" Math asked, and in spite of herself, she felt comforted. "What's worrying you, Elain?"

Of course it showed. She wasn't really of spy calibre. She'd never before had to be on a job so intensely, or for so long. She'd never fallen in love with a suspect before, either. It was hard for her to hide her feelings from Math.

She glanced around the room. Jeremy was on the other side of the kitchen, mixing something in the magimix. Vinnie had disappeared. She began hesitantly, "Has it ever occurred to you that—that someone might have started the fire in order to disguise the fact that they'd stolen the tapestry?"

If he'd been concerned before, he was staggered now. "What?" So far as she could tell, it was pure surprise. "The tapestry stolen? Why do you think so?"

"Because there's no other obvious motive."

"You can hardly call this obvious. Unless—what makes you think the tapestry didn't burn?"

She wished she could tell him the truth. "I don't know. The fire was started right under that room, wasn't it?"

He frowned as though what she said was really making him think. Then he shook his head. "It can't be. The loss assessor took samples of the burnt fabric. If it wasn't the tapestry, they'd know about it." He looked at her. "They can date the fabric, even though it's been burnt."

"Did the loss assessor tell you that?"

He shrugged. "He didn't have to. It's just something I know. It's the kind of thing archaeologists do, you know."

So at least he could not have hoped to fool the insurance company by stealing his own tapestry and then claiming it had burnt. He was innocent of that fraud.

"They haven't said any—" She broke off as Jeremy silenced his machine.

"Right, then! Here's the batter," he called, coming across the room with a big bowl.

"What are we having?" Elain asked brightly.

"Crêpes," said Jeremy. "Math's forgotten specialty, apparently."

They all sat at the round table again, as was the custom now on Mondays. It was Elain's fourth Monday, which meant she had been here exactly three weeks. She marvelled that a life could change so profoundly in three short weeks.

Math was beside her tonight, and she remembered that first night, when she had been so relieved not to have to sit beside him. She had been nervous of him, thinking him dangerous, not even guessing that she thought him dangerous because she was so powerfully attracted to him. She almost laughed now, looking at him, to think she could have been so blind. Math was so sexy, so warm, and his eyes were so full of promise when he looked at her. She must have taken it all in subliminally, but not a drop of it had reached consciousness.

It was ridiculous to suspect him of anything, and she knew it suddenly and clearly. For a start, if Math had had some reason to want to torch his own hotel, he would never have risked people's lives to do it. She knew that now. Except for these past few nervous days, she had always known it.

There was someone else. Some other reason. Whatever the logic of the situation said, and most of it pointed to Math, the logic was wrong. There was some factor she hadn't discovered yet, that was all.

She smiled into his eyes, eating the food he had cooked, and made up her mind. Raymond would bellow if he found out. He might fire her. But she didn't care. Tonight, she would tell Math everything. Maybe he had information she didn't. If they pooled their data, they might come up with something.

"So, we all take turns, do we, on Monday nights?" Brian Arthur asked ponderously, when they had finished dessert. He hadn't spoken much up to now. "I'm not a fancy cook, myself. Shepherd's pie, bangers and mash, I'm your man for that.''

"You'll be staying on, will you?" Elain asked sweetly, mistrusting his genial stupidity.

He looked at her, the stolid look that Raymond sometimes adopted, hiding his brain behind a surface slowness. "Well, you know, next week. You're here permanently, are you?"

Ouch. "Not at the moment," she said.

"Working girl, are you?" he pursued. He had the knack of rooting for information while looking as though he were only laboriously trying to make social conversation.

"Yes, I am," she said dismissively, smiling and turning to Vinnie.

But before she could open her mouth on a word, Brian Arthur said, "What do you work at, then?"

For a horrified moment, she thought he knew and was baiting her. Then she told herself that that was impossible. He was asking questions as she had done, to try and get a lead, somewhere to start looking her up.

"I paint pictures," she said flatly. "What do you do, Brian? I mean, you're a working boy, are you?"

Davina tittered nervously at the blatant hostility in her tone.

"Oh, this and that," he said, avoiding the answer with an ease that infuriated Elain. "You make a living, do you, painting?"

He was way ahead on points. Trying to see a way out of where he was heading, Elain felt herself getting tongue-tied.

Math stood up. "I've got a phone call to make this evening," he said, excusing himself. He squeezed her shoulder in a wordless signal that she knew meant he hoped she'd go to his flat.

She flicked a smile up at him and gave the most invisible of nods, but Vinnie was smiling away at them, so she doubted anyone was fooled.

Brian Arthur said his good-nights not long after, and Elain wasn't sorry. She didn't want to have to deal with him any more tonight. They all stood and began clearing the table, and Olwen came out and collected the trolley. People began moving in the direction of the sitting room, but Elain went on to the stairs.

She stopped at her room for a few minutes and then headed up the stairs. Mudpie was waiting at the door.

"There's no point rubbing my legs. There'll be no more whisky for you," she told the cat sternly. "It would be more than my life's worth."

Either the cat didn't believe her, or else bore no hard feelings for what was not Elain's fault. She purred ferociously and arched up on her back legs to rub herself against Elain.

The light was on in the sitting room. Math was already here. Calling hello, Elain paused to drop a few things in the bathroom, picked up a vociferous Mudpie, and then moved on to the sitting room, crooning and scratching the cat's ear.

He hadn't answered her. Frowning a little, but with no sense of foreboding, Elain rounded the corner into the sitting room. Math was sitting on the sofa, and he had some papers in front of him.

"Business?" she asked, smiling because she knew that whatever it was, he would stop now. She had that kind of power over him; that he would not want to be doing any more paperwork tonight.

Then Math looked at her, his jaw clenched, and she knew she was a child playing with a tiger. She had no power over him at all, and she never would have.

"Math!" she breathed.

He stood up, facing her. "Do you know a man named Raymond Derby, Elain?" he asked softly, and the look in his eyes was turning her to stone.

Chapter 16

"I can explain," Elain said desperately. But even if there had been something to say, she couldn't have formed the words. Not with him looking at her like that.

He closed his eyes as if to ward off a blow. He hadn't believed it, she saw. Whatever he had been told, he hadn't believed it until he heard her offer to explain.

"I'm sorry," she said. The cat leaped from her arms as she ran across to him. "Math, I—"

He opened his eyes then, and she stopped as if she'd run into one of the stone walls on the hillside. She stood in the dock of his accusing stare, motionless, her heart thudding. "Let me hear it straight," he said. "You're a detective? A private investigator?"

She swallowed, and the old helplessness came over her, tying her tongue in knots, as it had used to do when they made fun of her. "I was going to tell you tonight," she cried. "I was going to—"

"You're working for the insurer of the hotel?"

She was silent.

"Are you the reason they're refusing to settle the claim? Something you told them? Something you think you found out while you were getting me to spill my guts in bed?"

She swallowed, staring at him.

"Answer me, dammit!" he said harshly.

"No," she said. She coughed to clear her constricted throat. "No. They sent me because they suspected you already."

"Suspected me? Of what, for God's sake? A fraudulent claim? The place is gutted. They've seen it."

She had never seen anything so cold as his eyes. She had been wrong, they were all wrong. Hell was not a place of fire, but of ice. She had died and this was her hell—Math looking at her as if she had never touched him, as though he didn't think her human.

"Of arson."

There was silence as she counted her heartbeats. How amazing that it should still be functioning.

"Dammit to hell," he said, softly and precisely. "You've been waiting for me to confess to the arson of my own house? The place went up like bracken. It was pure luck the whole thing didn't go. We might all have died."

"I don't think you did it. I never believed you did—well, only at first. I've been trying to prove you didn't," she said desperately.

He was watching her levelly, but nothing was reaching him. "Innocence doesn't get proven, Elain. Only guilt. Or do the insurers feel otherwise?"

"No, I don't— Of course they think— But I—" She stopped. Nothing was possible. No explanation could excuse any part of what she had done. It stood revealed now in all its unforgivable detail. Even if she had confessed tonight, she saw, there would have been no way to justify herself. She had been dreaming when she thought there was a way out.

"Math, I love you," she whispered. "I do love you."

He gave a crack of laughter. "I'll just bet you do," he said.

She took her courage in both hands. "You love me. Don't you?" she pleaded, and she had never been more naked than she was now, under that black, raking gaze that stripped her down beyond skin, beyond bones, right to her heart. And it was being torn from its roots, with a pain that she had felt once before, long ago....

She knew what he had said before he said it. She had heard it in another lifetime.

"I do not love you," he said. "You little hypocrite, you want that, too?"

She had been staring at him all the while. Now she closed her eyes, dropped her head. She put a hand to her eyes and felt tears drop into her palm. Why didn't anybody ever tell you that a broken heart was real, not just a phrase, that it hurt so horribly? Why hadn't she been warned that the pain would make it impossible to speak?

"I love you," she sobbed. "Math, Math!"

He snorted furiously. "What the hell are you after now? Get out of here before I tear you apart with my bare hands. Get out of my hotel. Get out of my life."

"Where will I go?" she asked desperately, almost incoherent.

"Wherever people like you do go when your job is over or you've been found out. Back to the hole you crawled out of in the first place. Get out of my sight!" he shouted, as the tight rein he had on himself suddenly snapped, and then his fury was a very palpable, very frightening presence in the room. "I've had as much as I can take!"

She tore the door open and ran out into the void.

"And he threw you out? In the middle of the night?"

Elain hiccuped on a sob. She had run from him, run from the house, not stopping for anything except her handbag, where her car keys were. How she had driven the mile to Pontdewi without going off the track and down the gorge must be attributed to other hands than her own.

"Oh, how awful it all sounds." Sally's voice had pulled her back to sanity, her caring a lifeline. She had listened to the disjointed recital, not asking questions, though she could scarcely have understood more than the essentials.

"It is awful," Elain said. "I'm awful. What I did was awful."

There was no denying that, and Sally didn't try. "God, honey, what are you going to do?"

"I don't know, I don't know." She hiccuped again. She had pretty well stopped crying now, but it had been a long half hour of abandoned weeping before she had pulled herself into sufficient shape to phone. She had rung the club first, till common sense kicked in and reminded her it was Monday and Monday was Sally's day off. She had wakened Sally from the only good night's sleep she got in seven.

"God, what a mess! I wish I could—oh, what a mess! I just feel so helpless. He must be so angry, so hurt."

"He is as cold as arctic ice," replied Elain flatly.

"Where are you now?"

"In the phone booth in the village."

"Elain, it's so late. Where are you going to spend the night?"

"I don't know. I'll try the pub here, or go into Dolgellau. I must be able to find something."

"Hang up now before it's too late to find something. Call me in the morning. Never mind how early. I won't be able to sleep anyway, worrying about you."

"I'll be all right, Sally. Thanks for listening."

But it wasn't easy to find a place to stay at midnight in a small Welsh town in the high season. The pub at Pontdewi had no rooms, and in Dolgellau, the nearest town, most places were locked up for the night, and the one that wasn't was full.

She would have to spend the night in the car, and the thought terrified her. Crime was not so high in the Welsh countryside as in other places in the world, but a woman sleeping alone in her car overnight anywhere these days was a fool. She drove for awhile through the dark night, looking for some little haven where she might feel safe; then, like a homing pigeon, she was wearily forced back to the White

Lady. When she passed through the last gate, she shut off her headlights and drove as quietly as possible around the dark building, along the drive and over to the outbuildings. She pulled inside the doorway of an old barn, turned off the engine, dragged a rug over herself and, deeply exhausted and determined not to think, settled for sleep.

A harsh knocking on the window behind her head woke her. She sat up, confused for only a moment before everything flooded into her brain. Then she dropped her head forward, rubbing gritty eyes. It was morning. Her shoulders ached from her awkward sleeping position, her head ached with crying, but her heart, thank God, seemed numb.

The banging came again, and she turned abruptly. Math was bent impatiently over the car. "What the hell do you think you're doing?" he demanded, when she had rolled down the window.

"You said get out. I couldn't find a room anywhere."

He swore. "So you came back here?" he said incredulously. "You thought you'd be safe here?"

"I was afraid to—" She broke off helplessly.

He smiled the devil's own smile, cold, heartless. "You're a fool if you think yourself safe with me. Anywhere near me."

She knew that was no more than the truth. She said, "Anyway, I have to pick up my things, pay my bill."

"Honourable to the last, I see."

She was suddenly angry. "And I'm going to get cleaned up and changed before I go, so don't expect me to be out in five minutes. You'll just have to put up with me polluting your property for awhile."

"I'll be out for an hour," he said. "Be gone before I get back."

He strode away, and a minute later she heard the sound of hooves. Of course Balch was stabled in the other damn barn. She hadn't thought of that. Of course he had noticed her car on the way past.

* * *

"I didn't know you were leaving us today."

"No. It's a sudden decision."

Olwen looked sideways at her. "Math knows about this?"

Elain snorted mirthlessly. "Oh, yes, he knows."

"Well, there's nothing to pay anyway. He said you weren't to be allowed to pay your bill," Olwen told her with a smile. "He told me that a few days ago. See? I've marked it here on your card."

She had to hold herself together by main force. She looked down, pressed her lips together, then looked up again. "I think you'll find he's changed his mind about that," she said, as levelly as she could.

There was a short pause while Olwen absorbed that. "Oh, but shouldn't I—"

"Olwen," she said. "Just let me pay the bill and go. Please."

She looked at her, and Olwen knew that it was one of those times when one woman just has to listen to another.

"Will it go on your credit card?"

Elain nodded and handed over her card, then tucked the receipt away.

"Aren't you going to say goodbye to the others? Not even to Vinnie?"

Guilt smote her at the thought of how Vinnie would look at her if she knew. She had betrayed Vinnie, too, checking up on her, finding out things that were none of her business, none of anyone's business. "I'll write Vinnie," said Elain. "Tell her I'm sorry."

"Hell," said Raymond. "Who told him?"

"I don't know. He said he had a phone call to make, or coming in, something like that. Half an hour after that, he—he told me. He threw me out."

"Where are you now?"

"In Dolgellau."

"Right. Well, you'd better come back to town. They're going to be very sorry about this, but it's not your fault."

"Isn't it?"

"No. It's mine. I had a query from a prospective client the other day—I told him too much about you. I said you were on a job and wouldn't be available for a week or so. He wasn't a client at all, of course. It was somebody checking up, to see if you were working for me. Fool that I am."

"But who knew I might be working for you in the first place?"

"Ah, hell, anybody, Red. An old client. Your roommate, your friends. You're an artist, right? Tell anybody there you'd been to the Slade?"

"No—yes! But—" She started to speak and then stopped.

"Yeah, you leave a trail a mile wide, easy for a professional. Somebody probably went down and bought a drink for that roommate of yours, got her talking. Easy enough. I should have seen that one coming."

"Yeah," Elain agreed lifelessly.

"I'll get on to the client and tell them. You get driving. Come here as soon as you get in, yeah?"

There was a coffee shop close to the phone box in Dolgellau, and she went there to think. Something was nagging at her, and she wasn't going to start driving till she had it nailed down.

From the moment she had learned that the tapestry hadn't burnt, she had been looking at it from only one angle—that Math must be guilty of something. Fraud, if not arson.

Because nothing else seemed to make sense. If a thief had wanted the tapestry, he had only to take it. Indeed, he had successfully taken it, if the forensic experts were right. It was insane to think that someone would set fire to the hotel, with possible loss of life, in order to disguise the disappearance of something worth at most £50,000. Surely no one would risk a possible life sentence for that kind of money.

Why steal the tapestry anyway? It wouldn't be easy to pawn, like a diamond ring. Unless you had a client who had seen or heard of it and ordered it stolen. That would mean its going straight into a private collection; no need to disguise the theft, because no one but the new owner would ever see it. The thief wouldn't have to worry about being caught trying to sell it.

So why set fire to the place?

Only Math could benefit from both the disappearance of the tapestry and the hotel fire. That was why suspicion of him had been virtually forced on her—and, no doubt, on the insurance company.

But she knew that Math did not feel he had benefited from the fire. Things that he valued had been lost forever—like the seventeenth-century woodwork in the burnt-out rooms. She believed Math innocent. Her head had cleared. She simply knew that Math could not have risked human lives for personal gain, knew that he had not been lying to her when he said the tapestry had burnt. He had believed it.

And suddenly a very ugly pattern was emerging from what had been stupid confusion.

To set fire to a hotel with potential loss of life in order to disguise the theft of a tapestry worth £50,000 would be the act of a madman. So, unless they were dealing with a psychopath, the hotel had been torched for another reason.

Someone had wanted to burn down Math's hotel. But more than that. There was the tip-off to the insurance company. They also wanted Math suspected of arson. Suppose the tapestry had even been removed not because someone wanted it, but because they knew the insurers would discover that it hadn't burnt? Suppose they had taken the tapestry merely to cast further suspicion on Math?

They couldn't be expected to know that it was undervalued. But Math did. He'd had an appointment to have it valued by Sotheby's in October. If he was going to torch his own hotel for the insurance money, why wouldn't he have waited till the tapestry was valued for the full amount?

Someone had wanted to burn down the hotel. They had access through a secret tunnel that no one knew about. So, late at night, they had come down the tunnel, through the door, up into the kitchens. They had gone and collected the tapestry, carried it down into the tunnel. Then they had dragged the petrol cans through into the cellar and set some kind of timed wick alight. They closed the secret door, ran down the tunnel, stuffed the tapestry through the gap and climbed up inside the old fortress. Then they went over the wall and down the public footpath.

Did they go into the village, or the other way? In the other direction, where did the path lead?

Now they had the tapestry, and they had the hotel out of commission. And Math under suspicion.

If you looked at it that way, other incidents since the fire were more sinister. The burning coal on the carpet in the lounge, only discovered because of the dog. The broken tap, also discovered by chance before it could do real damage.

And those stupid psychic sisters, with all their talk of sinister ghosts, had blinded them all to what was really going on. Somebody was sabotaging Math, and didn't care whose life got in the way.

"I'm not coming back," she said.

"What? They want you to. They want to debrief you," Raymond said in surprise.

"Who's talking like a movie now? I don't care what they want. Something's going on here, and I'm not leaving till I find out what it is."

"What's going on is arson by the owner," said Raymond. "Clear as daylight. You keep your nose out, or I'll have an angry client on my hands."

"I'm here, Raymond, you're not. And I'm telling you, no."

He digested that in silence. "The client's not going to like it, Red. And they sure won't be paying your expenses beyond today."

"I don't want them to. I quit."

"Going over to the enemy? Be careful what you tell him. You're not above being sued for conflict of interest, you know."

"I'm not going over to anybody," Elain said doggedly. "I'm looking for the truth. Or isn't the client interested in that?"

"Very few people are, Red. Where are you going to be? Not still at the hotel?"

"No. At the moment, I'm driving around with my luggage in my car. I'll find somewhere, I guess."

"Let me know," said Raymond. "And Red..."

"Yes?"

"Keep me posted, eh? Call if you need help."

Something else had been bothering her, too. The only person she had mentioned the Slade School of Art to was Math.

The door opened, and he stood there, cold as justice, his eyes hooded. "What are you doing here?" he asked in soft savagery.

She quailed, but stood her ground. "I want to talk to you."

"No, you do not. Not if you know what's good for you."

"Oh, Mr. High and Mighty," she jeered. "'Dear Kettle, yours sincerely, Pot'?" She hadn't meant to say this. She had meant to outline her suspicions in a calm, reasonable way, convincing him. She hadn't meant to accuse him of investigating her as she had investigated him.

"Get away from me, Elain," he said steadily.

"Who asked someone to check up on me, Math? Who knew I'd been to the Slade? Who knew about Sally? Only you! You're the only way someone could have got a lead on me." She pushed past him, and he let her do it, closing the door after she was in. But he stood there, his hand on the knob, cold and still.

"I did not ask anyone to check up on you."

"They just did it off their own bat? They gave it to you as a friendly gesture? But you listened to the report, didn't you? You believed it!"

He smiled grimly at her, and she saw something terrible behind his eyes, but couldn't name it. "Are you suggesting it wasn't true?"

This was ridiculous. She was getting nowhere like this, shouting her hurt at him. "Math," she said urgently. "Don't you see something's going on? Don't you see there's danger? The tapestry was stolen, Math. It didn't burn in the fire, there was no trace of it. I'm not supposed to tell you that. Somebody's out to get you, or to get this place, can't you see it? I want to help!"

"Is that what you came to say?"

"Who told you about me? Who phoned that night?"

He was silent, gazing tiredly at her.

"Don't you see it's important? Whoever did it must have seen that I would find out the real facts if I carried on. They wanted to stop me. They want you charged with arson."

He looked resigned, like a man buttonholed by some intolerable bore at a party, waiting till she had finished and would move on.

"Who's Brian Arthur?" she said desperately. "Have you ever asked yourself that? What's he doing here? I can tell you, he's not what he says he is."

"Few people are, apparently."

Her heart was breaking all over again. She had tried not to hope before she came, but she knew now she hadn't succeeded. She couldn't stand him looking at her like that, his eyes and his voice so cold, hating her in that cold, terrible way. She threw herself against him with a pleading cry, and then gasped at the utter lack of response she felt in his body.

He was absolutely stiff, and his hands came up and clenched on her upper arms as he pushed her away from him with a slow, dreadful force that not all her strength could have overcome. His hands hurt; she knew she would bruise. Her skin bruised easily.

"Math!" she pleaded, when he had let her go.

"If you come near me again, I will not be responsible for the consequences."

"Math, I love you!"

He looked at her without a shred of response, and unconsciously her hand stroked the hair at her left ear. "I don't know anything uglier than you with that lie on your lips," he said, and that word was enough to drain all the blood from her heart, all the hope from her future.

She stood shaking, hopeless, helpless, as he opened the door. Her heart was stone now, unfeeling, but she knew when she was alone her heart would be flesh again, and she would feel the razor of his hatred cutting through her....

"Ah! What timing! I was just about to knock!" said Theresa Kouloudos. "You got my message, then. Hi, Elain."

"Oh . . . Theresa. Hi. I'm just leaving."

"Oh, don't do that! It's both of you I need to speak to. We've got a contract."

Theresa Kouloudos wasn't anyone you would want to meet in a dark alley, Elain thought. She let absolutely nothing get in her way. Somehow she was inside the flat, sitting at the table with them.

"But I've got the car loaded," Elain protested. "I can't do this just now. I'm going to travel around, do some painting." Any lie rather than tell her that Math had kicked her out. She looked at Math. Why didn't he say something to reinforce her? He didn't want her here.

But Math said nothing. He sat watching the two women as if he were at a play.

"I wonder if I could convince you to stay on just for . . . well, for however long it takes you to give them what they're asking for?" Theresa responded in a tone that made it clear she had no intention of letting anything else happen. "Henrietta wants to make this book part of a package she's offering the U.S. publishers, and she wants to go over there next month. The more complete the book we show them, the better chance there is of their buying it. Much as she loves the idea, Henrietta can't go into an expensive production like this on her own. She needs the Americans in on it."

"But—"

"I said neither of you had any prior commitments. I said you'd both get down to it and work flat out for the next few weeks. You haven't got anything pressing at the moment, have you, Math?"

Math's face was unreadable. "When does she want it?"

"She's leaving for the States on September 10th."

He shrugged. "All right."

Theresa glanced from one to the other, as though their lack of enthusiasm had suddenly filtered through to her. But she was not the type to let a little thing like a smashed love affair stand in the way of a book contract.

"Right, then," said Theresa. "We'll get Elain settled back in downstairs. You're going to need to be close enough to collaborate."

His face was without emotion of any kind.

Chapter 17

She moved back into Llewelyn's Room, and then sat staring at the walls. What was she doing here?

"I don't know anything uglier than you with that lie on your lips." Elain closed her eyes. It was true. She was ugly. She had always been ugly. Somehow she had believed otherwise for a couple of strange, dreamlike weeks; she had believed that love conquered all. But she was awake now. She would never be trapped into that seductive stupidity again. He had been less clumsy than Greg, but far more brutal. At least Greg had been honest with her. He hadn't pretended to think her beautiful, once he'd seen her deformity.

The wound he'd inflicted had been, she saw now, relatively clean: one good, deep stab. Math had got right inside before he started slashing her up. *I don't know anything uglier than you with that lie...* Would she ever forget the look in his eyes?

What was she doing here? He didn't want her, and she no longer wanted him. She didn't want anything except to crawl under the sheet and sleep. Sleep this life away and wake up being born into another life, where she would be strong and beautiful and invulnerable. Instead of weak and ugly and bleeding to death. *I don't know anything uglier than you... anything uglier than you...*

She did sleep, and woke feeling sick and groggy to find the sky overcast and the air thundery. She didn't go down to tea. She took a shower in the ancient bathroom and wandered around her room, unable even to concentrate on a simple task like unpacking.

She didn't look at herself in the mirror as she dressed. For dinner she drove down to the pub. The storm still hadn't broken. She ordered chicken and chips and sat in a corner by herself, letting the cheerful laughter and talk wash over her, putting up that protective shield she always carried, so that those who glanced at her with more than casual interest soon looked away again.

Only with Math had she let that shield down. She had enjoyed the freedom, the lightness that came with letting it drop. But it was second nature to her. She was scarcely aware of picking it up again. She was scarcely aware that it was this shield that constituted her prison. She only knew that she felt herself again. In control. Wanting no man.

The storm broke while she ate, but it was a small one of brief duration. As she left the pub to get to her car, she passed the phone box, slowed down and went in.

"You have reached Derby Investigations. There is no one to take your call at the moment. Please leave a message after the beep."

"Raymond, it's Elain," she began. "I just—"

There was a clatter of the phone being picked up. "Hi, Red," said Raymond. His business phone rang at home, and he screened his after-hours calls. "How's it going?"

"Nothing much is happening. I just called to let you know I'm staying at the White Lady after all."

"Ah." He didn't question that. But of course, he didn't know the full story. He didn't know how much of a personal betrayal she had committed.

"I guess I'll be there for a week or two. Until further notice anyway." And she would pay for it if it killed her to do it. She wasn't having Math subsidize her. "Any news with you?"

"Ah, yes, what was it?" She heard him flip over the pages of his notebook. "Right. Those two sisters. Esterhazy. We finally got a line on them."

"Did she write those books, then?"

"Not only did she not write them, Red, she's not in the business at all."

"What business? Writing? But I—"

"The psychic business. She's not a psychic, a channeller, a medium or any other kind of New Age charlatan. None of her friends has ever heard her use the word 'vibrations.'"

"What?" Elain demanded, her brain whirling. "What the devil does that mean?"

"She's faking it, Red."

"Yes, but why?"

There was silence for a moment. The pips started going, and she hurriedly shoved another pound coin into the slot. "Hard to say. The other one, the sister—"

"Rosemary."

"Rosemary Esterhazy is a schoolteacher. Teaches English and history at a girls' sixth-form college, medium posh. Due for retirement this year."

Well, she had certainly pegged that one. "I'm surprised it's not art."

"How's that?"

"Nothing. What does Davina do?"

"Keeps house for her sister. Used to be a secretary, but lost that job five years ago. Nothing since then."

"But it doesn't make sense, Raymond. They weren't even here when the fire started."

"They weren't at home, either. They left for an extended holiday the last week of May. Rosemary took leave of absence for the last term. Compassionate leave or something."

"The fire happened the second week of June, didn't it? They arrived here ten days later, I think. Is there any way we can trace their whereabouts during those three weeks?"

"Hell of a lot of legwork, Elain. And I've got no one picking up the tab now. What I just gave you is on the house. It's set me back a couple of hundred quid. Digby's good, but he doesn't come cheap."

"Couldn't you put it to them? Show them how suspicious it is? They'd be happier if it was arson, whoever the arsonist was, wouldn't they?"

"If they thought they could prove it, they might. All right, I'll talk to the client. I'll tell them I've kept you on it, too. Try to squeeze some funds out of them."

"It doesn't make sense, though," she had to admit. "Why would Rosemary and Davina want to burn down the White Lady?"

"I'd be guessing, Red. Oh, one more thing. You're right about Brian Arthur. He's a dick."

"Listen to me," she begged. "Just listen for five minutes!"

The look on his face was boredom. She might have been a vacuum-cleaner salesman. "You have nothing to say to me."

"I do! Please, Math! Just forget everything for a minute and listen. Five minutes, that's all!"

He let her in, and she led the way to the dining table. That had memories enough, but the sofa would have been intolerable. She sat down, dropping a small notebook in which she'd been making her notes. Math remained standing. He picked up the glass of whisky he'd been drinking, but he offered her nothing. There was a small fire in the hearth and a book open on the sofa. Bill was snoring gently on the rug. A cosy evening was all she had interrupted. He wasn't suffering. He didn't need her and never had.

She picked up her pencil and pulled the pad to her. "All right," she said. She wished he would sit down, but not for a continent would she have said so. "Would it interest you to know that Davina Esterhazy is not—never has been up to now—a psychic?''

"Not particularly.''

"But, Math—she's pretending she knows all about Jessica! She's—''

"There are a lot of sudden converts, especially this kind, at this moment.''

"But she says she's writing a book. She's acting as if—''

"The world is full of phonies, or hadn't you noticed?''

She sighed, dropped her head and blindly read her notes. "I'm telling you anyway. They've been away from their home since the last week of May.''

"I always knew that. That's why they didn't get our message cancelling their reservations.''

"Oh.'' That deflated her a little. She began again. "Jeremy Wilkes isn't related to Earl Spencer. And he's never been published under his own name as far as . . . as we can discover.''

This time he laughed. "Jeremy doesn't fool anyone. When you know him better . . . if you knew him better, you'd realize that no one here is fooled by Jeremy's fantasies.''

"Why does he stay here?''

He shrugged. "I suppose because he has nowhere else to go. Before the fire, we had a chambermaid here who was very impressed by his aristocratic connections. She always treated him like royalty. He can dream here, and no one rubs his nose in the truth. But if you're going to tell me he started the fire . . .''

"No. I'm just pointing out how—''

"How people aren't what they seem around here? I had noticed,'' he said drily.

She wasn't going to tell him about Vinnie. That couldn't possibly have any bearing on anything. "Brian Arthur is a private investigator. But no one knows who he's working for. Not for—not for the insurance company, I know that.''

"I see,'' he said, unmoved.

"*Do* you see?'' she exploded. "Do you see how suspicious it all is? Something is going on, and the target is you!''

"Yes, indeed."

"Don't you see? If we pooled our information—"

"I don't think so," he interrupted harshly. "Working with you on one project is more than enough."

She realized then that it was hopeless. He would never believe her, never be able to hear her clearly. He just wasn't listening.

She stood up, clutching her notebook and pencil. "You're a fool," she said angrily.

Math smiled, but not the kind of smile she wanted to see. "There's never been any doubt about that," he said.

She didn't think, she just moved close, put her hands on his chest and called his name again. His hands came up to her shoulders, and she knew he was going to push her violently away, or strangle her. But as he gripped her she felt him tremble. Then, amazed, she felt the control that she hadn't realized he was using, felt the strength of the control he had needed around her by the power of its snapping. Her heart soared as his hands moved, not to push, but to pull her tight against him, tight and hard, and her head went back and his mouth came fiercely down on hers.

She sobbed once under the touch, and felt his ruthless hands on her back, her arms, her thighs. Then her hips were against the table, and he was pressing against her, his mouth wild, savage on her own. She wrapped her fingers in his thick hair, drawing his head down, then tore her mouth away to catch a ragged breath. She felt his hand on her skirt, dragging it up, and his lips were on her neck, her throat, wherever he could reach.

She was fainting with the wildness of it, drowning in the passion of her own blood. "Math!" she cried, moaning and pulling at his hair, the knowledge of his strength melting her. His voice was in her ear then, as his hand tore at her briefs, slipped inside to enclose her in the heat of his palm.

Then he drew his head back, one hand roughly in her hair to hold her away from him, the other hand still enclosing her centre, and with what seemed to be superhuman effort, he fought for control. For a moment, he watched the passion on her face. Then he said hoarsely, "I'll have this for my revenge, shall I? You heartless little tramp, you think you'll get to me this way? You will not get to me, but I'll get to you, won't I? This is as deep as you go."

She was icy cold by the time he had finished this speech, but his hands were still on her, and he pulled her to him.

"No!" she said, panicked. "Not like this!"

He stopped and smiled. "Not like what? Not with the truth between us? You prefer the lies?"

"It wasn't lies! Not all of it!"

He laughed and let her go, and on his face there was nothing, not even contempt.

In the other direction from Pontdewi, the public footpath led, as she knew from previous experience, along a valley and up a ridge to a view of the estuary. She had been there and painted the view.

If someone had used the footpath to gain access to the tunnel, she thought, they would not have come up from the village. They could not have risked being seen. People did notice things in a village the size of Pontdewi. Either the arsonist had wanted the hotel to burn down, or for Math to be accused of arson. Either way, they would have expected a full police investigation, with people being asked questions about who had been seen in the village. The arsonist couldn't have risked that.

Elain took the footpath in the direction of the estuary, and before very long came to what she'd been looking for: a fork in the path. The left fork was the one she'd taken before, on her painting outings. The right one, scarcely noticeable as it branched off, led straight down the slope towards the main road.

And stopped far below, in a small lay-by, which had parking for about five cars. The kind of place built to provide public access to the footpaths.

So, they had driven here and parked, late in the night. Then they walked up the footpath to the stile, went over the stile, over the fortress wall, into the fortress, where they loosened the board over the entrance to the mine. Then down into the tunnel. When the task was done, they came out the same way, carried the tapestry to the car and were gone. Behind them, the flames must have been already leaping to the sky, while Math fought a brutal battle for his home and the lives of his guests.

They all knew about her now, though not by being told. It was as if the information had seeped out of the ether. The atmosphere was a little chilly.

"Do you think I'm a terrible person?" she asked Vinnie.

"Well, my dear, it's not as though you knew us before you took the job. I suppose it seems unpleasant to us because you had seemed to fit in so well."

"But that wasn't fake. That was real. That's what made it so . . . hard for me."

"But you carried on with it."

"Only because—oh, I wish I could make him—you— understand. I was trapped."

Vinnie smiled sadly. "I expect we'll all manage to forgive you in time. And of course, it's rather exciting to have been, however briefly, the subject of a professional detective's interest. I'm sure Jeremy will be painting you in very thrilling colours by next month."

"Do you—do you think Math will forgive me?"

Vinnie paused. "Well, of course, with Math," she said sadly, "you have history against you."

She sat up at that. "History?"

"I wondered if you knew. You didn't find that out then? Math's father was a judge, you know. The first of his family to rise so far. His wife—Math's mother—got a crippling disease early—oh, in her fifties, I think. They went on loving each other, but she wasn't capable of physical love."

"I didn't know any of this."

"No, it was in all the papers about fifteen or twenty years ago, but it's never been resurrected since. But I remembered it when I met him."

"Why was it in the papers? What happened?"

"Math's father—well, perhaps it's more common nowadays, or at least such things are more often made public than they used to be. But it was shocking enough then. His father had taken a mistress, my dear, as we used to call it. By all accounts he treated her very well. He told the girl the truth, that he loved his wife and would never marry her. He started an annuity for her, so that she would be financially sound for the rest of her life. It was an amicable arrangement. Then he got his knighthood."

Elain blinked. "Math's father was knighted?"

"He was made High Court judge, you see. A knighthood comes almost automatically, I believe, with the appointment to the High Court Bench. It was a tremendous achievement for him, coming from a family that had been farming for generations. But the lure of publicity was too much for the girl. When the next honours list was published, she sold her story to the papers."

"To the *papers?*" Elain repeated incredulously, though it was nothing new. It was happening every day.

"A scandal sheet—there were only *News of the World* and *The Sun* then, I think. Haven't times changed, though! Now they have a choice of half a dozen. It looked a very sordid story when down in black and white, and of course the judge had to resign. No one at all had known that Math's mother was sexually incapable, but it was all revealed. You can imagine in what terms."

Elain could only shake her head in horror.

"No doubt she had understood implicitly, if not explicitly, what arrangement her husband had made, but . . . she died of the shock within two weeks of the first press story. And the press being what it is, her death simply added fuel to the fire."

Of course it had. Elain could almost see the headlines. SHAME DEATH OF LOVE-NEST JUDGE'S WIFE.

"Oh, God," she whispered, suddenly seeing where all this was leading.

"Yes, it must have been dreadful. Math's father committed suicide two days after his wife's death."

She was silent with horror. "How old was he?"

Vinnie understood who she meant. "He was a teenager. Fifteen or eighteen."

"Where is the—the woman who—"

"As far as I know, she disappeared into oblivion." Vinnie's tart voice seemed to express that it was well-deserved oblivion, without saying so.

"I suppose that's why he writes under a pseudonym. So the story won't be resurrected."

"Perhaps," said Vinnie. "He has always struck me as a very private man. Perhaps he always was."

"And now he sees me as just another cheat."

"Oh, but the cases are so different," Vinnie said soothingly.

They weren't, though. From Math's point of view—from any point of view—they were far too alike.

She must concentrate on work, on *The Mabinogion*. Whatever happened, it was still a great chance for her. She'd be a fool to mess that up.

She pulled out all the sketches she'd made, the ones she had packed away the other night when Rosemary had come to her room, and hadn't looked at since. Perhaps if she set them out around the room, they would inspire her.

But they would never inspire her again. Someone had taken a black felt marker to them, defacing them with wide, ugly scribbles that all but obliterated each carefully drawn, delicately watercoloured sketch. And in the marks she read a violence of anger that was chilling in its intensity.

"Look," she said helplessly. "Don't you see there might be danger?"

"You're getting tiresome," he said. "What is it you want?"

The door was unlocked. She had walked in and found him at his desk.

"You wouldn't believe me if I told you. Have you thought about this at all—if it wasn't, as Davina keeps insisting, the

ghost who put the coal on the rug and broke the tap, who
was it, and why did they do it?'' She took a deep breath.
"And how did they get inside a locked room?"

"Accidents do happen."

"Did you ask Evan about that tap? I did. He said it had
been deliberately smashed. And tell me how an 'accident'
gets a burning coal five feet from the fireplace when there's
a screen in front of it."

"Leave it alone," Math said. "There's no reason for you
to concern yourself, and wouldn't your employers prefer it
if you concentrated your efforts on establishing me as the
guilty party?"

"I've quit. I don't have any employers," she said quickly.

"No doubt you are of less use without your cover."

"You may think so," she said hardly. "Someone else isn't
so sure." She lifted her hand and dropped the spoiled
sketches on the desk in front of him so that they spilled out
in all their grotesque ugliness.

His face was wiped of all expression as he saw them. He
cursed under his breath. "Unless you were the one who did
that," she said coldly.

He looked at her then, and she saw that this destruction
had shaken him as nothing else, perhaps, could have. For
one unguarded moment, she saw the real Math. Then his
eyelids dropped, his jaw clenched and his expression was
hooded again.

"Well?" he asked.

"Did you do it?"

For one minute, when she had first looked at them, she
had believed it, had thought of Math's fury and believed
him capable of this. But that had been her own guilt talking.

"No," he said coldly. "I did not do it." They were silent
for a moment, and his hands were firm on the thick pages
of the sketches as he gathered them up. His eyes rose to hers.
"Did you?"

She breathed as if he had struck her, reached out and snatched them back from him. "What would I do that for?" she demanded furiously.

"I don't know," said Math. "I don't fool myself any more that I understand how your mind works. But if you thought this would help you slip in under my guard, think again."

She had never come so close to hitting anyone in her life. Never come so close to hating. "Believe me, I do not want to get anywhere near you," she said, spitting the words at him as if they were poison darts. "I've had enough of that kind of lie to last a lifetime!"

He sat unmoved. The darts didn't get near him. "Good," he said. "I suppose if I've saved some other sucker, it ought to be enough for me."

Sucker. I guess I'm the sucker this time. Fury seized her. Without volition, her hand flashed up, but his own hand moved just as quickly. He stood, and her wrist was caught in a strong, lightning grip that sent all the sketches flying, his chair falling back with a crash. The cat skittered madly from the room.

"Don't even think it," he said, and at the look in his eyes now, as he stood so close over her, something in her shrank back in fear.

"If it came to a fight, of course you'd win," she said bitterly.

"Be sure of that."

For a moment they stood silent, unmoving, facing each other like adversaries. The sense of threat she felt was familiar, and she remembered what she had felt at the beginning—before she had fooled herself into thinking she loved him—that somewhere, sometime, he had been her enemy. She twisted her wrist out of his grasp and he let her go.

She was panting. She said, "I don't care what happens to you anymore. But I'll tell you this anyway. 'The Dream of Rhonabwy'—the tapestry watercolour—is missing from that." She indicated the swirl of vandalized sketches lying across the floor and his desk with a contemptuous jerk of her head.

He said nothing. She laughed without mirth. "I guess they were hoping I wouldn't notice. Quite a history your enemy has, of trying to disguise the theft of that tapestry with another crime."

Math said tiredly, "Why don't you leave it alone?"

She ignored that. "I guess they were afraid I'd give the sketch to the police. We were looking at it in the restaurant awhile ago, you and I. The restaurant was busy that night, but maybe if you think hard, you can remember who was there," she said coldly. "Because someone who was there that night and saw that sketch is your enemy. And whatever they're after, they haven't stopped yet, have they?"

She no longer knew what drove her. Not any desire to protect Math, not even any need to prove anything to him. She hated him now. He had lied as much as she had—more, and with less reason. He had said he loved her. He had said she was beautiful. That was worse than any lie she had told.

She had bought the most powerful flashlight she could find, another little pocket-size one, and a waterproof jacket and pants. And a strong rope. It was after midnight when she parked her car in the parking lot. No one was in sight anywhere. The summer night was warm, the sky full of stars, an owl hooting, a cow bawling. The moon was just off the full, and she climbed the footpath mostly without the use of the flashlight.

The fortress looked eerie in moonlight, its jagged edges misty white against the black sky. Its shadow seemed to move as a cloud scudded across the moonlight, and the trees were waving softly in the wind.

She was remembering Jess, and the woman who waited, and the rats. She did not want to be here, especially at night. But she was driven to find the answer, if only for the pleasure of throwing it in Math's face.

She had reconnoitred the entrance earlier in the day. More boards had been put up to keep people out, but she had worked a couple of them loose, and now they came away easily in her hands.

The Romans had dug this as an air shaft, perhaps, but they had carved steps into the rock, too. These were steep and sheer, and she needed the rope she had brought. She left it hanging just in case, although she had no intention of coming back this way. She could come back and clean up the evidence early in the morning.

There was water dripping somewhere, and she could feel the dampness on her face. The blackness was intense, and the beam of light seemed to do nothing more than create shadows. She walked carefully. The floor was rough and uneven, full of shadow.

Her foot kicked something loose, and it went skittering away with a high, tinny sound that had her heart leaping in terror and goose bumps running all over her body. It was much worse than she had imagined. She was terrified.

She went on again, playing the light around her at intervals. She didn't even know what she was looking for. Evidence that someone had been here? Proof that it could have happened the way she imagined? Or perhaps—some evidence as to why someone wanted to destroy the White Lady?

How many Romans had spent their lives down here? Someone had said they were slaves, all the Roman miners. Had some of them died down in the tunnels?

She had meant to explore them, but now, creeping along, she knew that it was impossible. She lacked the courage. This wasn't a place to be in alone at night, with the sound of dripping water and another sound, like the moaning of wind far away, deep in the tunnels.

What was she doing here? She must have been crazy. That terrible last meeting with Math must have simply fried her thinking processes. What could she possibly prove down here? Nothing—unless she ran smack into whoever was using the tunnels for whatever purposes they might have.

How easy murder would be down here. How easy to make it look as though someone had fallen and hit her head, or slipped and drowned in the water she could hear somewhere. . . .

Should she go back? She turned and trained the light back the way she had come. It didn't reach to the stone steps. Was she more than halfway? She must keep calm and continue to walk slowly. She mustn't allow herself to panic, to try to run. It would be so easy to fall and hit her head, and how long would it be before they found the note in her room?

She recognized the face of the rockfall with a feeling of drenching relief. The worst was over. The worst had been fearing that she wouldn't recognize the wall when she saw it.

It wouldn't be long now. She pressed her way through the niche, and stumbled up the tunnel and into the passage. Thank God she'd soon be in the kitchens.

The door into the cellar had been completely and solidly walled off.

She tasted bile in her throat, and her stomach was heaving with animal fear. No! She couldn't go back! She could not go back into that gaping central chamber, with its ghosts and rats and the lurking terror.

If she screamed loudly enough, would someone hear? Would someone come and break down the barrier and let her out? Once she let herself begin to scream, her fragile hold on her sanity would slip, she knew that. She would be reduced to the pure animal terror that was waiting to engulf her. And if they did not find her, if he didn't come . . .

Once he had come when she called, though she hadn't known she was calling. But he wouldn't come now. She could be screaming with all the hounds of hell at her heels, and Math would not come. She could be sure of that.

She had to go back. There was no other way. She must turn and walk slowly, one step at a time. She must not run, or cry out, do anything to shake her control. It wouldn't be long. She flashed the light over her wristwatch. Ten past one. She would be at the exit by twenty past, twenty-five past at the latest. Ten minutes, that was all. She could hang on for ten minutes.

She was shivering with nerves as she pressed her way back through the niche, cold and sick. She must not throw up. Not yet.

The darkness of the cavern terrified her now. She could feel another presence, as if her first passage had awakened the ghosts of the place; she was no longer alone. She stood for a moment unmoving, and peered around her, but it was useless to try to see anything. Her flashlight was half blinding her, casting huge rock shadows.

She should turn out her light, but she was incapable of that. She had experienced the total blackness of the mine. It had terrified her then; it would kill her now.

There was someone here. She could sense it, feel it, with every pore. If she left the protection of the wall, he might come up on her from any side.

She could hear him breathing. "Who's there?" she cried, her voice low and rasping, no more than a whisper.

There was no answer but the drip of water and the sound of hollowness, as before. Elain moved a little into the chamber, and then she heard it again. She froze, and turned the light wildly in all directions, trying to see, knowing that whoever it was had all the advantage.

Then, without warning, there was a huge, moving shadow, much, much closer than she had guessed. He was beside her in a split second as she screamed, and then there was an arm around her neck and a hand squeezing the wrist that held the flashlight, and against the strength she felt she knew she was helpless.

Chapter 18

Her scream had been involuntary, a purely animal response. She didn't waste time or breath on another, but devoted her energies to the battle. If she could get her wrist free, she could smash his head with the flashlight. Elain stamped wildly backwards, and felt the walking boot she wore connect with his ankle.

She twisted her wrist then, but there was no give in his hold. He squeezed her wrist more tightly and twisted until she was forced to open her hand. The flashlight fell and smashed against rock, and then there was pitch blackness and she knew she was going to die.

Fear gave a fury to her muscles that she did not recognize. She began to punch and swing at her assailant in the darkness, to kick and smash blindly, struggling so that she could not be held. He grabbed at her, and they tripped and fell to the hard floor. She heard him grunt as she landed on him, and used her advantage to smash a fist down. It landed all but uselessly on his chest or upper arm, and she punched again, and again, seeking his neck and head, all her terror released in the violence.

They fought in silence, broken only by grunts and the sound of gasping breath. He was stronger than she, but he could not afford to let go of her, for if he did she might easily escape in the darkness, and she knew that he did not want that to happen. And she had the animal strength that fear gives. Time and again she twisted out of his hold to land a kick or a punch.

She was hampered by her thick waterproof suit, but it gave her protection from the sharp stones that he did not have. At last he reared up, grabbing her, finding her arms, her wrists, holding her helpless.

Then it was as if time shimmered in the darkness, and some border was passed. She recognized him then, as an ancient, terrible enemy, and knew that this battle had been waiting to happen for whole lifetimes.

Dread seized her, for he was too strong for her. She fought, but he dragged her down, flattened her under him. Now it was a terrible, animal fight to the death. She twisted and writhed, tried to bite and kick, and all the while she felt him reaching out with one arm, groping for something. He was trying to find a rock, a stone, and he would smash her head as soon as he found it. She knew that these were her last seconds of life.

One second stretched out, and she saw, in the clear light that approaching death brings, that the only important thing in life was love. She saw, too, with awful heartache, how little she had loved. All her life she had hidden behind fear, protecting herself from the one urgent task given to humankind. How little store she had laid up for herself in heaven!

But at least she had loved Math, completely, wholly, from an overflowing heart. Perhaps that would weigh in the balance. Maybe love was so strong that ... oh, what she would give, now, for more time to love! For time to love him as she knew she could, through a life span and into eternity!

She dragged in air. "Math!" she screamed, loudly, desperately, stupidly, knowing nothing except that she loved him, and that she could not bear to leave him yet. "Math, help me!"

Her assailant went still on top of her, and she heard a wild curse. *"Elain?"* His voice rasped terribly, as if he were dying. *"Elain?* My God, what the hell is going on?"

"Math?" she whispered, her voice raw in her throat. "Math, is it you? Oh, God, oh, thank God!" She began to cry, tearing sobs of reaction. "Oh, God, Math! I thought I was going to die! I thought you were going to kill me!"

He said, his voice shaking, "I nearly did."

They made their way out using the small flashlight she had put in her pocket, then simply lay on the grass in the moonlight. For a long time they did not speak.

Nothing had ever been as sweet as the night air, and just being alive. "Where did you come from?" she asked quietly then.

"I saw you from the study window, coming over the wall. I thought it was ... whoever it is, going to make more mischief. But I knew he wouldn't get into the hotel. I went to wait for him. You're hurt. You're bleeding." His hand reached out to touch her face. It was trembling. "What were you doing there, Elain? What in God's name—"

"I don't know. It was just an—instinct I had, that there might be something down there, something that would prove something."

A helpless breath of laughter, but not of mirth, escaped him, and he shook his head. "Did you find anything?"

"No. When I got down there I was too scared to explore. I just wanted out. But you—the doorway is blocked."

"I didn't recognize you," he whispered hoarsely. "I thought you were a kid from Pontdewi and I was going to throw the fear of God into him ... and then it seemed as if you were someone else."

"Yes," she breathed. "My enemy. I felt that."

"If I'd found a stone, or the torch— I wasn't in control then. How hard would I have hit you?"

* * *

The moon was high, and they stood up to go. In spite of her oilskins, she shivered in the breeze. "We need a brandy," said Math. Then they walked in silence.

Suddenly, as they neared the hotel, Math grabbed her arm and hissed a warning in her ear. Elain stopped dead; the mystery and uncertainty of this night were all around her.

"Someone moving around in the lounge," he whispered in her ear, so softly she could hardly hear. "Get down."

They crouched down and moved into the shadow of a couple of trees. Now she paused to look. Through the arched leaded windows of the lounge, she could clearly see that there was a very dim light moving around. "What can they be doing?" she whispered.

"Let's find out."

He led the way carefully through the shadows, from tree to tree, and at last in against the inner wall of the burnt wing. He went quickly along the wall, and she silently followed, to the corner where the two wings met and along another few feet to the sitting-room windows.

Here they were no longer in shadow. Math slid up beside the window and glanced in, then came down again.

"What are they doing?" she whispered.

"Can't tell. Moving very erratically."

A passing cloud decided to obscure the moon for them, and they both leaned up to look inside. Someone in a white dress or robe was moving around the room, holding the tiniest of flashlights. The beam of light was just too faint to show them a face or any distinguishing characteristic. But Elain felt sure it was a woman. They ducked down again as the cloud went on its way.

"She's moving furniture!" Elain whispered. "That's what it looked like!"

Math was frowning. He slipped up for another look and came down again. "Moving the rug now."

"Math! Do you think—could there be a trapdoor in the floor? Something buried underneath?"

He shook his head. "Don't know. It's the cellar under here as far as I know." But with a house like this, built over time and on an erratic plan, it was hard to be sure of direction and dimension.

Another cloud came along, and they both crept up again. "Where is she? She's gone," Elain hissed.

"In the corner," said Math. "By the fireplace."

He was right. Elain found her just in time to see her raise an arm, white in the moonlight, and it seemed as if she threw something. Then there was a bright, white light and a loud, roaring explosion. When her eyes could see again, the woman was gone.

So was Math. He was inside the front door and running towards the lounge. Elain gasped and followed.

When she came around the corner, he was smashing his shoulder against the lounge door, and there was the sound of a door opening and footsteps and a call from above. With one huge thump, the door broke open under Math's weight, and his hand found the switch and flooded the room with light.

Elain noticed two things. The room looked as though a bomb had hit it, and there was no one in the room save themselves. "Where did she go?" she demanded. "Could she have got out this door and locked it, as fast as that?"

Math just put his finger to his lips. "People coming," he said.

There were more voices and footfalls overhead, and within a minute or two more, they came clattering down the staircase, Jeremy in the lead, with Davina close behind and Vinnie a poor third. Olwen came running along the hall, tying the belt of her dressing gown, Evan close on her heels. Upstairs they could hear Rosemary calling, "What is it? What's happened?" Then Rosemary and Brian Arthur arrived in the hall, making the numbers complete.

They all shoved their way into the lounge, gasping and exclaiming with shock.

"My God, what's happened here?" said Olwen in astonishment.

"There has been a psychic explosion," Davina said in a low, throbbing voice that, in spite of herself, sent chills up Elain's spine. "I can sense the energies. She has Tuhned now." Wearing a pair of dark pyjamas under a rather tattered red terry robe, her hair wilder than usual around her head, she was looking more like Madame Arcati than ever. She turned to Math accusingly. "I warned you!" she said.

"But what's she done? Dropped a bomb?" asked Jeremy.

That was what the room looked like, all right—except that there was no sign of burn. All the furniture seemed to have been blasted back from an epicentre a few feet in front of the fireplace. Chairs were tipped over, rugs were squashed up against the walls, pictures and mirrors had fallen, lamps and tables were overturned—but there was no black spot where the epicentre should be. There was no breakage, no fire, no actual damage. You might imagine that a presence with a huge force field had manifested in that spot.

If she hadn't seen what she had seen through the window, Elain would have been as chilled and shocked by the unearthly quality of the room as the others clearly were.

Looking at Math, Jeremy screamed faintly, "My God, were you here when it went off? You're wounded!"

Everyone looked at him then. His bare arms were covered with scratches and abrasions, and it was clear he would have bruises. "No," said Math.

"And Elain, too! Your face is bleeding!" Rosemary exclaimed in shock.

"We were not here," Math said. "Our scrapes have got nothing to do with whatever happened here."

They were all shaken; no one questioned that. They stood helplessly looking around, murmuring to each other in wonder. Elain began to watch them. Olwen was wearing a yellow nightgown, but she had too large and comfortable a figure. The ghost, Elain was sure, had been much thinner. Jeremy lit a cigarette, and put his silver case and lighter back into the pocket of a blue velveteen dressing gown with a trembling hand. Underneath she caught sight of striped pyjama cuffs.

Rosemary, surprisingly, seemed to be naked under her woolly purple dressing gown. Brian Arthur was still dressed, in chinos and a shirt. Vinnie was wearing a short tartan robe over a light cotton knee-length nightgown.

For one wild, uncomfortable moment, Elain began to think that they had really seen a ghost. After all, the woman had been dressed in white, and had disappeared without a trace. Then she remembered the little flashlight. Ghosts, she told herself, don't need the benefit of artificial light.

"There was a terrific blast," Jeremy protested from the far side of the room, examining one of the rugs where it was squashed up against the drinks dresser. People were beginning to recover. "It should have left a mark, shouldn't it, something that size? But there's nothing."

"You don't understand about psychic explosions," said Davina.

"No, we don't," said Elain suddenly. "Tell us what you think happened here."

How was it she had never noticed before how awkward Davina became when asked for specific details?

"Oh, my dear, I can hardly—the presence is still so strong—a psychic explosion is an explosion on the...the etheric level. There is light and sound and force, but not from an explosion of matter."

"And it's Jessica, you think?"

"Certainly some One, or some Thing, resident in this house. Perhaps a certain evil energy has been released by the opening of that passage in the cellar," she said darkly. "Which I warned against."

"Bollocks," said Math evenly. "Some sleight of hand is what we've got here. Right, would you all mind going back to bed? I'm going to lock this room and make it out of bounds. I'd like the police to have a look at it. This isn't the work of any ghost."

Rosemary had been looking around the room. Her face was white with shock now. "I hope you're right," she said doubtfully, and Elain was amazed to hear her voice actually trembling with fear. She looked as though she might faint. "Well," she said, her panic abruptly calming into decision. "I'm for bed, as Math says. I think we should all go. It's well past two, and this sort of thing is really too distressing at my age."

The headmistress tone in her voice was impossible to disobey entirely. They all began to shuffle awkwardly.

"Yes," said Math. "Will everybody go back to bed, please? We'll talk about this in the morning."

They obeyed reluctantly, glancing over their shoulders as they filed out of the room and up the stairs. After a few minutes, there were only Math, Brian Arthur and Elain left in the room.

"What did you see?" Math asked Brian Arthur softly.

The detective glanced at Elain and back at Math, who nodded. "This young lady is the only person who left her room after retiring for the night," he returned, his voice quiet, as though he thought someone might be eavesdropping. "The rest stayed in their rooms."

She gaped from one to the other. *"You?"* she whispered hoarsely. "You're the one who hired him?"

"You never guessed?" said Math. He was at the fireplace, looking for something. Suddenly his hand waved the other two to silence. "Right," he said loudly. "Good night, then. See you in the morning."

He reached down and seemed to catch hold of something, and stayed there. Elain crept closer. Between two of the antique wooden panels that covered the stone wall at the side of the fireplace, a piece of white fabric, triangular in shape and no more than a foot square, was caught on a rough piece of wood. Math had grabbed this and was still holding it. For a moment, Elain couldn't understand what it was doing there, what it was. Then her brain made sense of the image: the fabric was sticking out between the panels. Something was caught behind.

At his signal, Brian Arthur moved towards the door and said a loud good-night. Elain crossed the room with loud steps, out into the hall, and said good-night as Brian Arthur put out the lights. Then they crept back into the room before closing the door with a bang.

Moonlight flooded the room through the leaded windows, making the disorder seem even eerier and reminding Elain of what they had seen earlier. They stood in perfect silence for several minutes, while her eyes got accustomed to the darkness, and then there was a faint whisper, as of silk on sandpaper, and the piece of fabric Math was clutching began to disappear into the wall.

He held it tightly. It was clear a great deal of pressure was being exerted on it. Elain was gawking, her brain whirling. Someone was behind the panels, but how the hell had they got there, and who was it? Everybody had been in the room a moment ago, they had all gone out by the door.

Had the woman in white disappeared into the panels? And had she been there all the time, waiting to dislodge her gown and get away? Was there a secret door, a space big enough for a person, between the stone wall and the wood panelling beside the huge fireplace?

In spite of this ordinary possibility, she felt shivers up and down her spine when the shadows began to move in the moonlight, and the panel shifted, and a white hand reached out into the room, dragging at the fabric. The moment seemed to go on forever, but it could have been only a split second before Math's hand snapped out and grabbed the wrist.

There was a wild cry and a scream, and then the panel was thrust wide open with the person's struggles, and the lights flashed on.

"Well, Rosemary, hello!" said Math cheerfully.

Chapter 19

"Let me go!" Rosemary said furiously.

"I don't think so, just for the moment," said Math. "Why don't you come out of there?"

"Take your hands off me! This is appalling!" she shouted. But the typical Englishman's conditioned response to that headmistress's tone wasn't affecting Math.

"I think so, too," he said. "You might have killed someone. You nearly did."

He dragged her out by main force, while a voice from above cried softly, "Rosemary?"

She was clutching a torn white nightgown. Math gave Rosemary into Brian Arthur's hold, then put his head into the space that had been revealed in the wall and looked up. "Why don't you come down, too, Davina?" he invited.

"Is it a staircase?" Elain demanded in shocked delight. "A secret staircase? How amazing!"

"Not amazing at all," said Rosemary contemptuously. "Not even unusual. Just a priest's hole, almost standard in houses of this age. The staircase makes it slightly more elaborate than the general run, of course."

"Of course, you'd know that, wouldn't you?" Elain couldn't resist saying. "You teach history, so you'd know all about priests' holes."

"Anyone with any kind of education at all knows about priests' holes," Rosemary said, putting Elain in her place.

Of course, that room was called The Chapel, Elain reminded herself as Davina appeared, gingerly clambering down the rickety ladder from the room above. She remembered, too, how unwilling the sisters had been to be moved somewhere else.

Davina was crying. "Oh, I knew it would come adrift," she said, wringing her hands.

"You didn't know any such thing, you silly woman," said Rosemary. "Shut up."

There was a tap on the door, and Jeremy poked his head around. "I say, I thought something was up!" he exclaimed in his Famous Five voice. "Mind if I join you?"

Math rolled his eyes but didn't say anything, so Jeremy came into the room. He righted a couple of chairs and then sank into one, looking around expectantly. "Good grief!" he said when his gaze fell on the fireplace. He got up and moved to the space, poked his head in and looked down. "Leads down into the cellar, I suppose," he said.

At this, Elain leaped to the priest's hole and peered in. On the right, there was a hole in the floor and a ladder leading down. "But where does it come out?" she demanded.

"Is that you, Elain?" called a voice. She looked up. Vinnie's head was framed against the square of light on the floor above. "Isn't this fascinating? To think I'd been living with this in the house all these years, and never knew it!"

Clutching her robe around her, she came rather nimbly down the ladder. "Well, well!" She beamed into the room. "This solves a lot of the mystery, doesn't it? Now we know how the burning coal got onto the carpet. Rosemary simply came in this way when there was no one in the room, and went out again the same way."

"Be careful," Elain warned. "There's another opening just by your feet. It goes down into the cellar."

"But how thrilling! I suppose this is how Jessica's lover got into the house and how he disappeared when they thought they had him."

"I suppose," remarked Jeremy, who had lit another cigarette, "it's also how the tap in the sink upstairs got broken. While being blamed on poor Jessica!"

"It explains a lot of the how," Math agreed quietly, and the authority in his voice caused them all to fall silent. "But none of the why." He turned to where Rosemary was, now sitting in an armchair, Davina hovering beside her. "Would you care to make that clear?"

"Give me one of those, please," Rosemary said to Jeremy, reaching for a cigarette and bending towards him for the light he offered. She took a deep draw and exhaled. "Well, I suppose once you've got this far..." She drew and exhaled again, carelessly flicked the ash, and sighed, shaking her head. "I suppose you've been through the tunnel and found the passage," she said to Math.

He inclined his head, while the others made noises of astonishment.

"There's a passage?"

"Where does it lead?"

"Why didn't you tell us?"

"Did you understand what you saw?" Rosemary asked disdainfully, ignoring them all.

Math grinned at the tone. "A Roman mine, I thought."

"That's right," said Rosemary. "A Roman mine. Do you know what they were mining?"

"Lead?" Math wrinkled his forehead and then astonishment relaxed all the muscles in his face. "Surely not!" he said. *"Gold?"*

"All we wanted was to make you decide to sell, to take a lower price than you'd paid. Something we could afford. We didn't really mean to burn the place down. We had no idea it would burn so quickly...." Davina was still crying, her face in her hands. "We only wanted to put you out of business. When we heard someone had only just escaped being killed, we were horrified!"

Math wasn't impressed. "If you set fire to a building with sleeping people in it, you can count yourself damned lucky not to be guilty of murder."

"Yes, I see that now, but—we thought, well, it's not high season, the place isn't full.... Rosemary came up and did it all. I was afraid of the mine, you know. We parked and came up the hill, and Rosemary went down and set the fire. Oh, Lord! There was the most terrible explosion! I was horrified, standing there watching it go up, and Rosemary hadn't come out yet! But then she came—"

"Bringing the tapestry," interjected Elain drily.

Rosemary turned on her. "Don't you talk to me in that arrogant fashion!" she snapped. "You're a horrible little spy! You needn't feel so pleased with yourself, you sneaking, snooping little liar! I don't know how you can look at yourself in the mirror! You have no idea of fair play or honour whatsoever!"

Elain could feel herself blushing under the assault of words. She wanted to answer, but as usual, nothing came to her.

"And you do?" asked Math pointedly. "Elain did what she did to uncover a crime. Who has Elain hurt, or tried to hurt? You did what you did for personal gain."

"That isn't the point!"

"I think it is. Go on. You came out with the tapestry after setting the fire, and drove to wherever it was you were staying. Where is the tapestry now?"

"I don't know anything about any tapestry."

"Oh, Rosemary, what good is it?" Davina said tremblingly. "It can't do any good now." She looked at Math. "We've stored it away. You see, we'd seen the tapestry when we were here last year—well, we saw it the first time we came, too. But it wasn't until last year, when we found the passage..." She began to babble almost incoherently. "It wasn't quite by chance, because Rosemary said there ought to be one in a house this age—we had no plans then, except to show it to you if we found it—but then there was so much more to it. And Rosemary was sure it must be a gold mine."

"What made you think there was still gold there?"

"I didn't *think* it!" Rosemary snorted. "I took some samples and had them analysed. There is at least one healthy vein down there. Do you think I did all this for a dream? There are mines in this area that weren't abandoned until the early years of this century and are now being profitably worked again! This mine hasn't been touched since the Romans, as far as I can see."

"I'm rich then," Math said drily. "So you made your plans and came back this year as newly unveiled psychics. Did you really think a ghost story would make me want to sell up?"

"Well, if things kept happening, you see—and we thought, word will get out, and you'll have no guests at all—people wouldn't want to stay where there'd been one fire and a lot of accidents...." Davina, once started, was unable to stop. "And especially if we said the ghost was becoming sinister and evil—we thought you wouldn't be able to survive, you see, and then you'd sell up."

"Crap," said Math without emotion. "You were hoping to force me to default on the mortgage. If I had no customers and couldn't pay, you were figuring that the bank would foreclose. What hope would I have had of finding a buyer at the eleventh hour for a burnt-out place in this market? You were hoping to get it at a bank auction, for about ten per cent of its value. And you would have, if the whole place had burnt."

Davina watched him like a frightened sheep.

"And when it didn't," said Elain, who had recovered her calm, "you figured that if the insurance company didn't pay the claim, Math would be in financial trouble anyway. So you called the insurance company with an anonymous tip that he was guilty of arson."

"No!" Davina exclaimed, but as Rosemary made a noise of fury, she turned to her sister. She seemed to recognize that the look of cold rage Rosemary was directing at Elain meant she was guilty. "I didn't know that," she amended.

"You don't know it now!" snapped Rosemary. She turned to Math. "What are you going to do?" she demanded, a woman who would ask no quarter and give none. She was only asking for facts.

Math said slowly, "Most of what you've done hasn't had the effect you were after. But there's one thing you did that's unforgivable."

She snorted. "Oh, really, how melodramatic. What have I done that's unforgivable? Tried to rob you? People do that every day and are forgiven."

He said, "Yes, I think they do. But you did something more than that. You destroyed Elain's paintings."

"Oh, no!" exclaimed Vinnie. "Surely not!"

Elain sat mute, staring at him, feeling as though her eyes would catch fire if they stretched any farther.

"A few stupid sketches! She's lucky I didn't do more, the interfering, busy—"

"Shut up," said Math evenly, and Rosemary swallowed and went silent.

"Well!" said Jeremy. "It's certainly been one for the books!"

"I wanted to be a writer, you know," Rosemary said conversationally. "They wouldn't let me. They sent me off to teacher's training." No one said anything, and a silence fell on the room.

Brian Arthur, who had left some time before, came back and nodded to Math.

"The police are on their way," Math said.

Davina gulped and began to sob. But not Rosemary. "Really, how pathetic you all are. You've been sitting on a gold mine for fifty years, between you. It took me to find it, me to discover the way in. You ought to thank me. You can sell this place now for a fortune! And you're turning me over to the police? There's gratitude."

The whine of the police siren came up the valley on the wind.

"So you were suspicious all the time?" Elain asked.

It was nearly dawn. "It was clear there was something going on."

"And...you did ask Brian Arthur to check me out?" she asked, half hoping it was true. If they had each mistrusted the other, there might be room...

"He did that on his own. It just didn't occur to me. But as he said, he likes to be thorough."

Ah, well. She might have known. "I know you can't forgive me," Elain said. "I know I'm ugly. But I'm—I just want to say I'm sorry."

They had climbed the stairs together and walked along the hall to her room. The back stairs led up another flight to his flat.

Math looked down at her, unsmiling. "May I come in, Elain?" he asked quietly.

Her heart kicked against her ribs. "What do you want?" she whispered.

He breathed once. "Just—not to let you out of my sight. Just to hold you and know that you're breathing."

They explored the passage the next day, Elain and Math and Brian Arthur, climbing down the hidden staircase to the cellar. There, with the push of a large rusted latch, the wall opened, and they were in the secret passage where the wartime supplies had been stored.

"The mine was abandoned when the Romans withdrew, was it?" Brian Arthur asked. "I'm not much on ancient history."

"When the Roman Empire began to collapse, they pulled their garrisons out of the conquered territories," Math said. "Later, a fort would have been built over the Roman site—they'd built here before the Romans, too. I suppose they found the tunnels useful, especially in times of attack. They could store supplies and water and animals there, and maybe they could even go through the tunnels to come out behind the enemy. We don't know how many entrances there might have been."

"And when the fortress was built, it incorporated the tunnels, too," Elain suggested. Last night, they hadn't talked, they hadn't made love. They had just lain holding each other till they slept.

Math nodded. "The house was begun in the time of Henry VIII. Henry was the one who demolished the monasteries and made Roman Catholicism illegal. So the house, like so many others, as Rosemary said, was built with a priest's hole and with the passage leading to the mine."

"And Jessica knew about it," said Elain. "And told her lover how to use it."

"No doubt."

"I wonder what got walled up to keep out Jessica's lover?"

Math shrugged. "Maybe the rockfall was caused deliberately. Or maybe it was just a part of the myth. Or it may be that the walled part was opened again later. Certainly the stairs and panelling have been kept in good order well into this century."

And then, after all those centuries, the secret had been lost. Elain sighed. "I'm glad it was found again. But what a pity it had to be Rosemary who did it."

Later, Math and Elain walked on the hill among the trees, the fortress behind them. The sun was bright, the birds were singing, it was a perfect day. They didn't talk. Something had changed, so that it seemed they might never need words.

They climbed to the fortress, and Math led her inside the old keep. The sun was high, pouring through the open roof onto the grass floor.

She leaned against a stone wall and turned her face up to the sun's rays, closing her eyes. When a shadow came between her and the sun, she opened her eyes. Math was leaning over her.

"Do you remember the day you climbed these stairs, and I came in on Balch, and you came down to me?" he asked.

She caught her breath at what she heard in his tone. "I remember," she whispered.

"I knew that day," he said. "That's how strong it was for me. I'd felt it before—even when I saw you at a distance on the day you arrived, I was driven by something. And when I spoke to you, somehow I had to keep you here. But that day—that day I knew. I thought you knew, too."

"Yes," she said, her heart pounding. "I thought it was that other woman, the watching woman, but it was me, too. It was me, wanting to run to you. Only I was so afraid."

His eyes went dark. "I wanted to make love to you then as I have never wanted to make love to any other woman. I knew you'd think me crazy if I said anything. I've never needed control the way I did then."

But she knew there had been another time, later, when he had needed control not to smash her into the ground. When he had looked at her with icy hatred.

His right hand came up to caress her cheek; his left arm embraced her. He said, "Last night, I might have lost you. By my own hand I could have sent out of this life the only thing I want from it." His voice trembled. "Then I saw how impossible it would have been to live without you."

She asked, "Do you—think we were enemies once?"

Math shook his head. "I have no explanation for things like that. But if we were, we never will be again." He bent and kissed her neck, and she felt the passion trembling in him.

She sobbed once. "I'm so sorry for what I did," she cried hoarsely. "I didn't—just didn't know what to do, falling in love with you and spying on you and—"

He kissed her lips gently, stopping her words. "No," he said. "Rosemary called you spy and cheat, the kind of words I had used, and all I could see was how stupid and ridiculous those words are, used to you. You're not those things, you're not that person."

"Who am I?" she whispered.

"You're my woman, my wife," he said. "You're everything to me. And what I said last night was the truth I would have seen before, if I hadn't been so insanely angry. You never tried to hurt anyone, or did anything you did out of self-interest. You were trying to do what was right."

She blinked because her eyes were swimming. "Do you trust me, Math?"

"With my life. With everything I am and have. Last night you said to me, 'I know I'm ugly,' and I knew I was the one who had made you think so. You are so beautiful that my heart is torn out every time I look at you, but because I was hurt, I uttered an unforgivable lie. That lie was worse than any you might have told me. Will you forgive me, my love?"

She felt tears on her cheeks. "There's nothing to forgive," she said.

He pulled her to him then, and kissed her mouth. And as his hungry, seeking hands ran over her flesh, her body began to sing for him.

"Well, we're a little reduced in numbers these days," said Jeremy. "I hope you'll get the repairs done and some people in before the season is entirely over, Math."

"So do I." Math grinned.

"No comment on the present company, of course. Elain's omelette is delicious. And eating by candlelight is always charming, whether the electricity is down or not. No, it's only that one is rather tired of the *erratic* quality of the Monday night meal."

"There's always the pub," Math said heartlessly.

Jeremy shuddered. "No, really, Math. Chicken in a basket!"

"You mustn't be so ungracious, Jeremy," said Vinnie reprovingly. "I am so glad everything is over, and that all those ugly things have stopped happening, I don't care what I eat. Not that the omelette is not delicious, Elain."

"Thank you."

"And what a relief it is not to have to share it with Rosemary. I did get so tired of her always complaining about our Jessica! I found it very hard to be polite sometimes."

"Didn't we all."

"A most unpleasant woman. And when you look at the intelligence that went into it all, it certainly makes one uncomfortable. It was all so well planned and executed. I, for one, would never have dreamt Rosemary had a hand in any of it. They were always so obviously not here when anything happened."

"Yes, Rosemary is not stupid," Math agreed. "And she has very cool nerves. I imagine her real weakness was Davina."

"Do you remember the day the coal got on the rug?" Vinnie said to Elain. "How they went off with their picnic? When they came back—the fuss they made at the door, being too wet to come in, and needing towels. It was very well executed."

"Of course, Bill helped with the fuss." Elain grinned.

At the sound of his name, Bill pricked up his ears.

Jeremy began to giggle. "Bill has really been the only one of us to express his opinion of Rosemary fully. I admire that, I do, indeed."

They all laughed, and Bill, recognizing their approval, sat up, his mouth open in a broad grin. Elain slipped him a piece of cheese.

"How *did* they execute it, exactly?" Jeremy asked tentatively. "I've never quite followed."

Math tore off a bit of his French bread. "On that occasion, they went out by car, drove eventually to the car park that services the public footpath, walked up to the fortress and came down through the tunnel to the lounge. I assume Rosemary had chosen a rainy day so that there would be fewer people on the path to notice them."

"And because there was more chance of there being a fire in the lounge, no doubt," said Vinnie.

"I remember thinking how muddy Rosemary's oilskins were that day," Elain mused. "And of course, the day I went down the tunnel, she recognized that same particular greasy dirt on me. That's why she came to my room that night—to try to learn what I had found out."

"She must have been terrified that someone else would realize that it was a gold mine," said Jeremy. "I said so, you know. I guessed it without realizing. If only people had listened."

"And then she saw my sketch of the tapestry, and must have been really scared. She couldn't have known why I'd painted it."

"I suppose when we found out you were here as a private investigator, Rosemary was the least surprised of us all," Vinnie said.

Elain glanced at Math then, but he only smiled at her.

"Well, of course, some of us suspected *something*," said Jeremy archly. "You just aren't quite one's image of an artist."

Elain smiled. "But I *am* an artist."

"Yes, that's not what I mean. I mean you're not the *image* of an artist."

"But—"

They were all momentarily silenced, as usual after one of these confusing declarations. "Well," Jeremy went on, "I must say, it's good to have Jess back again, isn't it? I didn't at all like thinking that she was 'turning,' or whatever they called it, and wanting to kill us all."

"I never did think it," said Vinnie. "It was a ludicrous idea."

"But all those tricks—didn't it make you wonder? There didn't seem to be any other explanation."

"Jess was no explanation," Vinnie insisted. "I've lived with her for nearly fifty years. Those things were not her at all. Her tricks were always humorous, always. Puncturing someone's arrogance, or—"

With a little gasp of understanding, Elain's brain suddenly made sense of something it had unconsciously been puzzling over for some time. She put down her knife as the other three turned to her expectantly.

"I've just figured it out!" she told them. "I see what happened! There were Rosemary and Davina blaming things on Jessica, and each time, something occurred to prevent their horrible tricks causing real damage. Right? When they put the burning coal on the carpet, Bill went crazy till Math shoved him into the lounge. And when they broke the tap in their bedroom, my paintbox fell apart and my turps broke all over the floor."

They were looking at her a bit blankly. "Yes, we know this, dear," said Vinnie. "But I don't see—"

"Don't you see that it's *those* tricks that are like Jessica? Whenever Rosemary got rude she blew smoke at her or something. See? *Jessica* knew all the time who was doing it. And she sabotaged every attempt. *She* spooked Bill—ghosts can do that to animals, can't they? And she made my paintbox come open—maybe even made sure I took the back stairs that day!"

"I believe you're right," said Vinnie happily. "Of course Jessica would have wanted to protect her reputation. Why didn't we think of that long ago?"

Math was grinning. "And that's not her best trick, either. What caused Rosemary's nightgown to catch on the wood panelling that night? Without that, we might not have caught her."

Jeremy choked. "Poor Rosemary! Can you imagine her caught in that little space and tearing her way out of her nightgown? Then running up the ladder mother naked and throwing a robe on before rushing out pretending to have been awakened by the explosion?"

They all burst into laughter. "Like Superman in a telephone box!" Elain gurgled. "Oh, if only we could have seen that!"

"I suppose Jessica saw it all," Vinnie said, wiping her eyes. "I hope she got a good laugh. I'm sure you're right, Math. That's down to Jessica, too. She never did like Rosemary, you know, and that's very like her sense of humour."

"I'm sure she enjoyed it," Math said. He picked up his wineglass. "That calls for a toast, I think." With murmurs of agreement, the others picked up their glasses. "To Jess!" said Math. "Wherever she is."

Slowly the candle flames faded and died. They gasped and then laughed, and the sound of silver laughter joined their own faintly on the night air.

"Jess" they said, and drank.

* * * * *

Silhouette celebrates motherhood in May with...

Debbie Macomber
Jill Marie Landis
Gina Ferris Wilkins

in

Three Mothers & a Cradle

Join three award-winning authors in this beautiful collection you'll treasure forever. The same antique, hand-crafted cradle connects these three heartwarming romances, which celebrate the joys and excitement of motherhood. Makes the perfect gift for yourself or a loved one!

A special celebration of love,

Only from

Silhouette®
TM

—where passion lives.

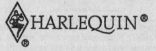

Kathleen Creighton's

RITA Award-winning author Kathleen Creighton
brings Midwest charm to the Intimate Moments
lineup in her ongoing miniseries, "Into the Heartland."
A WANTED MAN, IM #547, introduced Lucy Brown to
readers in February 1994. Now meet Lucy's brother,
Wood Brown, in ONE GOOD MAN, IM #639, coming
your way in May 1995.

Wood Brown had been to hell and back. And no
one knew his pain better than physical therapist
Christine Thurmond. But as she healed his battered
body and soul, she yearned for some loving all her
own. And only one good man would do....

The Browns—one sister, two brothers. Tragedy changed
their family forever, but never their spirit—or their love for
the heartland. Look for Rhett Brown's story in 1996 and
venture once again "into the Heartland"—*because
sometimes there's no place like home*—only in

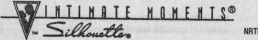

Five unforgettable couples say "I Do"... with a little help from their friends

Always a Bridesmaid!

Always a bridesmaid, never a bride...that's me, Katie Jones—a woman with more taffeta bridesmaid dresses than dates! I'm just one of the continuing characters you'll get to know in ALWAYS A BRIDESMAID!—Silhouette's new across-the-lines series about the lives, loves...and weddings—of five couples here in Clover, South Carolina. Share in all our celebrations! (With so many events to attend, I'm sure to get my own groom!)

In June, **Desire** hosts
THE ENGAGEMENT PARTY by Barbara Boswell

In July, **Romance** holds
THE BRIDAL SHOWER by Elizabeth August

In August, **Intimate Moments** gives
THE BACHELOR PARTY by Paula Detmer Riggs

In September, **Shadows** showcases
THE ABANDONED BRIDE by Jane Toombs

In October, **Special Edition** introduces
FINALLY A BRIDE by Sherryl Woods

Don't miss a single one—wherever
Silhouette books are sold.